The Clay Remembers

To Renee,
So glad you came to
Saddle Brooke and glad
you enjoyed my book,
Can't wait to show
you the park and the
Romero Ruin, the setting
for the Ramirez Ruin.

Sharon

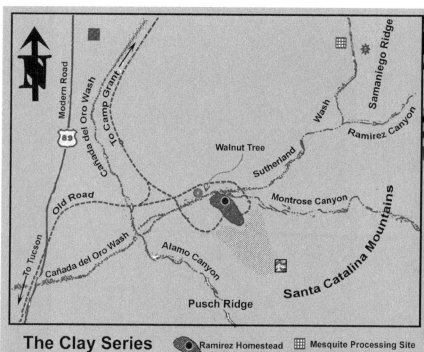

The Clay Series

The Clay Remembers
The Clay Endures
The Clay Sustains

Note: State Route 77 (Oracle Road) was US Route 89 in the 1980s

Ramirez Homestead Hohokam Village
Terraced Hohokam Agricultural Fields

Mesquite Processing Site
Two Ravens Ranch
Tonrai's Sun Sign
The Ramirez Well
Rock Shelter

THE
CLAY REMEMBERS

BOOK 1 IN THE CLAY SERIES

Sharon K. Miller

Buckskin Books
Tucson, Arizona

To Jim, my best friend and my love, who always believed in me,

and

To Victoriana Romero, whose life on a desolate ridge in the 19th century is the mystery that fired my imagination.

The Clay Series

Book 1: *The Clay Remembers*
Book 2: *The Clay Endures*
Book 3: *The Clay Sustains*

Contents

Acknowledgments viii
Note to Readers xiv
The Story 1
Chapters 1 through 37
Epilogue 286
Preview: *The Clay Endures* 289
Author Notes 294
Archaeological Site Etiquette Guide 299
Glossary 303
References 314
Book Club Discussion Questions 323

Reader/Reviewer Comments

A beautifully composed novel, *The Clay Remembers* was a pleasure to read and review. Ms. Miller has done a great deal of historical research on a unique topic, all the while weaving together a fictional story surrounding it. I loved the romantic undertones as Anna learns to accept  others into her life.... I look forward to reading the next book in this series. The author should be immensely proud of this work of art.

> Heather Osborne,
> Readers' Favorites Five Star Review

[Anna's] empathy, her bond with our forebears, is a gripping metaphor for the need of women down the years for recognition of their joy, skill and creativity, which enrich the lives of all. Sharon K. Miller shows how pressing that need can be, ranging against Anna a belittling archaeologist husband whose family is incapable of seeing beneath the surface, and whose greatest talent, ironically, consists of burying secrets.

> David Neilson, Author

Sharon K. Miller masterfully builds tension in her debut novel, *The Clay Remembers*. I'm looking forward to reading Book 2 in the series.

> Bliss Addison, Author of *A Waning Moon*

An interesting combination of contemporary Tucson living and Native American history/culture.

> Karen Lingelbach

Miller does an excellent job of creating a character that not only rediscovers herself through her work as an archeologist; but also as a new human being. The story is loving and moving and the plot will keep you immersed.

> Suzanne Kirby

If you have never been called a
defiant, incorrigible, impossible
woman..., have faith.... there is yet
time.

Clarissa Pinkola Estés, *Women Who*
Run With the Wolves: Myths and
Stories of the Wild Woman Archetype,
1992

Acknowledgments

Above all, I need to express my deepest gratitude and love to my husband, Jim, who never gave up on me and constantly encouraged me to keep going, even when this book was the last thing on my mind.

In 1999, when I began toying with the idea of writing this book, my plan was to write the stories of two women: a fictional tale of a nineteenth century woman who lived at the site of Romero Ruin north of Tucson, Arizona, and a twelfth century Hohokam woman whose village was on the same site. Both of these women struggled for survival during their time there, and I envisioned their stories connected through an ancient pot made by the Hohokam woman. To write these stories, I needed to know more about the Hohokam and about archaeology.

That came about with the instruction of Dave Stephen, Helen O'Brien, Leah Mason-Kohlmeyer, Buff

Billings, and the crew at Pima Community College Centre for Archaeological Field Training. I enrolled in a number of courses and participated in field activities to learn what I needed. The first time I picked up a potsherd, I was focused on the exterior surface and the faded design that was painted on it. When I turned it over, my thumb was resting in the thumb print of the potter. At that moment, I felt the presence of the woman who had made the pot more than 900 years before. It's an otherworldly feeling that many archaeologists admit they, too, have experienced. In that moment, my character, Anna, was born. It is this type of experience that guides Anna into archaeology as a career. Her story introduces the series; it is she who draws together the stories of the two other women.

Of the experiences I had taking archaeology classes, there were three that stand out as exceptional. The first pit house excavation I was involved in uncovered a full, human skeleton, an unusual find, as the Hohokam generally cremated their dead. At another excavation, I uncovered a tabular knife that was likely used to cut various plants for food or for weaving materials. And, because I intended to have my character reconstruct a pot, I was given the opportunity to try doing it myself. I spent many hours in the lab trying to join the broken pieces of a pot. Unfortunately, not all of the pieces were available, but I learned the techniques, and I actually had an experience very like the one Anna has in Chapter 17 when the pieces came together almost magically.

I would be remiss if I didn't also acknowledge some of my classmates at PCC. Among them were Ginny Dean and Margy Shaw. As serious archaeology students, they had much to teach me, and teach me they did. Margy and I spent a semester together in Exploration 2. We had completed Exploration 1, learning how to locate and map sites in the desert, but

Margy needed the second level in order to transfer to the university. I hadn't intended to take the course, but Dave told her she could not take it by herself because it involved hiking out into the desert to locate sites, update maps, and report their condition to the Arizona State Museum. It would be foolhardy to go alone. Margy asked if I would sign up with her. I did, and it was a wonderful experience.

If it hadn't been for my very first, primitive GPS, we might still be lost in the Tortolita Mountains. Several times, we drove into the foothills, left the Jeep along a dirt road, and hiked into the desert, sometimes climbing nearly vertical hills and dodging wandering javelinas, leaving a GPS "bread crumb trail" behind. There were many times, coming out, that we would not have found the Jeep if it weren't for that little trail of crumbs on the screen.

I owe my deepest appreciation to Byrd Baylor, whose work was the inspiration for the title of this book. Many of her stories and poems describe the powerful, spiritual connection between the desert of the American Southwest and its people. Her children's book, *When Clay Sings*, is a lyrical depiction of the legacy of the Hohokam, a legacy manifested through the broken and scattered remains of the pottery they crafted thousands of years ago. She emphasizes the importance of respecting each fragment because "every piece of clay is a piece of someone's life," and every piece of clay carries within it a song—like Anna, we only have to listen for it.

I am indebted to Deborah Swartz and Homer Thiel of Desert Archaeology, Inc., for their guidance with several archaeological details. Homer is responsible for the scene where Anna and Nick see Esperanza's wedding picture. I had included the crucifix in the story, but it was Homer who grabbed a book and showed me a photograph of a woman from the same time period who was wearing a beautiful crucifix. Thus, the wedding photo was born.

I'm also grateful to Deborah Swartz for some initial thoughts, and Linda Gregonis for the expertise she applied to the manuscript, setting me straight where I erred with Arizona history and archaeological theories, processes, practices, and terminology.

I've had the pleasure of hearing Allen Dart, of Old Pueblo Archaeology, present several programs about the Hohokam and the archaeological history of the Southwest. Touring Los Morteros, in Marana, Arizona, with Allen provided me with the setting for a critical moment in the story. Pottery making workshops with Andy Ward at Old Pueblo Archaeology helped me understand the ways ancient peoples created the ceramics we have inherited from them.

Andy's workshops taught me how the Hohokam, in particular, made their pots. We took a field trip to gather clay, and we learned to process and temper the clay for our work and to form vessels and pots using coils and the "paddle and anvil" technique used by prehistoric people. We fired our pots in the old way, building the fire from dried cow dung. In reality, the Hohokam probably fired with mesquite wood, which we did in a later class. My efforts to create a beautiful replica of "the pot" for this story were abject failures, but it was fun.

Retired Tucson Police Detective Milan Murchek provided invaluable advice about handling a police investigation that crossed city and county jurisdictions.

Frank and Vickie Pitts, at Pusch Ridge Stables, introduced me to horseback riding in the desert, one of the most spiritual connections to nature that I have ever had. The desert scenery and the paths that Anna and Nick travel in the story are there for anyone who ventures out by horse or hike. And my beloved Paco, who carried me many, many miles through the desert and into the foothills of the Santa Catalina Mountains, I still miss you, but you will live forever in this story.

Herminia "Minnie" Valenzuela, teacher and Yaqui storyteller, was the inspiration for the character of Minnie. She introduced me to Yoeme culture and the concept of Sea Takaa in 1999 at the University of Arizona English Department's Spring Conference.

Felipe Molina, a Yaqui/Yoeme scholar, provided me with an in-depth education on Yoeme history and culture in 2014. I am grateful for their contributions to the spirituality of Anna's "excursions into the past." In addition to his cultural expertise, Felipe also corrected my use of the Spanish language where it occurs in the book.

My deepest appreciation to Kim Campbell, my tireless and persistent reader, who offered me the best kind of criticism—she was brutally honest when she needed to be. Other readers, Judyth Willis, Linda "Lucy" Fernandez, and my sister, Betty Anne Hood, all provided exceptional guidance when the story needed a tweak or a sledgehammer.

My "critters" at Scribophile (www.scribophile.com) were invaluable. Wendy Barnes, Debbie Kozlovich, Kristen Kooistra, Marguerite "Markie" Madden, Bliss Addison, Ann James, and Cormac O'Hugh offered excellent critiques on several chapters. Fellow "critter" David Neilson was kind enough to critique the entire novel. Much of what is good about this book, I owe to his skills at offering a constructive critique with superb suggestions for improvement.

I am very grateful to my pre-publication, advance readers for their feedback and for catching little gremlins in print: Charlie McKee, April Hobson (and her girls at school), Ginny Moran, Kim Campbell, Suzanne Kirby, Linda Murphy, Linda "Lucy" Fernandez (her second reading), Jeannie Waters, Karen Lingelbach, and those Scribophile "critters" who stepped up for a second helping: Markie Madden (whose eagle eye spotted several missing quotation marks), Bliss Addison, and David Neilson.

Many thanks to the folks at www.99Designs.com and the wonderful designers who competed to design the cover for this book. Most especially, I want to thank Juan-Carlos Negretti B for his tireless efforts and his commitment to providing a cover that expressed exactly what I was aiming for.

And to my friend and editor, Heather Severson: you inspire me, and we nourish each other. Carol Sletten, my beautiful friend, I'm pleased to have you as an advisor and cheerleader.

Note to Readers

Nothing in this book is intended as a guide for amateur archaeologists to interfere with existing sites throughout the Tucson Basin.

The Arizona State Historic Preservation Office, a division of Arizona State Parks, provides a set of guidelines for those who are interested in visiting archaeological sites throughout the state. These guidelines are located in the back of the book as a service to readers.

The sun site petroglyph described in Chapter 30 is fictitious. Readers who set out to look for it will be disappointed. The human remains and many of the artifacts uncovered and collected in the story are the products of the author's imagination. The likelihood of such artifacts, other than potsherds, actually existing at local sites is extremely remote.

There is a glossary in the back of the book that provides explanations of events, people, places, words, and archaeological terms that may not be defined in the context of the story.

I hope you enjoy reading Anna's story as much as I enjoyed writing it. Thank you for joining me on Anna's journey.

There are desert hillsides where ancient Indian pottery still lies half buried in the sand and lizards blink at other dusty lizards that were painted on those pots a thousand years ago...Indians who find this pottery today say that everything has its own spirit—even a broken pot.

They say the clay remembers the hands that made it.

When Clay Sings, Byrd Baylor

Evanston, Illinois, May 1986

He stood beside her on the patio, drawing her against his tall frame. She forced herself to relax, to breathe steadily between sips of wine, and to focus only on the shifting colors of the dying day, her last sunset here.

When she tried to step away, Foster tightened his grip.

"Sweetheart, I have to turn the steaks." Anna struggled to keep her voice soft and even.

He chuckled and released her. At the grill, she kept him in her peripheral vision; he stood tall, shoulders back, left thumb hooked in his belt, watching the darkening sky push the last light behind the tree-lined horizon.

He will be furious when he comes home tomorrow and reads my note.

Anna had prepared his favorite meal: filet mignon with balsamic glaze, steamed asparagus, and baby red potatoes. Her stomach churning, she had forced a casual greeting at the door, standing on her tiptoes, giving him a quick kiss on the cheek and handing him a glass of red wine.

"Well, well," he said, pulling his necktie loose and unbuttoning the top button of his shirt. "Candles? Wine? What's the occasion?"

"Nothing special, Foster. I thought it would be a nice treat with the pressure of final exams." She was surprised at how easily she could lie.

"Anna...," he began, looking skeptical, his eyes darkening, but she turned toward the kitchen before he could finish.

"Give me a minute to check the asparagus."

❧❦

Foster watched her disappear into the kitchen. He welcomed this change in her behavior. He walked into the den, pulling off his tie and setting his briefcase on the floor. He took his handkerchief from his breast pocket and polished the bare desktop. Nothing rested on the mahogany surface. Not a desk pad, pencil holder, or lamp.

He looked at Anna's desk, pleased to note that for once, it was almost neat. Her tendency to clutter annoyed him.

He would have to say something about the way she was dressed. She had met him at the door in an oversized Wildcat sweatshirt, leggings, and slouch socks. Her ponytail was held by a purple scrunchie. She was no longer a student and didn't need to parade around in purple like a simple-minded co-ed. She was his wife, and she damn well should dress appropriately, even at home.

He turned toward the bedroom where he hung his tie inside his closet. With ten ties on the rack, it would be two weeks before he wore today's tie again. Tomorrow would be the navy blue with red stripes. That meant the navy blue suit.

He hung his gray suit jacket in its place among the others and brushed it with the brush from a hook next to his tie rack. At his dresser, he removed his cuff links and polished them with his handkerchief. He slid them into place in the leather jewelry box with the other four pairs. It would be a week before he wore them again.

He rolled the sleeves of his starched shirt three turns, smoothing each layer as he folded the next. He stopped on his way out of the bedroom to check his reflection. He tugged the sleeves, smoothed the folds again.

"You've come a long way, Tommy Robinson, a long way."

ؘ扶

In the kitchen, Anna leaned against the counter.

It was too much... stupid, stupid. Candles? What was I thinking?

She had been planning her escape since February. Everything was ready. Had she ruined it by going overboard with this dinner?

She rattled a pot lid and went to the sink and washed her hands.

She looked at her reflection in the window. She wore no makeup, even though Foster often told her she should make some kind of effort to hide the freckles on her nose—even at home. Her clear skin was unblemished except for a chicken pox scar on her cheekbone, just below the outside corner of her left eye. He had told her to cover that, too. She put her finger on it. It was a habit, as if she were remembering the childhood itching.

When he came into the kitchen, she turned around. "Time to put the steaks on." Carrying the plate and a pair of tongs, she went out the back door.

Foster walked to the door, his broad frame filling the space. He disappeared for a moment and then came out, carrying his wine along with hers. She took her glass from him and turned to look out across the yard at their last sunset.

∂∾∽

They had a mostly pleasant conversation over dinner, something that hadn't happened very often in the past few months. Anna kept herself under tight control and managed to smile and nod at the appropriate times. She did her best to keep her finger off her scar. Foster knew about her nervous habit, so it took all of her will power to leave it alone.

They chatted about his day at the university and the exam schedule for the rest of the week. He told her that one of his students had submitted a research report applying post-processual theory to the mound builders' culture at Hopewell.

"It's a radical idea, questioning our interpretations of past cultures and how they lived. After all, the artifact record makes it all pretty clear."

"Foster, surely you don't still believe that our interpretations of the artifacts and the data in the archaeological record are infallible, do you?" They had had this discussion before. Anna was open to the theory that archaeological interpretation is subjective, and Foster always defended the objectivity of archaeological analysis and interpretation.

He frowned and put down his fork. "You're starting to sound like a feminist again. I suppose now you want me to believe that prehistoric women made their own stone tools and even went hunting."

"Why not?" She took a drink of wine and leveled her gaze at him. "Face it, theories are changing. It's time to get on board or be left behind."

He didn't answer. She was taking a chance by pushing his buttons now.

He frowned again and his eyes darkened. "That's what I've been trying to tell you all along, Anna. You have this romantic notion of archaeology that will never serve you well in the field. You'll make a fool of yourself and it will reflect poorly on me. You need to understand your limitations."

She looked down at her plate, saying nothing.

"Don't you ever try to tell me what is true about archaeology again. You really don't know how little you know."

Anna picked up a bowl from the table. "Would you like more asparagus?"

౿ೲ

Later, when they went to bed, he was gentle in his lovemaking. Anna was surprised at his sudden tenderness and almost disappointed that her body betrayed her, giving in to the pleasure he so rarely offered any more. But then again, maybe he was rewarding her for being the dutiful little wife tonight.

Afterwards, she lay in the dark, thinking.

She had seen him lose his temper before, but until Aztalan, he had never aimed his fury at her. The first incident was not long after they started dating. They had gone to dinner in Chicago and, afterward, when the valet brought his Mercedes around, he accused the boy of mishandling it. He grabbed him by the shirt and practically lifted him off the ground, yelling profanities and threatening to break his neck. She was relieved when the manager intervened. In the end, the manager apologized to Foster and the valet was fired.

She was visibly shaken by his behavior. On the drive back to Evanston, he apologized. He said he didn't know what had come over him, that he had never done anything like that before. He promised her she would never see that behavior again. It was not a promise he would keep.

She thought about how he had treated her then. He pampered and spoiled her, something new to her. He had made her feel special, precious, telling her over and over how lucky he was to have her. That's how he said it: "I'm so lucky to have you."

Now, she understood. She was his possession, something he owned. Just like his red Mercedes, which he always parked well away from other vehicles to protect it from parking lot dings and dents.

She didn't think he could imagine what she was planning. If he noticed she was preoccupied and distracted from time to time, he probably suspected she was thinking about getting another job. She hoped she was right, because he would be confident she wouldn't act on it. He had made it clear that he would never share her with anyone, not *anyone*. He no doubt believed that her humiliation at Kimmswick and what he had done after Aztalan had brought an end to the matter of her working. She knew he would tolerate no disobedience.

2

Evanston, Illinois, February 1986

Rhinehart Wilson had invited Anna to join his excavation team at Aztalan. She expected Foster to oppose it, and he did, but she was determined to make her own decisions. She refused to let him control her every move.

She and Foster had worked with Rhinehart in summers as undergraduates. He had been managing field schools throughout the Midwest for over thirty years, and subcontracting archaeological projects for state and federal agencies. He was an outstanding educator and field archaeologist. Because she had learned so much from him, she jumped at the chance to join him, not as a student, but as a professional archaeologist.

She kept the job a secret for as long as she could, postponing the argument she knew would follow. Her stomach churning, she finally told Foster that she was going to Wisconsin to work with Rhinehart at Aztalan. She hoped he would approve because it was only two hours away, and she would come home on weekends.

"I know you don't want me to work, but I'm an adult and a professional archaeologist. I don't need your permission, just your approval."

He folded the newspaper carefully and deliberately before looking at her, his dark eyes becoming even darker. "Damn it, Anna, aren't we done with this foolishness yet? I thought we put this to rest after Kimmswick. You still don't get it? I'm telling you no. You can't go."

"Foster, you can't tell me no. You're my husband, but you can't make me into something I'm not. You knew I was an archaeologist when you married me, and you knew I planned to work while you were still at the university. On top of that, you've made it clear that I'll never... we'll never... " She couldn't continue the thought, so she simply said, "I'm taking this job."

He unfolded the newspaper and went back to reading, saying nothing further.

It was the first time she had stood up to him, and she thought his silence was reluctant agreement. All of her life, she had avoided conflict by going along with what others wanted, even when she didn't want to. This time she refused to go along to get along. She thought she had won this round.

But the evening before she was to leave, he watched her pack her field bag and suitcase. "I'm warning you, Anna. Don't leave this house."

"You're *warning* me?" She tucked three pairs of socks into the suitcase with an extra pair of jeans and her long-sleeved shirts. "I'm telling you that I'm going. You need to understand that you don't own me just because I'm your wife." She slammed the suitcase closed and set it on the floor. She picked up her dig kit and checked to make sure everything she needed was there—trowels, brushes, whisk broom, compass, protractor, gloves.

Foster stood there with his arms crossed, watching her. When she turned and walked out of the room, he didn't follow. He was still standing there in his signature "I'm in charge here" posture when she came back. She put her field book, calculator, and pencils into the kit, closed it, and set it down with her suitcase.

❦❦

In the morning, at breakfast, he was still angry. He didn't apologize for forcing rough sex on her the night before. Normally, he would beg forgiveness for the bite marks on her breasts and the bruises on her body, making hollow promises. He left for the university without saying a word.

In the car, she rolled the windows down and let the frigid wind blow through her hair. She didn't mind the cold for the time being. She turned the radio on and sang with Dionne Warwick and laughed when Steve Martin sang "King Tut."

When she arrived at the site, Rhinehart left the gathered crew and limped over to meet her, giving her a hug and wrapping her hand in both of his. She was surprised at the warmth of his greeting, but it made her feel good.

He was a little shorter than Anna and slightly built with long, gray hair hanging down his back in a thin braid.

"Anna, it's good to see you."

She marveled at his energy. Even at sixty-two and with his limp, he kept up with his crew.

"It's good to see you, Rhinehart. I'm looking forward to working with you again."

He took off his sunglasses and stood back to look at her. "You're pale. A little sunshine'll do you good." He hesitated. "Is this okay with Foster?"

She smiled. "Not really. He's very angry with me, but he'll just have to get over it. I made it clear I was taking this job."

"Are you sure he won't... ? I mean, do you really think... ?" Anna saw something in the older man's eyes that she couldn't quite read.

"It's okay. Everything will be fine."

"I hope so." Still holding her hand, he walked back to the group and introduced her.

To the group, he said, "The university has discovered a number of new habitation sites here recently. There's some thinking that they're not related to the original mound structures, so our job is—"

When he stopped mid-sentence, looking over her shoulder, Anna turned. Foster had just parked his car in front of hers.

My God! He's going to do it again.

He got out of the car, leaving the door open. When he was within earshot, he pointed at Anna. "Get your gear. You're going home."

"Wait a minute, Foster." Rhinehart stepped in front of Anna and held up his hands, palms out. "Can we talk about this?"

Foster stepped within inches of him and said, "Stay out of this, Wilson. I told her she was not taking this job, but she refused to listen. If you end up short handed it's her fault."

Silence fell over the site. One of the crew stepped out of the group and took a position next to Rhinehart. He was as tall as Foster, but nowhere near as heavy. "Mr. Wilson, can I help you?" He kept his eyes on Foster while he spoke. Another young man came forward to stand on the other side of the older man.

"Thanks, Rob, but I don't think that will be necessary." To Foster, he said, "Look, are you sure you want to do this?"

"It's none of your god damned business what I want. She's my wife and she belongs at home."

Anna had been too stunned to speak, but she found her voice. "Foster, I'm staying here. You can't make me go home. And you can't come here and push me or Rhinehart or anyone else around."

He glared at her. "Don't underestimate me, Anna. I'll do what I have to do."

When he reached for Anna's arm, Rhinehart again stepped in, but Foster shoved him. He would have fallen if Rob hadn't caught him.

As Foster started to drag Anna to her car, Rob followed them. "Hey, man. I don't care if she is your wife, you can't treat her like that."

Foster let go of Anna long enough to turn on Rob. "I'll break your fucking neck if you come any closer." When Rhinehart started toward the two men, Foster turned and pointed at him. "And I'll kill you if you ever talk to my wife again about a job."

Anna had never seen him so enraged, and, although she didn't want to believe his threats, she was afraid he was fully capable of following through. She needed to shift his attention back to her. "You can't do this again, Foster. Can we talk about this?"

"Yes, I can do this again, and there's nothing to talk about." He grabbed her arm and headed toward the cars. He stopped behind the Toyota and turned on her. "You need to make a choice, Anna. You can get into your car and follow me home, or I'll put you into mine and we'll just leave this hunk of shit sitting here."

He hated that she had her own car; more than once he had insisted she get rid of it. She couldn't leave it here.

"All right, Foster, but this isn't over. You have no right to come here and threaten Rhinehart or me or anyone. I won't be bullied like this again." She got into her car and, before he could get into his, she started hers and slammed it into gear, speeding around him, spinning dust into his face and pelleting him and his precious car with gravel.

扩

When she pulled into the driveway behind his car, he was waiting. He yanked open her car door and dragged her into the house.

"Let go of me." Anna struggled against his grip.

Once inside, he turned around and slammed his fist into her face. A bright light exploded in her skull. She wasn't sure how long she lay on the floor. When she tried to get up, he was standing over her, his eyes blacker than she had ever seen them. She couldn't believe what had just happened. It was her father all over again—almost. She had never seen him use his fist.

On his way out of the room, he turned to her. "There will be no more talk of getting a job. Now, get up off your ass and get my dinner ready."

She struggled to stand up, discovering that she could barely hold her weight with her right arm. She must have hit the coffee table before hitting the floor. Every movement hurt.

That night, he apologized and begged her to forgive her. When he touched her swollen, black eye, she turned her face away. "I'm sorry, darling. I didn't mean to do that. I wouldn't hurt you for the world, you know that."

She might have laughed if she wasn't in so much pain.

3

Evanston, Illinois, May 1986

Her independence day had arrived. Everything was ready, but her stomach was tied in knots. She put on her sweats and running shoes while Foster got ready to go to the university. She wanted it to look like a typical morning.

After a quick, but silent breakfast, he kissed her cheek and went out to his car. She watched him from the door, remembering the good times they had had together—in France, exploring those stunning, ancient caves, here in Evanston walking along the shoreline, watching nightfall over Lake Michigan. They often had dinner in Chicago and went to the theater. On weekends, they joined crowds on the Navy Pier and wandered through the shops.

We laughed a lot. What happened to the laughter?

A tear slid down her cheek. There were some good memories. They were the ones she wanted to keep. When it was good. She wiped the tear and pressed her finger against the scar.

This was the right decision—it was her only choice. She couldn't ask him for a divorce; her conversation with the attorney had made that clear. There was no way he would agree to it. She shuddered to think what he would do if he even thought she wanted to leave. She had to go now so she would be safely out of his range when he got home and found her gone.

She was reclaiming herself and her career goals. She put the diamond necklace and earrings he had given her on his dresser next to his leather jewelry box. She wrote a short note telling him she knew he would never understand, but she could not live as he expected her to.

She gathered up the last of her things and slammed the door behind her.

 ~

"Would you like something to drink?"

Anna looked up from her book, startled. The flight attendant leaned across the woman next to her, putting a small napkin on the tray.

"Apple juice, please." She pushed her book to one side as the drink and a small package of peanuts were placed in front of her.

She looked at her watch, closed her eyes and rubbed her scar.

What am I doing? What if he finds out where I am? What will he do?

Out the window, the land stretched out behind her, increasing the distance from Foster and her old life. After the verdant Midwestern farm fields, the plane rose above the clouds shrouding the changing landscape in mystery. Over New Mexico, the sky cleared and she examined the contours of low mountain ranges and broad valleys. They were punctuated by an occasional patchwork of green, cultivated fields, as well as a pattern of circles, some green from irrigation and some brown and lying fallow. Roads—long, pale, straight lines—stretched across the flat open spaces going from somewhere to somewhere else. Anna wondered where they led. Ribbons of green marked the paths of rivers and, along the contours of low mountains, drainages, like feathers, drifted down the slopes to the land below.

Everything was changing.

On the approach into Tucson, she was startled by the increasing ruggedness of the landscape below. She had always thought of mountains in terms of the rolling Appalachians or the Rockies or even the Alps. They had honeymooned in the French Alps, studying those 50,000-year-old cave paintings at Lascaux and speculating on the culture of the people who had left them there. Because the Alps were so spectacular, with snow-covered peaks and dizzying heights, they had defined the romantic notion of mountains in her imagination. These mountains, though, bore little resemblance to the Alps.

The city below, with its pattern of streets and highways, this city that would be her new home, did not distract her from the compelling view of the mountains as they slipped by the window. Deep canyons cut into the rock slopes. She was surprised by the amount of vegetation that covered their southern flanks; it was green, but scattered broadly, accentuating the grays and browns of the rocks and mountain slopes.

Even though she had seen pictures of the American Southwest, these mountains caught her off guard. There was a strange familiarity. A powerful surge of nostalgia overwhelmed her. It was as if she had seen these mountains before, as if she had been here before.

The plane banked, and Anna saw another, smaller mountain range with scattered, rough peaks thrusting upward from narrow valleys. When the plane banked for its final approach, the mountains dropped from sight. Anna found herself looking into a cloudless blue sky, more brilliant than any she had ever seen.

She had been holding her breath, but not because she was nervous about the landing. As the plane leveled and the city below drew closer, she breathed out slowly and allowed herself to watch the ground rising up to welcome her.

I'm home.

Home. The word had come unbidden and newly formed in her mind, bringing with it an emotional connection she had never experienced. *Home.* She remembered something she had read in school—was it Robert Frost? *Home is where, when you go there, they have to take you in.* At fifteen years old, the thought had consumed her with adolescent angst. To have to go home and for them to have to take you in would be unthinkable. Once she was able to leave, going back was never an option. Just like Howard. Her brother left the day after he graduated from high school and he never came back, not even for their parents' funerals. For a long time she had been angry with him for leaving her alone with them and then expecting her to take care of their end-of-life details. But eventually she understood. She shared his pain.

Later, when she married Foster, she hoped they might build a life she would be glad to come home to. Sadly, that hadn't happened. With Foster, home became a prison; home was where she had to be twenty-four-seven. There when Foster left for the university and there when he came home.

But now she was free of him. She would never have to deal with him again.

At least that's what she told herself.

4

Tucson, Arizona, June 1986

She dragged a box up the steps to the landing, swearing at herself for taking a second floor apartment. When she stopped to catch her breath, a striking, dark-haired woman with a complexion like golden honey came out of the neighboring apartment. Smiling, she handed Anna a large glass of ice water.

"Thanks." Anna smiled and took the glass, gulping the water. She had not realized how thirsty she was.

"I'm Anna."

"Hi, I'm Minnie. Here, let me help you." Minnie bent over, hoisted the clumsy box from the landing, and turned toward Anna's door. "Well, don't just stand there, kid. Get that door open."

She was standing there gaping at this stranger, but Minnie's command propelled her to action. Once inside, Minnie took the box directly to the kitchen.

"Gotta be kitchen stuff–nothing else would weigh that much."

Minnie came back, took the glass from Anna's hand and refilled it at the sink. Then she handed it back to her. "You have to drink more."

Anna shook her head. "Thanks, but I'm fine now."

"You live in the desert, you drink lots of water, even when you're not thirsty. Especially when you're new to it. Don't drink enough, you get sick. Drink." Clearly, Minnie would not take no for an answer. Anna drank. Minnie smiled again.

Anna looked self-consciously at her sparsely furnished apartment; she had leased only a few pieces of furniture and shipped very little from Evanston. She had filled the car with personal belongings before turning it over to the transport company. Most of what she and Foster owned she had left behind. None of it was hers anyway. Plus, if she was going to make a clean break, she had to do it quickly and quietly. It was a coward's choice, to be sure, but it was all she could do.

"It's not much, but I guess it's home now." There was a slight quiver in her voice, especially on the word *home.*

"You'll be all right here." Minnie's voice was reassuring, and when Anna looked into her dark eyes, she believed it.

After Minnie left, Anna opened her suitcase and found the shadow box and seven projectile points that had first aroused her interest in archaeology. She hung the shadow box on the wall between the kitchen and the living room. She unwrapped each of the points and restored them to their positions. When they were all in place, she stood back and thought about what those seven points meant to her.

When she was about thirteen, she had found these points in the plowed field behind her house. During summers when school was out and her parents were at work, she was likely to be walking in the woods, climbing a tree, or digging in the field. On weekends when they were at home, she spent as much time as possible away from the house. She had found the first point, turned up by the neighboring farmer's plow, so she kept digging to see what else she could find. She loved to kneel in the soft, warm soil, sifting it through her fingers looking for hidden treasures, never discouraged when she came up empty, always believing that something important was just inches away.

She had taken the first point to school to show her science teacher, who told her not to call it an arrowhead because it could be from any kind of throwing weapon, like a spear. He said the proper term was "projectile point."

She told him where she had found it and he nodded thoughtfully.

"If you found one, there are probably more there. That's an area of early Indian activity. Most people have no idea what treasures lie just below the surface." He loaned her some books about local prehistory and archaeology. He encouraged her interest and often asked her about her finds.

She didn't tell him about the strange sensation she experienced when she picked up that first point. She imagined she was living in a different time, using a piece of deer antler to chip away at a stone to fashion this point. It felt so real.

From then on, she was hooked; she would be an archaeologist. Over time, she had found the other six points, and along with the first, they were in a shadow box that she had fashioned out of scraps she found in their garage. Each find had triggered the same sensation she had experienced with the first one—she was thrilled to have what she thought was a good imagination, but she never told anyone about it.

She went back to her unpacking, hanging her clothes in the closet of her very small bedroom. She was glad to be out of the motel room and into a more permanent place. She made the bed and then stood back to survey the room. It was not much bigger than the double bed, with a nightstand on one side and a chest of drawers against the wall next to the closet. *It's not small. It's cozy. And it's mine.*

Her stomach growled and she looked at her watch. It was nearly five-o'clock and she was starving; she had not eaten lunch. In the kitchen, she opened the refrigerator and decided a ham sandwich would hit the spot. Just as she reached for the ham, there was a knock on the door.

When she opened it, her new neighbor was standing there holding a steaming casserole.

"I figured you'd be hungry by now." Surprised, Anna stepped back and Minnie made a beeline for the kitchen table, where she deposited the casserole. "I'll be right back."

Anna watched her out the door and then looked back at the casserole. The most delicious aroma made its way to her nose, and her stomach growled appreciatively. When Minnie returned, she had two wine glasses in one hand, a bottle of red wine in the other.

"My goodness. You didn't have to do all of this."

"No problem, kid." She shrugged. "I have to eat. You have to eat. Why not do it together?"

Anna choked up. It had been years since she had a meal with anyone besides Foster. "You have to let me repay the kindness, though."

Minnie nodded and poured one glass of wine, and then looked up. "Oh, geez. I forgot to ask if you drank wine. I'm sorry. Sometimes I'm too pushy. If you don't want... "

"It's all right. I'd love some."

Minnie poured the second glass and then handed it to Anna. She lifted her own glass and said, "Welcome to Tucson."

Anna tapped her glass lightly against Minnie's. Someday she would tell her how much this meant to her.

At the table, they spooned big portions of cheese enchiladas in red sauce onto their plates and Anna learned more about her neighbor. Minnie told her that she had grown up in one of Tucson's historic barrios and that her father was Mexican and her mother Pascua Yaqui. Anna decided that would account for her honey-colored skin and black hair, which was pulled back and twisted up on her head and held loosely by a barrette.

"Pascua Yaqui? I don't think I know about them. 'Pascua?' Why does that make me think of Easter?" Anna scooped another helping of enchiladas. "I can't believe how hungry I was. These are delicious."

Between mouthfuls, Minnie continued. "It's the Spanish word for Easter. My mother's people converted to Christianity a few hundred years ago in Mexico when the Spanish missionaries arrived. Easter has become one of the most important celebrations in Yoeme culture."

"Yoeme?"

"That's the original cultural name of our people."

"It sounds fascinating. I love history."

"What brings you to Tucson?"

Anna hesitated. "In part, it's that love of history. I have a job with Southwest Archaeological Associates that begins next week."

"Archaeology. I teach my third graders Mexican history along with the history of our people and the Tohono O'odham. That's another Indian tribe in the Tucson area. Every year, I take the kids on a field trip to Camp Cooper, the school district's outdoor education center. It would be great if they offered an archaeology experience for the kids."

"That sounds wonderful. Third grade? That would make them about eight years old. Such a fun age."

"True, but some of them are older because of being held back or because they didn't go to school in Mexico before they came here. Most of them are Mexican, Yaqui, or Tohono O'odham and some don't speak English very well. Minnie scraped the last of the enchiladas from the casserole. "I have to concentrate on getting them ready to succeed in an Anglo world. Sometimes it's tough."

"I believe it."

"So tell me about you. Where are you from?" It occurred to Anna that this was a question she would hear often.

"I'm from the Chicago area. I studied at Northwestern, and this is my first real job since I graduated." She hoped that would suffice.

"Maybe sometime you could come in and talk to my students about archaeology."

"I'd love to. Thanks."

After dinner, Minnie offered to wash the dishes, but Anna refused.

"It's enough that you shared your dinner with me." She began to choke up again and wondered if Minnie noticed.

"You're tired. Get some rest tonight. I'll catch up with you again soon."

After Minnie left with the wine glasses and empty dish, Anna cried for the first time since leaving Evanston. Everything was suddenly so different—

there was someone she could talk to and share a meal with. That hadn't happened for a long time. She dried her tears and washed the dishes with a smile on her face.

࿇

Anna tried not to think about Foster and what was happening in Evanston, but she couldn't help imagining what he had done when he got home. Her note would have infuriated him. She shuddered to think about it.

First, he would have been angry that her car was not in the driveway. The car had always been a flash point with him. With the car, she had a little freedom from his control. She was pretty sure he was embarrassed to have his wife driving around in an old Toyota. Once he had insisted on buying her a new car, but she refused. The Toyota was hers and hers alone. Something had told her that she needed to keep it. It had been her lifeline.

After Aztalan, if she wasn't there when he came home from work, he would fly into a rage. It didn't matter what had delayed her. No excuse was good enough. The last time she was late, he had rifled her desk, apparently looking for any indication that she was looking for another job. When she came in the door, he was going through the drawers, throwing her papers over the den.

"Where the hell have you been?" He stood up and grabbed her arm.

"Let go of me!" She jerked her arm away from him and looked around the room at the mess he had made. "What are you doing?"

"Never mind that. I asked you where you have been."

"I was at the grocery store. My car got blocked in by a fire truck and an ambulance. An elderly man had the nerve to have a heart attack in the parking lot. I couldn't exactly go to the paramedics and demand that they move because my husband's unreasonable demands are more important than a man's life."

When he narrowed his eyes, she said, "Okay. How about this? I was abducted by aliens but they let me go when I told them what you would do to me if I was late."

"Very funny." He stalked out of the room, but turned around in the doorway. "And clean up this mess—now."

Her car being gone would have him primed before he ever got into the house. Finding her note probably sent him around the bend.

Aztalan had taught her that the behaviors she thought were out of character for him were, in fact, totally in character. In public, he was composed and refined. But at home, whenever he feared Anna might be asserting herself, he lost control.

She imagined that whatever was left in her desk or in her closet had been destroyed by now. She was thankful for the post office box. That kept her communication with Rhinehart and her plans secret. She was certain she had left nothing that would give her away.

She thought about the print from the Cave of the Bulls in Lascaux. It was on the wall over their bed. When they visited that cave on their honeymoon, she was so enchanted by the drawings that he had purchased a print at a local gift shop, had it beautifully matted and framed and shipped home as a special surprise for her. It probably did not survive his rage.

Her deception had kept her safe. As much as she wanted to believe she would remain safe from him, at times she was uncertain.

5

Tucson, Arizona, June 1986

These thoughts had haunted her for days, but she tried to dismiss them on the morning of her interview with Jonathan Lomax. She was nervous.

What if he doesn't like me? What if he thinks I'm not qualified?

Knock it off. It'll be okay.

She had argued with herself until her stomach was tied in a knot.

When she got into the car, the heat inside was oppressive. In Chicago, she hadn't much cared about the air conditioner, but it was a necessity in Tucson.

She checked the city map and headed out to find the offices of Southwest Archaeological Associates.

She wouldn't be here without Rhinehart's help. He had contacted his old friend who agreed to give her a job even without knowing her story. Rhinehart had assured him she was a talented archaeology student who had a gift for the work. That, along with the fact that she needed to get away from Chicago.

Driving north on Campbell Avenue, she passed the University of Arizona and the University Medical Center, taking note of their locations. She turned east on Grant Road, following it to the archaeology office. She was so focused on finding her way that she didn't get a good look at this part of her new city. That would come later.

She parked her car in the small lot, got out and looked around. The rugged expanse of the Catalinas was closer here, and she was comforted, feeling the familiar kinship. She was beginning to get used to that feeling. She inhaled the hot desert air. As hot as it was, it renewed her. When she entered the office, a petite, blonde-haired woman looked up and smiled.

"I'm Maggie. I assume you are Anna?"

"Yes. Thank you." Anna shook her hand firmly. "Anna Robinson."

"Max will be with you in a few moments."

"Max?"

Maggie smiled. "Everyone calls my husband Max. From Lomax, you see."

Just then a tall, red-haired man stepped through the open door of an adjoining office. He shook her hand and smiled.

"Glad to meet you, Anna. I'm Max. Rhinehart spoke highly of you."

"Thank you. I'm glad to be here. I can only hope I live up to Rhinehart's recommendation." She liked this man right away—his hazel eyes sparkled and deep laugh lines animated his face. He looked to be somewhere in his early forties, long and lean, with freckles dotting his tanned face. He was wearing jeans and a lightweight, long-sleeved khaki shirt unbuttoned at the collar.

Before escorting her into his office, he put a gentle hand on Maggie's shoulder. "Have you heard from your mother?"

Maggie laughed, looking up into Max's eyes. "No, and I really don't expect to hear anything until they get back from their honeymoon."

He laughed with her. "You're probably right."

Anna watched this affectionate exchange a bit enviously. Max was at least a foot taller than Maggie. Maggie turned to Anna and laughed, "My mother just remarried at the grand old age of seventy-two, and she's having the time of her life." Anna laughed with her.

In Max's office, she noted diplomas and certificates testifying to his education and expertise, along with photographs of projects and artifacts. He gestured her into a chair and he sat behind his desk.

"Rhinehart tells me you graduated from Northwestern—good program."

"Yes." She handed him a folder with her résumé, transcripts, and letters from a number of her Northwestern professors. She watched as he leafed through them, nodding thoughtfully from time to time.

He asked her a number of general questions about the experiences she had listed on her résumé. She expected him to ask what she knew about Southwestern archaeology, so she had done some recent reading on the subject. She was determined to make good on Rhinehart's recommendation.

"Tell me what you know about the Hohokam."

She looked down at her hands, clenched together in her lap, and then up at Max.

"Unfortunately, I didn't have a lot of coursework on archaeology of the Southwest at Northwestern. We had a survey of American prehistory, so I did get a glimpse of the work of Emil Haury, for example, at Snaketown, along with some of his other achievements, but, frankly, I don't believe it's enough. Since I arrived in Tucson, I've been to the library to find resources, and I've tried to learn more about the archaeology of the Tucson Basin."

Max waited.

"As I understand it, the Hohokam were an agrarian people taking advantage of the agricultural promise of the Sonoran Desert. Most sites that have been excavated over time have shown farming activity and the early presence of pit houses, followed later by platform mounds and walled compounds." Anna relaxed a little when Max nodded. But again he waited.

"I think it's curious that much of what we know about the Hohokam is possibly dwarfed by what we don't know."

"Such as?"

"Many archaeologists speculate they arrived in southern Arizona around two-thousand years ago, possibly from Mexico, and then disappeared around five-hundred years ago. No one really knows why they disappeared or where they went, and if they assimilated into other existing peoples.

"You would think they were a highly organized society, especially considering the extensive irrigation canals they built, which I understand are still in evidence in the Phoenix Basin." Anna was just getting warmed up. Her hands were no longer clenched in her lap, but actively gesturing along with her descriptions of the Hohokam.

"The physical area of Hohokam communities is huge, and there appears to be evidence that there was trade among the villages throughout that range. The presence of ball courts at numerous sites probably suggests intercommunity activities throughout much of the area."

Max asked several more questions. Anna thought she answered them well. He reached behind his desk and handed her the preliminary mapping report for their current project along with other materials about archaeological activity in Arizona.

"Our current project is a collaboration with the community college to provide excavation experience for their archaeology students. The Tortolita Mountain range has hundreds of habitation sites along its base. Right now there isn't a plan for development, but because it's prime desert land, it won't be long.

"Before you leave today, Maggie has some papers for you to fill out—all the standard employment information. Do you have any questions for me?"

"I don't think so at the moment, but I suspect I'll have a dozen after I go."

"Time enough for questions when they arise—don't be afraid to ask me or the others on the team anything you need to know."

When he stood, Anna did, too. He reached for her hand. "Welcome to Southwest Archaeological Associates, Anna."

"I can't tell you how much I appreciate—" Her voice caught in her throat and she blinked back tears.

"Not at all."

For the moment, Anna couldn't say anything beyond the simple thank you she managed.

He reminded her to drink plenty of water before leaving for the site and to bring water with her. Since it was June in the desert, they could count on a very hot day of work. "Hydration is important, and we don't want to have to call an ambulance for a greenhorn, so take it seriously. You'd be surprised at how fast you can dehydrate."

"I'll remember, Max." She promised herself that she wouldn't compromise Max's archaeological goals by doing something stupid.

❧❦

Max had said to meet the crew the next morning—before dawn—at the Lariat in the village of Catalina. The early start was important so they could work before the June heat that would come later in the day. When she told Minnie where she was meeting the crew, Minnie told her it was a legendary saloon. "Don't worry, kid, it's been years since anyone got shot there." Anna wondered if she was kidding.

Shortly after she arrived, Max drove up in a white Suburban. A couple of crew members were with him. When she got out join them, other vehicles pulled in. Several people got into Max's truck along with her, and two more vehicles carried the rest.

They crossed the highway onto a primitive ranch road, driving toward the small range. On either side of the road, the land was flat and strewn with large boulders. There was an occasional depression around which foraging cattle gathered in the hope of finding run-off water. Today, those depressions were dry, and the cattle seemed indifferent to the vehicles passing by.

At the site, the crew and the students piled out of the trucks. It was clear that everyone knew what to do. They drew the tarps off their excavation areas and set up the levels at the primary and secondary mapping datums, along with other equipment for recording the elevation and provenience of anything they might uncover today.

Anna was a little lost at first, but excited; Max led her to a sprawling mesquite tree where several crew members had gathered to watch the students get ready for the day's work. Coolers, backpacks, and field bags were scattered in the shade, and Anna added hers to the collection. Among others, he introduced her to Nick Anderson, the forensics anthropologist on the team, and to Margy, his crew chief.

It was a whirlwind at first, and Anna thought she wouldn't remember any names. Except for Nick Anderson. He was slim, but muscular, about half a head taller than she, with the greenest eyes she had ever seen. He was wearing a pair of worn Wranglers, cowboy boots, and a blue chambray shirt with the sleeves carelessly rolled up to the elbow. She stared for a moment at his sleeves, thinking how different they were from the way Foster rolled his sleeves. He wore a battered, sweat-stained cowboy hat that was pulled low over his forehead, but when Max introduced them, he pushed his hat back and looked into Anna's blue eyes and smiled.

She broke eye contact with some difficulty, feeling unsettled. She would have to be careful around those eyes.

Margy, a lithe young woman with a long, blonde ponytail, smiled at Anna. "I'm glad to meet you, Anna. Max asked me to orient you to the project. You'll be working with me for a while." Anna smiled in return.

Margy took her on a tour showing her the major features. "The site sits at the entrance to Rattlesnake Canyon, so it's called the Rattlesnake Site." Margy must have seen her eyes widen. "Don't let that worry you, though. So far, we haven't seen any rattlesnakes, but it's important to keep an eye out for them. They are definitely out and about." She swept her arm around the site. "This is a major floodplain for Big Wash, the primary drainage for the Tortolitas." She laughed. "I guess you're already aware that most of our rivers and washes don't carry water except in monsoon season."

Anna laughed with her. "I've heard that when the rivers have water, people come out to see it."

"That's true. In Tucson, rain is a spectator sport. But be warned. Many roads don't have bridges across small washes, and during monsoon, they can be treacherous. It doesn't take a lot of water to wash a car away."

"Thanks for the warning."

They walked on. "There is a wide variety of features here besides the pit houses. There are rock alignments, food processing areas with bedrock grinding stones, roasting pits, a check dam, and trash middens. Up there," she pointed, "are agricultural terraces. I'll show you some of the other features later on. For now, we're going to work here." She stopped at one of the pit houses.

"Our objectives are to remove fill to the floor, collect artifacts, record their provenience in our field manuals, bag and label them properly, screen all of the soil—" Margy stopped. "I'm sorry. I'll bet you've done this lots of times. I forgot I wasn't talking to a student."

"It's okay. Always good to have a reminder."

Margy stepped down into the feature. Much of the interior had been excavated to various levels, but none had reached the floor. There were two students already at work and another screening the soil. Margy introduced Kristen, David, and Kim. "Kim is screening today and recording information on the lot form. We rotate roles so the students have experience with everything."

Anna pushed her brushes and trowels into her back pockets, put her bucket and whisk broom into place and stepped into the feature. She knelt down, sat back on her heels, and set to work beside Margy, removing layers of soil centimeter by centimeter.

At first, she focused solely on the soil in front of her. She was excited about the work, and soon fell into the routine, recording the location of the artifacts she uncovered, collecting them, and keeping her field book up-to-date. Margy was an excellent mentor, helping her to feel at home and giving her space to demonstrate her skills.

They knelt together in the pit, each concentrating on her own work, when Anna suddenly rose up to her knees and looked around.

"Is something wrong?"

"Um ... no ... It's nothing, Margy. I thought I heard someone call my name." For a moment, she was sure she had heard Foster's voice.

His voice continued to intrude throughout the day. *Get your gear. You're going home.*

Each time, she shook it off and went back to concentrating on her work. She found several pottery sherds, mostly red-on-brown. She asked Margy to confirm her thinking. "Red-on-brown?"

"Yes, that's right. We've found a good bit of that, along with some plainware."

At the end of the day, Max walked with her back to the truck. "Margy tells me you did a good job today."

"Thanks. I loved every minute of it." She was tired, but at the same time energized by her contact with the soil and the work.

The next day they picked up where they left off, this time, with Anna screening the soil. When they broke for lunch, she sat under a tree with Margy.

"Tell me about Max. Is he a pretty tough boss?"

"Oh, yeah. He is. But he's the best. Do your work and he'll treat you right. Slack off and he'll let you know soon enough."

Anna promised herself that he would never regret hiring her.

At the end of the day, walking back to Max's truck, Nick Anderson caught up with her.

"Anna, welcome to the team. I'm sorry I didn't get a chance to speak with you yesterday." He took off his cowboy hat, revealing sun-streaked brown hair that had been pushed into riotous directions from the heat and the hat. She thought it was charming.

She smiled. "I'm looking forward to working with you. Margy told me they've found some interesting bone fragments here."

"We did." She wondered if he was self-conscious about his hat hair because he kept running his fingers through it. "There was a small piece of a human cranium near that rock alignment over there." He pointed. "We also found a piece of carved bone, something that might have been used as an awl." When he looked directly into her eyes, she had the sensation she was swimming.

She shook the feeling off. "It's a fascinating site." She turned and climbed into Max's truck.

After Max left her at her car, she drove home, feeling better than she had for a long time.

Two good days behind me and no Foster.

She was going to be fine. She was free.

6

Evanston, Illinois, February 1981

He's such a hunk," her friend Debbie had said one day over lunch in the dorm cafeteria.

"He is that," Anna agreed. "Tall, dark, and handsome—just what we dreamed about in high school." In fact, she thought he was the handsomest and most interesting man she had ever met. He was broad and tall, well over six-three, towering over her small frame. His dark hair, brown eyes, and good looks drew others to him, and many young women at the university jockeyed to be wherever he was, giggling and fawning over him.

"Have you noticed how people react to him? Even men find him interesting. And the women? They're falling all over themselves to get near him—including yours truly. When he walks into a room, people notice. It's not just his height and good looks, though. He has that—what's it called?" She paused for a moment to think. "*Savoir faire?* That's it. He's suave, sophisticated and so polished." She stretched out the word "so," and Anna nodded. Debbie sighed and leaned closer to her, whispering, "I hear he's rich."

"Does that really matter?"

"Does it matter? Of course it matters, Anna. What's wrong with you? If a man like that were interested in me, I'd play it for all it's worth. Just think, you'd never have to work and you'd have servants to wait on you night and day and you could dress in the finest clothes and furs and go to the most expensive restaurants and the theater and—"

"Enough, Debbie." She laughed. "I get the picture. But I want to work. I plan to have a career. Marriage is the last thing on my mind, and I'm certainly not going to marry for money."

"Okay, if you say so. But if Foster Robinson is interested in anyone here at school, my money's on you."

Anna dismissed her friend's comment as just silly girl talk. She couldn't imagine someone so sophisticated would be interested in a girl like her. She was from a modest, rural background, coming to Northwestern on a scholarship. She didn't dress fashionably—in fact, her wardrobe was pretty limited. Other girls worried if they wore the same sweater or skirt more than once in a week, but she barely had enough clothes to make it through a week without repeating something. Besides, she wasn't in college to show off; she was here to learn about archaeology.

Following her conversation with Debbie, she began to see that he was paying attention to her. He would often catch up with her after class and walk with her even if he wasn't heading for the same class.

When he joined her and Debbie in the campus café one day, Debbie jumped up and made an excuse about needing to hurry to an appointment with her advisor. When she turned back and winked at her, heat rose in Anna's face. She was embarrassed to be blushing with this handsome man at her table.

When he asked her out on a date, she was flattered, but cautioned herself not to make too much of it. She had never had a steady boyfriend in high school, although she had dated a few times. She had never allowed herself to trust any of the boys that had asked her out, so she didn't get a lot of second dates. It was something she owed to her relationship with her father and her fear that he was typical of the male member of the species. Boys didn't hang around long.

She could hardly believe it when Foster asked her for a second date. It wasn't long before he was seeing her exclusively. Although she wanted to proceed cautiously, he came on strong, pampering her and making her feel special, telling her he had never been more in love with anyone in his life. She was shocked that he was talking about being in love so soon after they had begun dating, but she couldn't seem to resist his charms.

He was the consummate gentleman who held doors open for her, moved to the outside of the sidewalk to create a protective barrier between her and the traffic; he insisted she wait in the car for him to come around and open her door. He sent her flowers for no particular reason, always with a sweet note. It wasn't long before Anna, so overwhelmed by an almost fairy-tale courtship, began to trust him and acknowledge her own feelings toward him.

≈⚬

As their relationship deepened, she saw that Debbie's assessment was right. He did have a certain presence that drew people to him. She could see how he used that presence to his advantage.

"I need to be sure the department chair knows who I am, Anna. I need him to notice me because I don't intend to leave the university until I have my PhD. I have my sights set on becoming the director at the Field Museum. It's a prestigious position—just right for me."

"That's very ambitious, Foster. I just want to get out and dig in the field. I'm not really interested in going that far. How do you propose to attract his attention, as you say?"

"There's a reception at the Field Museum on Saturday night—black-tie affair. It's a fund-raiser for a partnership between Northwestern's School of Anthropology and the museum. Father arranged for me to get an invitation."

"I'm impressed; I'm sure you'll enjoy it."

"You should be impressed, darling," he said. "But I'm not going alone."

"What do you mean?" On the one hand, she was afraid he was going to tell her he had another date, but on the other, she was terrified he expected her to go with him. "Who's going with you?"

"You are, darling. Who else?"

"Foster, that's impossible. I can't go to a black-tie affair."

"Don't be silly. Of course you can."

"No. No, I can't. I don't have anything to wear and I would be completely out of place."

"Of course you'll have something to wear. I'll see to it."

Even though she protested, he took her to Marshall Fields, where they went up to the top floor. He told the receptionist they needed something for the lady that would be suitable for a formal reception. They were escorted into a lounge where they were seated on a sofa in front of a platform with three mirrors arranged at angles behind it. A waiter appeared with three bottles of wine for Foster's review. He made his selection and in a few minutes the waiter returned with two glasses, a plate of various cheeses, fruit, and crackers, which he placed on the coffee table in front of them. He poured two glasses of wine.

Anna was so astonished she was sure her mouth was hanging open, making her look like the country bumpkin she believed she was.

Before she could say anything, a sales lady walked in with three dresses that she hung on a rack near the platform. She brought each one over for Anna's review. The first one was gold lamé, gathered in the front so the sides of the skirt flared and opened slightly at floor length. The second was a form-fitting dress of clear blue silk with long, ruched sleeves and jewels that circled the neckline. The third was a pink sequined number, low-cut and form-fitting with the most outrageous puff sleeves Anna had ever seen.

"Perhaps Madame would like to try one on?" The sales lady pursed her lips and waited for an answer.

"No. No, thank you." The woman turned to hang up the pink dress.

"Foster, I can't wear any of those dresses. They're awful." She said it quietly for fear of offending the sales lady.

He frowned. "What's the problem? They're not good enough?"

"That's not it. They just aren't me. I'd feel like a circus clown."

Foster frowned again and started to say something but the sales lady interrupted.

"Perhaps Madame would prefer something simple, yet elegant?"

"Yes," Anna answered. "Simple would be good. And not floor length."

"Of course." The saleslady wrinkled her nose and carried the offending dresses out of sight.

Foster looked at her. "I need you to wear something that will impress them. I don't know what was wrong with any of those dresses."

"I couldn't wear any of them." She looked down at her hands, folded in her lap. "Maybe you should go without me."

"Don't be silly. You are going to this reception."

The sales lady returned with a black silk dress, its square neckline edged in silver lamé. The skirt was street length, slightly gathered at the waist and flaring nicely. The three-quarter length sleeves were simple and edged with a narrow band of silver lamé.

"That's lovely. I'll try that one on, thank you."

In the dressing room, Anna insisted that the sales lady remove the shoulder pads. She complied reluctantly. When Anna came out for Foster's opinion, he said nothing. She turned around and looked into the three-way mirror. She liked it; she could wear it and feel comfortable.

"Shoes." Foster looked at the sales lady and said, "Bring shoes."

After Anna told her the size, the sales lady turned and Foster called after her, "And jewelry. Bring jewelry."

Anna stared at him.

"Well? You need shoes and the right accessories, don't you?"

When Anna was properly outfitted with the dress, a pair of black suede heels with silver lamé trim, a half-carat diamond on a simple platinum chain, and diamond studs for her ears, she felt completely overwhelmed and guilty that he had spent so much money on her. She had tried to talk him out of the jewelry, but he kissed her and told her, "Nothing is too good for my Anna."

She had not seen price tags, but she did see the final bill. It was more than her mother had ever made in a year. As they were leaving the store, he told her he had made an appointment for her on Saturday afternoon at Giorgio's La Bella for the "full treatment: hair, facial, nails and makeup—the works."

"Foster, that isn't necessary, is it? Can't I do my own hair? And I don't wear makeup."

"To answer: Yes. No. And you will on Saturday night."

She wondered why Cinderella wasn't as terrified as she was about going to the ball.

7

Chicago, April 1981

They often cruised along Chicago's Lake Shore Drive in his red, 1981 Mercedes 500 convertible, a car that he told her had cost nearly fifty thousand dollars. For her, riding in a fancy sports car, going to the theater or dinner, was far removed from any of her experiences.

She wondered if she would ever get used to it. Certainly the reception at the Field Museum was beyond anything she had ever done, but she actually enjoyed hearing about the plans for new exhibitions that the university would sponsor. And Foster was pleased that she had garnered a number of appreciative glances from those in attendance.

When he took her home to meet his parents, she was terrified. He didn't make her feel any better when he just laughed at her.

He told her his father was an executive at Arthur Andersen, one of the "Big Five" firms that provided accounting and auditing services to some of the country's most powerful businesses. He said his father was the force behind a new consultancy division, and under his leadership, their clients' revenues skyrocketed. He had tripled the accounting firm's profits. Foster told her that his father had found a golden goose, and life could only get better.

He turned off Lake Shore Drive and slowed to a stop in front of one of the many brownstones that populated the street. It was a five-story home built of stone, the first three stories with large bay windows projecting outward toward the street. The top story had a large arched window crowned by a stair-stepping pyramid of stone trimmed with white bricks. Foster explained that it was built in 1888 by the famous developer, Potter Palmer, who reclaimed swamp land from the lake shore and established one of the wealthiest subdivisions in the country. She didn't know who Potter Palmer was, but she was suitably impressed.

Foster drove around the corner to the alley behind the house. He reached into the glove box and pulled out a small, rectangular gadget. He pushed a button and the garage door lifted. Anna had never seen an automatic garage door opener. Her father's garage was little more than a long shed with no doors. The ceiling lights came on as Foster drove in and parked behind his father's black Mercedes, and the door closed behind them.

He got out of the car and came around to Anna's door. She was surprised at how bare this garage was. Her father's garage had been a riot of tools, both useful and useless, and the smell of gasoline had hung in the air all the time. Here, there were no tools, nothing remotely related to a vehicle. She got out and looked around, noticing the absence of any odors. Except for the presence of two cars, no one would know it was a garage.

The walls were clean and white, interrupted only by a few block glass windows that allowed in natural light, and a door that apparently led to the interior of the house. There was a large fan above the automatic door that came on just after Foster turned off the car. The faint smell of the car's exhaust quickly dissipated through the fan to the outside.

It was the fourth wall that caught Anna's attention. There were guns—rifles and shotguns—six altogether, hanging on the wall next to a tall metal cabinet that looked like a safe. Next to the display of guns were several framed photographs of various sizes.

Foster saw her looking at the guns. He smiled. "My father is the president of the Gold Coast Gun Club. It's a skeet-shooting club, but twice a year they have live pigeon shoots. Father holds the record for the most kills in an hour."

"Live pigeons?" Anna was appalled.

"Of course, darling. There's not much sport in shooting clay pigeons. They fly in a predictable pattern, but the live ones can go any direction. It takes real skill and precision to win that competition." He walked over to the display of guns.

"These," he said, pointing to several guns on the right side of the wall, "are his skeet and pigeon guns— all shotguns." He turned to look at the ones on the left side. "Now these, these are his rifles. This one—" He touched it reverently. It was sleek and polished. "This one is a real beauty. It's his big-game gun, a Weatherby 9-Lug Mark Five."

Anna had no idea what he was talking about, but he continued without noticing.

"Father allows me do some pistol shooting with him—the handguns are locked in the gun safe." He nodded toward the big cabinet. "But he's very particular about his rifles. He only allowed me to shoot the Weatherby once or twice. He believes it will be a collector's item and very valuable." He drew his hand along the smooth stock. Anna was a little disturbed by the intimacy of the gesture, but she shook it off.

He turned and pointed to the largest picture. "That's Father in Africa when he brought down an elephant with the Weatherby."

Anna looked at the picture, a large black and white print showing an elephant lying on its side in the jungle with a man posing beside it with a gun. Foster might be proud, but the sight made Anna nauseous.

Foster mistook her reaction for nerves about meeting his parents. "Relax, darling." His smile gave her strength. "My parents are going to love you just as much as I do."

He led her into the house, pausing only to say that the maid lived on this level. Before she could digest that, they had climbed up to the next floor. The dining area and living room were combined into a huge room with a polished wood floor. The walls were faced with carved walnut wainscoting.

The dining table, big enough for twelve people, was set for four with delicate china, an extended number of silver utensils on both sides of each plate, and three crystal goblets at each place setting. Anna's stomach clenched at the thought of trying to figure out which utensil to use when. She would rely on the maid to fill the proper glass at the proper time. A chandelier, modeled after an old-fashioned gas lamp, hung above the table.

At the other end of the room, the floor was covered with an oriental rug, and an antique claw foot table stood in front of the bay window. On the table stood a lamp with a beautiful stained glass shade that reflected the afternoon light. Anna had never seen anything so beautiful. The sofa and side chairs were covered in damask—*damask? How do I know that?*—and arranged artfully on the colorful rug before a large fireplace.

She looked up in time to see a tall woman coming down the stairs. Foster's mother made a grand entrance. She was wearing a floor-length, open-front red taffeta skirt over a black, street length sheath dress, with black hose and black spike heels. The red skirt flowed behind her on the stairs. Sparkling gems hung from her earlobes—real diamonds, of course. Her hair was swept into a French twist with studded combs on each side of her head. She looked at her son and spoke.

"Foster, darling, I'm so glad you've brought your little girlfriend to meet us." She took both his hands and kissed the air beside each cheek before turning her attention to Anna.

In her high heels, Grace Robinson was almost as tall as Foster; she easily had six inches on Anna. After greeting her son, she looked down at Anna without lowering her head, her smile failing to reach her eyes. She held a bejeweled hand at her neck, perhaps to show off the rings or maybe to hide the wrinkles.

"I'm so glad to meet you, Mrs.—." Anna reached out to shake hands, but Mrs. Robinson had already turned to walk away. Foster took her arm and they followed his mother to the dining table, where he immediately seated Anna on one side. Anna was surprised at the speed with which they would dine; she had expected informal conversation and opportunities to get acquainted. She was certain his mother was less than impressed with her, and dinner didn't change her mind.

Foster's father joined them, coming wordlessly down the stairs and taking his place at the table. Like Foster, he was tall, but he had combed his thinning hair up from the sides and across his head to provide the illusion of hair on the top. He was dressed in a suit and tie. He spoke courteously to Foster, barely acknowledging his wife, and only nodding at Anna when Foster introduced her. Once he was seated, the maid entered with a tureen on a tray. She set the tray on the sideboard, where elegant china in various sizes and shapes was stacked. She picked up a pitcher and filled the large goblets with ice water. Anna waited to see what everyone else did. And she waited. No one picked up a goblet. Everyone appeared to have their hands folded in their laps, so Anna did the same.

The maid placed a smaller plate on the large plate in front of each of them—she would learn later the large one was called a charger, and no food ever touched its surface. Next, the maid placed soup bowls on the smaller plate, and carried the tureen to the table to set it on Mrs. Robinson's right. She ladled a pale yellow consommé into the soup bowl from a silver ladle. She repeated this for each of them, moving the tureen from person to person and serving the same amount to each.

The soup had a few mushrooms and what looked like chives floating in the broth. Mrs. Robinson kept her hands out of sight until all at the table had been served. Then she picked up the outermost spoon and dipped it into the soup, sliding the spoon away from herself before lifting it carefully to her lips. Anna followed her lead and breathed a sigh of relief that she had, perhaps, not yet embarrassed herself, and especially that she had not embarrassed Foster. There wasn't much flavor to the broth, and she saw that Mrs. Robinson did not allow a single mushroom onto her spoon. Foster and his father both had eaten theirs.

She had actually allowed some mushrooms to pass her lips and wondered if eating the mushrooms was not lady-like.

Mrs. Robinson, having eaten about one-third of the soup, placed her spoon on the plate under the soup bowl, and looked pointedly at Anna.

"Tell me about your family, Anna. What does your father do?"

Anna put down her spoon just as Mrs. Robinson had, and tried to swallow her fears. "He was a construction engineer, Mrs. Robinson. He operated heavy equipment on construction sites. He died about six years ago."

The older woman, cocked one eyebrow and said, "I'm sorry to hear that. And your mother?"

"She was a receptionist in a doctor's office. She died two years ago." Mrs. Robinson cocked the eyebrow again and looked thoughtful.

The maid came in to clear the first course, and Mrs. Robinson watched every move she made. Anna wondered if the maid's work was satisfactory or not. When she returned to the kitchen, Mrs. Robinson turned back to Anna. "Oh, you poor child. Do you have any family?"

"I have a brother who lives in South Carolina."

"Well, I suppose that's something." She looked up as the maid re-entered the room with another tray, which she placed on the sideboard. "Edna, do be careful with that platter. It's irreplaceable." She smiled indulgently at Anna who wondered if she was expected to commiserate with the problem of clumsy servants.

During the entire dinner, neither Foster nor his father said anything. Anna looked from one man to the other. They were focused entirely on whatever had been placed before them. They never glanced in her direction, but they didn't appear particularly uncomfortable either. Mrs. Robinson kept up a continuous chatter about the ladies in her bridge club and Gold Coast gossip that Anna knew nothing about. The men merely grunted from time to time when it seemed she was waiting for some kind of reaction from them. Anna felt very alone at this opulent table. She was relieved when Edna brought out what was surely the final course.

After dessert and the after-dinner drink—the *digestif*, as Mrs. Robinson called it—Foster stood and came to stand behind Anna, who had managed to choke down the brandy without too much embarrassment. "Mother, may I be excused to show Anna the house?"

"Of course, darling. You children go ahead."

As Foster escorted Anna up the staircase, Mrs. Robinson said to her husband. "Interesting young woman, don't you think?" If Mr. Robinson answered, Anna didn't hear it, but there was a sharp edge in the question.

If Anna had been overwhelmed by the main floor, she was unprepared for Foster's room—or rooms. The fourth floor was like a separate apartment. There was a sitting room toward the front of the house, much like the one downstairs, with another oriental rug on the polished wood floor and an oversized leather sofa and chair arranged before a marble and walnut framed fireplace.

"Foster, *this* is your room? Or should I say rooms? This is bigger than any place I've ever lived."

Foster watched as she wandered around the room, looking at photographs of him on the wall and among the books on shelves. None of the pictures showed him much younger than about fourteen years old.

"Have you lived here all your life?"

He laughed. "Actually, no. We moved here when I was in eighth grade, just before I started at Lake Forest Academy. Father got a promotion and a big bonus. Mother decided we should be able to entertain in style, and so here we are."

"Don't you have any pictures from before?"

His eyes clouded over. "No, darling. Life before Elm Street was a very different time—a very different story."

She was curious about what he meant, but because he didn't elaborate, she didn't ask questions.

Like the living and dining rooms two floors down, Foster's living room blended into the dining area with a full-sized kitchen and a fully stocked wet bar at the top of the stairs. The appliances looked like they belonged in a commercial kitchen, and there wasn't an empty rack in the wine cooler.

The staircase had continued beyond the entrance to Foster's rooms. "Your parents' room—or rooms—are up there?" She pointed.

"Yes." He laughed again. "They have the top floor, our 'penthouse,' with access to the roof patio."

"What was on the floor we passed?"

"The guest suite, darling. You don't think that we would allow guests to pass by our private residences, do you?"

"Guest suite." Anna no longer raised her comments as questions; she repeated Foster's announcements, with barely disguised awe and a little discomfort at what she began to see as snobbishness.

She wandered toward Foster's bedroom, passing a half-bath immediately to the right. When she stepped farther in, she saw that there was a full bathroom as part of the bedroom suite.

When she came back into the kitchen, she said, "You have a bath and a half?"

"Of course, Anna." He gestured to her with two wine bottles. "Red or white?"

"What? Oh, yes—white, please."

He popped the cork and poured them each a glass. He handed the crystal goblet to her and lifted his own as for a toast. She responded and touched her glass against his. "To us," he said. After they had each taken a drink. He took her glass and set it on the counter with his own.

Taking her hand, he led her into the bedroom where he took her into his arms and kissed her. She put her arms around his waist as he kissed her on the neck. He slid one hand down her back and pulled her hips hard against his body. He pushed her sweater up and began to explore her breasts, unhooking her bra. He kissed her hard on the mouth. When she attempted to resist going any further, he wrapped her tightly in his arms, pinning her arms against her sides so that she could barely move.

"Foster." Anna tried to turn her face, but he covered her mouth again with his own, probing past her lips and teeth with his tongue.

Finally Anna was able to push him away. "Foster, don't. I can't do this here. Your parents are downstairs."

"So what? They know the score. It's no big deal."

"It is to me. Please. I don't want to do this here."

"C'mon, Anna," he whispered. "You can't resist me."

Anna struggled against his grip. "Please, Foster, don't make me... Please..."

Foster pushed her away. She nearly fell. "Jesus, Anna. Don't be a prig. It's not like I haven't fucked you before."

She cringed. She wondered where these occasional outbursts of profanity came from; they were out of character with the refined, sophisticated gentleman he projected to the outside world. She hated it.

"That's not the point, Foster. Will you take me home?"

8

Evanston, Illinois, June 1983

They were married just two weeks after completing graduate school at Northwestern. Falling in love had not been in her plans, but the fact that she had found such a wonderful man who practically worshiped her added to her happiness. She had earned both her Bachelor's and Master's degrees in archaeology and would soon embark on a career that she had long dreamed about. All of her dreams were coming true.

Well, almost. She didn't get to plan her own wedding. If it had been up to her, she might have talked Foster into something small and private, but there was nothing that was up to her. His mother orchestrated the entire wedding, rarely consulting her about anything.

Anna was surprised at the energy Mrs. Robinson put into the wedding, because she had been worried that her future mother-in-law would try to talk Foster out of marrying her. Surely she couldn't approve of a poor, country girl for her son. Instead, his mother appeared enthusiastic and excited. She had insisted that the Chicago social scene be properly enriched by her son's wedding, which included a number of pre-wedding "appearances" in public with Foster and his parents. To that end, she spared no expense, even taking Anna shopping for a "proper" trousseau.

Anna was grateful that her mother-in-law had better taste in fashion than the sales lady at Marshall Field's before the museum reception. She tried to persuade Mrs. Robinson not to buy so much, but it was futile. Anna decided her future mother-in-law was enjoying herself. Maybe she just liked spending money. They went to all of the best stores. She outfitted Anna in two traveling suits, several dresses, skirts and sweaters—cashmere, of course—slacks, and shoes for dress and for walking.

Fortunately, Anna was able to draw the line on lingerie. Her girlfriends at Northwestern had thrown her a bridal shower before graduation, which provided her with an embarrassing variety of underthings, so she didn't have to go shopping for lingerie with her mother-in-law..

In terms of the ceremony, Anna got through the ordeal with her dignity intact, just giving in to Mrs. Robinson's demands without an argument. She nearly stood her ground on the wedding dress, but because she wasn't buying it herself, she chose to go along to get along. The only thing that mattered was that she and Foster were getting married. She wouldn't argue with her future mother-in-law about the hideous pile of lace and brocade that Mrs. Robinson had insisted on.

The best part of the wedding was that her brother came. She had asked him to give her away. Her guest list was very short: only her girlfriends from Northwestern, two of whom were her attendants, and Howard. Like her, he had wanted to get away from their toxic household as soon as possible. He enlisted in the army and made it his career. Most of the time, she wasn't even sure where he was stationed; they didn't correspond very often. He was married with two children and had worked hard to put his painful childhood behind him. They had communicated infrequently, exchanging pictures now and then.

When she picked him up at the airport, she had an uncomfortable moment. Should she hug him or not? He was almost a stranger.

He made the decision for her, pulling her into his arms and hugging her. "Anna, it's been so long." Then he hugged her again. "How are you?"

"I'm fine, but just a little intimidated by the wedding plans and all of the events that my future mother-in-law insists on."

"You're a survivor. You'll make it."

On the way into town, he asked, "So tell me about your fiancé. You met him at Northwestern?"

She gave him a quick summary, finishing with, "And he's wealthy."

Howard looked at her. "You snagged a rich guy? Way to go, Little Sis."

Anna laughed. "It's not like that. But I do need to prepare you. Since graduation, I've been living at Foster's parents' house, and you'll stay there, too."

"They have extra guest rooms, I take it."

She laughed again. "How about a guest floor? The second floor of their brownstone is for guests."

Howard whistled. "Nice."

"Well, yes, it is nice, but I'm not altogether comfortable in such opulent surroundings, what with maids and housekeepers and a cook—"

"You're complaining?" Howard laughed. "I think I'm going to enjoy the next few days."

"Tell me about the kids and Fran. How are they doing?"

"They're great. Jeff's going into third grade and Cristy starts first grade in the fall. Frannie's planning to go back to teaching now that they'll both be in school."

The rest of the way into town, they caught up on each other's lives. Once Howard was settled in at the Robinson's, the whirlwind of wedding preparations swept him along with Anna.

Foster's parents were pleasant enough with Howard, but Foster was distant and cool. It reminded her of her own first meeting with Foster's parents, but she couldn't understand Foster's behavior toward her brother. Howard told her he would leave for the airport right after the wedding instead of spending another night at the Robinsons' without Anna there as a buffer.

At the reception, just before he left for the airport, he danced with the bride. "You look happy enough for a new bride, but something's bothering you."

"It's just…. this fancy reception… and this dress… " She leaned toward him and whispered, "I hate this dress, but Mrs. R. insisted. Who was I to argue?"

Howard frowned, "Anna, you're the bride, of course you could argue."

"No. You don't know my mother-in-law." Then she laughed.

He didn't laugh with her. "Watch yourself, Little Sis. You're going to have to watch out for yourself."

"What do you mean?"

He shook his head. "Nothing. Nothing at all." When the music stopped, he kissed her on the cheek and said goodbye.

When he got to the door, he turned and smiled at her and was gone. She stood in the middle of the dance floor alone, wondering why she was crying on her wedding day.

❖

They honeymooned in France, visiting Lascaux, and in Italy, visiting Pompeii. Of course, they went to Paris and to Venice. For Anna, seeing the places they had read about and studied in the university was a thrill. Nothing they had seen firsthand in America rivaled the age of those sites.

When they got home from their honeymoon, Foster surprised her with a house he had bought in Evanston, not far from the university. She had expected to move into his Evanston apartment until they decided what they wanted to do. Not only had he bought the house without consulting her, he hired a decorator to remodel, paint, and furnish it. Everything was finished and ready to move in, down to the wallpaper, oriental rugs on hardwood floors, paintings and pictures on the walls, kitchen ware, and landscaping. He had given the decorator freedom to choose everything and an unlimited budget. Anna was speechless when he told her the house was theirs.

He had even arranged to have all of Anna's things brought from his parents' house, where they had been stored since she moved out of the dorm. He didn't just buy the house and have it decorated, but all of their clothes had been hung up in the closets or placed in the dresser drawers. It took her weeks to find out where everything was.

She did her best to hide her disappointment at not having the chance to choose furnishings and home decor that she liked and would be comfortable with. It wasn't that the house wasn't gorgeously decorated, it just wasn't her style.

She didn't complain. She smiled and thanked him for creating a beautiful home for them. She would just have to get used to the floral prints and heavy draperies on the windows. The one thing in the house that she was happy about was the print that the decorator had hung above their bed. Foster had bought it for her when they were in Lascaux as a surprise. When she saw the print for the first time, she threw her arms around him and wept. It was the best gift he had ever given her. She would forgive him for not letting her decorate her own house—their home.

∽۞∽

It was time for Foster to start his doctoral program, and she was ready to start a career as a professional archaeologist. She had a gorgeous husband who loved her, and life was good.

As a teaching assistant, Foster was required to be on campus for his coursework and teaching schedule. His field experiences were also dictated by the program. Through the first year of his assistantship, whenever he had any field assignment, he arranged for Anna to join him. She loved being in the field, helping him gather the data he needed for his research. That he had been insistent that they always work together didn't strike her as a problem at first, but she got restless when there was no fieldwork.

Every time she suggested she wanted to get a job, he found reasons to discourage her—not the least being her need for his help. "You need me, darling; you don't quite understand how difficult the work is." At first, she was pleased that he wanted to be with her, but she grew more and more uncomfortable with his condescension and the limits he wanted to put on her.

"Foster, I don't know why you think I need your help. You know I'm a capable archaeologist and I've never had any difficulty doing the work. I can haul wheelbarrows full of dirt to be screened, and I can even operate the backhoe for trenching. What is it you think is too hard for me?"

He sighed, a bit impatiently, Anna thought. "It's not the physical work that concerns me, darling. I want to help you learn more about the work, to make you a better archaeologist." He smiled. "You do want to get better, don't you?"

She gave up arguing with him about it, sometimes wondering if she really didn't know enough about archaeology. She wanted to feel good that he cared so much about her, but it wasn't always easy.

Finally, since he didn't want her to work, she suggested they could start a family; she had always wanted children. While he wasn't very enthusiastic, she thought he agreed. She had not yet learned that Foster's silence on an issue signaled firm dissent. She stopped taking birth control pills, but over several months she had not conceived. Her doctor assured her she was perfectly healthy, and it would happen in its own good time.

Even being attentive to ovulation didn't help. In fact, Foster complained when she told him it was "time," telling her he didn't want to "perform on a schedule." And he made it clear that he did not want Anna to initiate sex. He told her he wouldn't have his wife behaving like a slut.

9

Evanston, Illinois, January 1984

Finally, she decided if pregnancy wasn't in the cards, she would work on getting a job.

Besides, maybe taking their minds off conception would be good luck.

She applied for and accepted a fieldwork assignment at a site called Kimmswick, south of St. Louis, Missouri. She had been excited about it because some years ago, a Clovis point had been uncovered in association with mastodon bones. One of her former professors, well-acquainted with Dr. Stephen Doyle, the archaeologist in charge at Kimmswick, had recommended her and urged her to accept; she was thrilled at the prospect of working with Dr. Doyle. Foster had asked her not to go, but he hadn't insisted.

He kept telling her how much he was going to miss her and that he wished she would stay. "I can't believe I'll come home to an empty house," he said over and over, each time pulling a sad face. By way of reply, she'd stand on tiptoe and give him a kiss on the cheek and laugh, never quite believing he was serious. She was foolish enough to think that he would get over his fit of pique; besides it was less than 300 miles away and she'd be able to come home once in a while for a few days.

At Kimmswick, she was happy. She loved digging and scraping the dirt centimeter by centimeter uncovering artifacts that offered silent witness to those who had come before. On the third day, she was kneeling in the pit, concentrating on lowering the hole by no more than four centimeters, focusing on each bit of earth collected. Even though she had found nothing significant, she took her collected soil to the screen for sifting. You never knew when a tiny bone fragment might turn up, the signal of a larger find just below. Whenever she found an artifact—maybe a stone tool—she added it to those already in the brown paper collection bag. Each bag was marked with the pit level and provenience for her area of excavation.

She sat back on her heels, wiped sweat from her forehead with her sleeve, and reached for her water bottle. It was then she saw him. Foster, dressed in his best gray suit and risking dust on his trousers and Italian leather shoes, was standing about ten yards away talking with Dr. Doyle. They both looked her way. Dr. Doyle nodded his head, shook Foster's hand and walked away. Puzzled, Anna climbed out of the pit, being careful not to disturb the perimeter. She was uneasy, believing something must be terribly wrong at home for him to drive five hours to get here, without even changing his clothes.

"Hi, honey," she said, accepting his kiss of greeting. "Is something wrong? What are you doing here?"

Foster smiled and put his arm around her, turning and guiding her away from the pit. "Anna, I couldn't stand it, not having you at home. I've missed you so much."

"But I've been gone less than a week, Foster. And you know I'm coming home for a few days on Sunday. It couldn't have been that bad." She extracted herself from his arm and turned to look at him. "What were you talking to Dr. Doyle about?"

He smiled. "I told him that I needed you to come back to Chicago tonight. He was very gracious about letting you out of the job."

"You told him *what?*"

Foster's smile faded and his voice was firm. "You knew I didn't want you to go, Anna, but you wouldn't listen. I need you at home."

"You need me at home?" Her voice rose and others turned to watch. "You need me at home, Foster?"

"Anna, you're making a spectacle of yourself. Calm down." He took hold of her arm and pulled her away from the rest of the crew.

She yanked her arm from his grip. "I can't believe you did this, Foster, I'm not going back to Chicago. I'm staying here."

She was angry and on the verge of tears; she hated that she could be reduced to crying whenever she got mad.

"You need me at home? To do what? Wait all day for you to come home from the university? Fix your dinner? Clean the house? I can only stand so much of that. It's not enough. I'm not cut out to be a *housewife.* I need to work."

Gentle again, he ran his thumb along her cheek catching the first tears. "I want you to work, you know that, but now is just not the right time, not when I can't come with you."

When she was shouting at him moments before, she had heard her mother's voice. She heard the yelling that always preceded what she and Howard had called a knock-down-drag-out. Her resolve faded. She couldn't let her marriage dissolve into the kind of domestic conflict and fighting that she grew up with. She would go along with him now, but she would just have to persuade Foster that she needed to work.

After she apologized to Dr. Doyle and turned her collection over to one of her pit mates, she had packed her field bag and followed Foster to the car. Alone in her car following him home, she allowed her tears to flow, first, feeling sorry for herself, then angry for allowing him to drag her away from a job, and finally trying to convince herself that Foster was right.

She had been embarrassed, but she refused to believe that he wouldn't ultimately understand, that she would finally be able to persuade him to let her work. She was restless and wanted to get her hands in the dirt and dig.

❧❧

When she saw the announcement in an issue of *Archaeology and Anthropology in America*, she leaped at the chance, thinking this time she would persuade Foster that she could go. She showed him the ad, hoping that he would finally be supportive because, after all, it was Rhinehart. They had both worked with Rhinehart Wilson several times during summers and in field schools.

He was silent on the matter, and in spite of what had happened at Kimmswick, she once again took his silence as assent. This time would be different. She went ahead with the application, making sure he was aware of every step she took.

He still said nothing. So she looked forward to hearing from Rhinehart, thinking Foster finally approved.

When, after two weeks, she had heard nothing back from her old friend, she became concerned.

"I can't imagine why I haven't heard from Rhinehart about my application." She had just returned from the store and he joined her in the kitchen. She put her purse and a bag down on the counter by the door and opened the refrigerator.

"Oh, yes–Rhinehart, he called on Monday. Forgot to mention it. Sorry." Foster's voice was casual as he went to the cabinet and reached for the plates. "Shall I set the table?"

Forgot to mention it? Rhinehart called on Monday? Four days ago? Anna turned around and stared at him, her mouth open to speak, but nothing came out.

Sometimes he was the most exasperating man, changing the subject in mid-conversation, dismissing her with the wave of a hand or turning the conversation in a totally different direction. She rarely stood up to him. In the past she had permitted him to change the subject, to force his will upon her, but not this time.

"Foster, what did he say?"

He turned his back and carried the plates to the table, not meeting her gaze. "I told him you had changed your mind about the job."

"That's not true! You know I didn't change my mind."

"Yes, darling, but you remember that ugly situation at Kimmswick, don't you? It's best for you to wait until I can go with you."

Anna was infuriated. She had never been this angry at him. *How could he do this?* Saying nothing, she walked out the back door, leaving the refrigerator open, its harsh light and chill air filling the space she had left behind.

On the patio, she watched the blood-red sun slide below the trees. She pressed hard against her scar and rehearsed the words she wanted to say. She would run back into the house and tell him he couldn't treat her this way. She would tell him just how much he hurt her every time he dismissed her like this, or when he dragged her home against her will. She would tell him she was capable of making decisions for herself, that she wasn't a child. She would remind him that she was a skilled archaeologist in her own right and could have her own career, that she didn't need him to help her do the work. She wanted to say all of this, but she wouldn't. Her anger dissipated, leaving a dull ache in her gut.

She took a deep breath and walked back into the house. Foster had finished setting the table. He glanced up at her. "There's some leftover chicken in the fridge. How about that?"

"Sure." Why couldn't she say what she wanted to say? Would it really be all that bad to sound like her mother? Why shouldn't she stand up for herself? Why should she let him continue to try to undermine her confidence?

She was afraid her marriage was unraveling.

That night, in bed, Foster pulled her into his arms. He stroked her cheek and kissed her neck.

"You're mine and I love you, Anna. You don't know how much I love you and I need you to be here for me."

Even though she didn't want to hear it, and she truly didn't want to make love, not after the way he had treated her, this was not a good time to argue with him.

"Come on, baby, relax, let me love you."

In spite of herself, she yielded to his sweet promises.

⤚•⤚

Afterwards, alone and crying in the bathroom, she thought about what had just happened. Foster was capable of being a gentle and generous lover. He knew how to give her pleasure, but whenever she had somehow displeased him, or he needed to remind her who was in charge, it was always like this—the promise of pleasure and the promise broken. She could see now how skillful he was at cruelty in bed. She could see it in the bruises on her thighs and the bite marks on her breasts.

10

Tucson, Arizona, August 1987

When Max's company won the contract to survey the site and do the archaeological testing for the new Catalina State Park and to excavate the Ramirez Ruin area, he was delighted. The park had been dedicated in 1983 after a contentious battle between legislators, local environmentalists, and developers. It was an archaeologically important site since it was both prehistoric and historic. Max would need to demonstrate the significance of the site to all stakeholders.

On the way to the site, Anna was struck by the stark differences between the desert landscape and the lush, shoreline of Lake Michigan that she had left behind. Driving around the point of the mountains— where the Catalinas abruptly end—the rugged back range of the mountains rose to the east. Long finger ridges, dotted with trees and desert scrub, spread across the land beneath the mountains. Saguaro cactuses of all sizes, some with arms pointing in every direction, stood mostly on the south facing slopes. She marveled at the extent of vegetation and how beautiful it was.

Anna parked her car near the others and got out, reaching for her field pack and water. It was already hot this morning with a promise of more heat to come. At the lower level, she noted the variety of desert plants. She was proud that she was able to name so many of them. There were creosote bushes, and trees like paloverde and mesquite. She expected to see Mormon tea and hackberry on the upper ridge. She walked to the Sutherland Wash, dry now, which, a short distance to the west, joined the Cañada del Oro Wash, coming from the north. From examining the map Max had given her, she knew that on the east side of the ridge, Montrose Wash added to the network of water sources that made the ridge an ideal site for an ancient agrarian people to build a village.

She easily spotted the ancient walnut tree, with its double trunk, twisted and black on the north bank that Max had said to look for. It looked like a tree that she would have climbed when she was a kid. It was eminently climbable. Maybe she would give it a try sometime. She smiled to think about the trees she had climbed and even hidden in growing up. Those trees had been her friends.

The trail passed the tree and crossed the wash, then wound up the ridge to a broad view of the peaks, canyons, and bajadas of Pusch Ridge, a rugged expanse of rock towers and pinnacles that make up the western end of the range. She paused to take a drink of water and to take in the view. Broad alluvial fans spread out below the ridge, blending into the lower hills and peaks. Pusch Ridge sweeps to the east, colliding with a deep canyon that cuts through the range, the contour changing dramatically beyond the canyon. Samaniego Ridge stretches northward and Mount Lemmon rises behind it. The steep slopes of Samaniego Ridge, with a scattering of green even now in summer, had its own rugged character with shallow, vertical canyons and rocky palisades along its peaks.

On the path, she spotted a few scattered potsherds. She picked up a small piece about the size of a quarter. When she turned it over she noted the red lines that decorated it. *Tanque Verde red-on-brown—Classic Period Hohokam?* Along the broken edge, mica glittered in the sunlight...

> *The sky above was suddenly a brilliant blue. The path before her narrowed; the slopes in the distance rose somehow differently. She looked down at the small jar, brown with red lines, in her copper-colored hand. On her left wrist was a shell bracelet, the bulb etched with a frog. The seeds inside were precious, and An-at would be waiting.*
>
> *Around her, the high-pitched whine of the kohtpul rose from the bushes as she hurried along the path.*

From the desert scrub, a high-pitched whine emanated, getting louder and louder. Cicadas. One began, and several others joined in the chorus, until a powerful hum filled the air around her. Just as quickly as it began, it quieted. She looked at the sherd in her hand—her own hand now—and reverently returned it to the ground where she had found it, turning it over so the decorated side was down. That way, it wouldn't attract the attention of hikers who might innocently compromise a site. Or worse, it could attract the attention of vandals and pot hunters who could destroy a site and make it impossible to learn the stories the land holds in those places.

Small lizards darted across the trail in front of her and a larger lizard with a dark collar did push-ups on a rock by the trail. As she passed, he stopped and cocked one reptilian eye at her, regarded her with mild interest, and then resumed his exercise. The leathery creature reminded her of Foster's mother, and she laughed.

She continued along the trail, taking in the panorama of the mountain range from this perspective. She had seen it from Tucson and she had seen it from the Tortolitas in the distance, but here, along this part of the back range, because it was so much closer, it was different.

It was a perfect location for a prehistoric habitation because of the promise of flowing water on three sides of the ridge. The agricultural terraces could not be far, probably toward the south. Anna had continued to study everything she could find about the prehistoric peoples in the southwestern desert, so she understood the sophisticated farming system that provided food and sustenance.

She rounded a curve in the trail and saw a cluster of people out in front of her. Max, Nick, Margy and the others were already gathered there.

"I'm sorry, Max. Am I late?"

"A little."

She hoped he wasn't upset with her.

She pitched in to get the primary site datum and the secondary one set up. It would be from the primary datum that all data—horizontal distances as well as vertical measurements below ground level in each excavation area—would be measured.

Again, students from the community college were part of the crew. Max called them together and told Anna he wanted her to join the group and hear what he had to say.

He welcomed the students, telling them that they were embarking upon an important project, one that would preserve an important prehistoric and historic site.

"We are fortunate that this site is destined for preservation. The Ramirez Ruin and the prehistoric site it sits upon will be preserved for generations to come. And much of it will remain unblemished, something that is not often the outcome of our work." He looked around the group. "How many of you students have participated in an active excavation before?"

About half of the students raised their hands.

"For those of you who have not been involved in an excavation, there are some important things you need to understand. Number one: Archaeologists are a destructive breed." He waited for that to sink in. "Does anyone know what I mean by that?"

A lanky young man in the back of the group raised his hand tentatively.

Max nodded at him.

"I think you're saying that the work we do changes a site. It's no longer what it was before we started and it won't ever be the same again."

"Good. That's exactly right. Thank you." To the whole group, he said, "I want you to remember that once disturbed, a site is forever altered. Its existence transfers from the land to the written record and artifact collection. That's why we make careful and accurate records of any data and artifacts we find.

"The second thing I want you to understand is that with our work here, we have a rare opportunity to write the story of this site, but also to preserve the reality of the site on this land, where much of its history will be undisturbed."

He continued. "My job is to prepare a report for the state when our work is finished. The park has already been established, and preparing the site for the interpretive trail across the ridge is part of the work we will all be involved in over the next several months." He looked at the group gathered before him. "Beyond that, we want to answer several questions about both periods of habitation. What can we learn about the Ramirez occupation? What evidence is there besides those stone walls?" He pointed at the remains of the small house Armando Ramirez had built. "What can we learn about the time of the Hohokam here? Especially here inside the compound walls. Do you understand the importance of this work?"

In general, the students nodded their heads.

"I hope so. One last thing. Because it's still monsoon season, we have to pay attention to the weather, and be prepared to leave the site at the first sign of lightning. Keep an eye on the clouds as they form over the mountains. Look for areas around the mountains where the rain has started. We don't want to get stuck here if the Sutherland begins to flow." He looked around the group to see if everyone understood. "Your crew chiefs will give you your assignments."

Their plan was to excavate selected areas that included both prehistoric and historic dwellings. By examining these particular areas, they would be able to develop a clear profile of the two periods of habitation. Interestingly, they had found few historic artifacts during the surface collection. There had been the occasional piece of rusted metal and some Tohono O'odham sherds. The scarcity of historic artifacts was thought to be the result of treasure hunters over the years, since legends about lost gold had spread about the site.

It remained to be seen if anything of historical interest lay below the surface. Max told them anything they could uncover would be a bonus.

⤳⤳

Anna knelt, removing layers of soil centimeter by centimeter. She was so focused on her task that she was unaware of the buzz of activity surrounding her at the site. For her, every bit of soil she lifted with her trowel and dropped into the bucket held a story. Someone long ago lived here, walked here, and worked here—maybe even died here. It was her job to find their stories. Her light brown hair was pulled back in a ponytail that had been threaded through the back of a baseball cap reading, "I Dig Archaeology."

Margy and Jesse, a younger crew member, were in the same pit, doing the same thing, while Lee was sifting the soil through a screen looking for small artifacts that might have escaped notice.

The project involved excavating four different areas of the site. Max had tasked Anna and Margy with focusing on the historic features in and near the ruins of the Ramirez house and what might be considered the yard. The other areas, the ones where historic evidence was likely to be more rare, would move more quickly to the prehistoric level. Margy's team would continue down to the prehistoric level after their work at the historic level concluded.

One crew was excavating a rectangular pit house that was inside the old compound walls. Another crew was working at the trash pit—some distance out along the ridge—and the last crew was at a circular pithouse outside the compound walls. With the exception of Margy's crew, all focused directly on the prehistoric level.

Max didn't expect to find much at the historical level, since the surface collection had yielded so few artifacts. However, he didn't want to miss anything that might be of importance that could offer insight into the Ramirez occupation.

When she and Margy were setting up their work in the area of the house, Max asked Anna what she anticipated finding.

"I was thinking, not just about the Ramirez occupation, but don't forget the gold hunters when they thought this was the Lost Mission of *Cirú*. We might find some artifacts from the prospecting." Anna looked from Max to Nick and back to Max again for a response. "In fact, Armando Ramirez had come out here with a friend looking for the gold before he registered his homestead claim here."

Nick grinned at Max. "Yeah, maybe we'll find the lost gold."

Anna laughed. "Don't be silly, Nick, I'm serious. If there's anything related to the treasure hunting, it will be a bonus, but we should get some real insight into the Ramirez occupation. The documents at the Arizona Historical Society about their time on this ridge aren't first hand. And the history is confusing and contradictory. How long were they here? The surface structures and the collection suggest not long, and what remains of their house indicates it was a fairly primitive building.

"The patent for the land was later granted to their heirs—I found a copy of it at the historical society." As she talked, she became more and more animated and enthusiastic. "Homesteading required a five-year occupation to qualify for ownership. If they lived here that long, why wouldn't the house have been improved? She swung her arm around to encompass the two-room rock-walled enclosure. "Do these remains suggest a five-year occupation? I know if my husband had brought me here to live, sometime in those five years I might have demanded that he at least put some plaster on the walls. There doesn't appear to be any plaster or any flooring except the packed dirt. There might be remnants of woven mats on the interior floor, which would suggest some effort to raise the level of comfort. Maybe we can find something concrete to give us insight into their time here."

Max nodded. "You're right. Those are some important questions. And they all relate to the questions posed for the project." He turned and walked away.

She looked at Nick. "He was testing me, wasn't he?"

"Yep." He grinned. "And you passed the test."

"Thanks, Nick." She smiled at him. "Now, let's hope I find something."

"I hope so, too. Good luck." He turned to catch up with Max and she stood for a moment watching him walk away.

She was relieved that she hadn't disappointed Max with her speculations.

Even so, she scraped the layers of soil meticulously, putting it in her bucket. Then, barely below the surface, her trowel met some resistance—a potsherd. As she removed the soil from around the sherd, she could see that it was a pretty good-sized piece. She began to find several others in close proximity to the first. She picked up two of them and brushed the dirt from them, noting that they appeared to be two pieces of the same vessel. There were several more fragments of pottery still embedded in the soil.

"Max!" Anna raised her head and looked toward the group by the tree. In a moment, Max and Nick stood by the pit looking down.

"Could be a pot break. Red-on-brown." She held up two sizable sherds that were clearly red-on-brown.

When she held them up for Max to see, she showed him how they fit together like pieces of a puzzle. "They don't belong here—this close to the surface."

Red-on-brown pottery dated to the prehistoric occupation on the ridge, so it was curious that such sherds were found at the historical house. Finding a pot break was exciting because there was always a chance it might be reconstructible. Max removed his sunglasses and squatted near the edge of the pit, watching. She painstakingly cleared the soil around the still buried sherds with a soft brush, her trowel set aside for the moment. She uncovered at least two exposed rim sherds.

Archaeology requires patience, and even with her rising sense of excitement, Anna forced herself to take her time. She paused in her work, and with Margy's help, she measured the elevation and provenience of the find, recording the data in her field book and on the bag that would hold the precious pieces of pottery. Margy took pictures.

She went back to brushing the dirt away from the sherds, removing them one by one and placing them carefully in the bag. As each piece presented itself, Anna became more and more excited. If this was, indeed, a pot break, and if she could find all of the pieces, she might be able to reconstruct it in the lab. When she uncovered an angled piece that was clearly not a rim, and then uncovered a similarly angled piece, she said, "Margy, I thought it was a bowl, but I think these are shoulder pieces—it's a jar." Margy nodded, and reached for her camera. She took several pictures of the collected sherds and the edges that peeked out of the soil.

With each sherd, it was clear they were all red-on-brown, and the faint designs suggested they were from one piece of pottery. She examined the last piece, a curved one, perhaps from the shoulder, with visible decorations on the outside. She turned it over and brushed the soil away. She licked her thumb and rubbed it gently along the inside, revealing a plain, brown interior. Her thumb came to rest in a very slight indentation that matched the size and shape of her thumb. She imagined the potter's thumb resting in this same spot as she worked the clay, and for a moment... there was no Max, no Nick, no Margy.

She cupped her hands around the jar and, strangely, her loneliness lifted. She turned it around and around in her hands, brushing the dirt away from the sides and using her apron to wipe the dirt from the inside. She carried it to the shed where she rinsed it in the horses' water bucket. She gently scrubbed the outside, revealing red lines and geometric scrolls encircling the pot. She ran her fingers along the inside of the rim and the shoulder, feeling the slightly uneven surface that had been smoothed by another woman's hands. She slid her thumb into the rim and turned it over, taking note of how perfectly round it was except for the neck that tucked in and rose up to a slightly flared rim. The round bottom was plain. She rotated the jar, sliding her thumb along the interior of the shoulder while she examined the lines and scrolls on the outside. She felt the slightly uneven interior surface and when her thumb came to rest in a small depression—she knew it was the thumb print of the potter.

In that moment, she knew the woman who had made it had also struggled for survival in this place. This jar was a gift....

She looked up, expecting to see only the mountain ridge, but instead, she saw Max and Nick watching her. Anna placed the sherds in a bag and then took her bucket of soil to the screen to sift out smaller pieces that might have escaped notice. Nick walked with her.

"Wouldn't it be great if I could reconstruct this vessel?" She was excited.

"That would be good. But what do you make of finding it so close to the surface?" She wondered if Nick was a little more than just curious.

"My guess is that Esperanza Ramirez found it and used it while she lived here."

"Mm-hmm. Could be." Nick took the bucket of soil from her and dumped part of it into the screen and watched her pull it back and forth looking for small sherds that might match the others. She found several and added them to the bag. She looked up at Nick and found him looking intently into her eyes.

"What?"

"I was just wondering... " He hesitated.

"What? What were you wondering?"

"Watching you in the pit. Something happened that I can't quite put my finger on."

"What do you mean?" Anna gripped the edges of the screen and shook it a little harder as Nick dumped a little more soil into it.

"I don't know for sure, but it looked like something came over you when you found those sherds. Maybe it's just that you are so intense when you are working." He reached into the screen and picked up a few small sherds to add to her collection.

She nodded. Nick handed her the empty bucket. As she walked away, she suspected he kept his eyes on her and her stomach did a little involuntary flip.

When she returned to the pit, Max was waiting. "What do you think?"

Anna thought for a moment. "Well, it's red-on-brown which probably dates it to the Classic period, but it definitely has a historical provenience. My guess is that Armando Ramirez's wife found it while they were living here."

"Maybe."

She wondered when she might finally win Max over. It was Esperanza Ramirez, but she had nothing to go on except her instinct.

There was no doubt Anna was in her element when she was in a pit. And here, in the southwestern desert, she had never been more at home. In fact, there was no place she had ever lived—even as a child—that had really felt like home. That she had been here more than a year and had heard nothing from Foster, that she had found this place and these people, she believed was nothing short of a miracle.

11

Tucson, Arizona, August 1987

Among the crew, there was always excitement when something important had been found. Anna's pot break stirred interest, but it would be a long shot if it could be put back together. Even so, at the end of the day, Anna was excited because she wanted to tell Minnie all about it.

Every time she got into her car, she silently thanked Rhinehart for making it possible to keep her car when she came to Tucson. He had not only gotten her the job, he had lent her four thousand dollars—no questions asked, no repayment schedule, just whenever she could get on her feet and start paying it back. She had gone to her post office box one day and there was a letter from him with a money order. It meant she could leave sooner, rather than staying with Foster over the long term. Since arriving in Tucson, she had begun making payments, and she was determined that she'd somehow find a way to repay his kindness.

She also thanked the city of Tucson for being laid out in a grid that was fairly easy to navigate. Minnie had given her a brief lesson in the geography of Tucson. She had pointed out that the mountain ranges create a frame around the city, so she would always know which direction she was going. The Santa Catalina Mountains, Tucson's signature mountain range, wrapped around the northern boundary of the city, with Mount Lemmon in the center, rising to more than nine thousand feet. She had developed a special relationship with those mountains.

East of the city, loosely connected to the Catalinas, were the less eroded Rincon Mountains. They rose upward, tucking northeast Tucson into a corner bounded by the two rounded peaks of the Rincons and the broad stretch of the rugged Catalinas. Minnie told her that *rincon,* in Spanish, means corner.

"The Tucson Mountains on the west are a crazy jumble of small points and peaks that just rise straight up out of the desert," Minnie had told her, "and the larger Santa Rita Mountains are several miles to the south."

Anna hadn't noticed that each of the ranges was very different.

"Once you can recognize each range's profile, you will never get lost in Tucson, because each mountain range is a compass point. Catalinas to the north, Santa Ritas to the south, Tucsons to the west, and Rincons to the east. Simple, huh?"

"Okay," Anna had said. "From now on I'll never get lost."

Minnie laughed. "Well, maybe. Unless, of course, you try to drive on a road that doesn't cross one of the rivers or washes. Tucson hasn't been that attentive to building bridges. You might run into a dead end at the Rillito someday."

"I'll keep that in mind." Anna loved everything about Tucson. She remembered the day she arrived, and how Minnie had become her friend—her first friend since Foster had taken over her life. She saw that as a sign. It was another indication that she had made the right move.

Usually, Minnie was home from school before Anna got back from the site, and they often got together over a glass of wine and a simple meal. Minnie had introduced Anna to southwestern cooking—her own combination of Mexican, Yaqui, and Tohono O'odham cuisine.

Minnie poked her head out of her apartment when she heard Anna on the landing. "Hey, kid! I was wondering when you were going to get home. Big day at the dig?"

Anna pulled off her baseball cap, shaking her hair loose and launching into an excited re-telling of finding the pot, but Minnie held up her hand.

"Hold on! This sounds like something that's best told over dinner and wine. I'll be right back."

Minnie came in with the wine and the glasses, set them down on the table and, as usual, rushed back out.

Anna thought that it was high time she bought wine glasses.

Minnie returned with a steaming casserole of green corn tamales with *salsa verde*. Anna put together a simple salad and told Minnie about the find while they ate.

Anna's blue eyes fairly danced with excitement about the prospect of reconstructing the pot.

"I've never done that before, Minnie. So it will be a new experience. We learned how to do it in class, but

I've never done the whole thing. I hope Max will let me try it."

Minnie thought for a moment. "I'm guessing that he will. I would be surprised if he hasn't seen how you relate to the work."

"Do you think so?"

"I do. I see it, and I've never even had the chance to see you kneeling in a hole in the ground, excavating stories. I don't have to see you in action to know that you are nourished by the earth and the stories it holds."

"Excavating stories. Yes, I think that's it." She hesitated. "I feel driven to figure out the stories in each fragment of pottery, each stone tool, each layer of soil."

"It's not about figuring them out. The fact is that each fragment of pottery, each stone tool, each layer of soil *has a story to tell*. There's a difference. You aren't figuring out the stories from archaeological evidence. The stories are already there. You *hear* the story as it is and as it has always been. You hear the songs in a reality that is yours, much like my ancestors heard the same songs and celebrated the earth."

"I've never thought of it quite like that, but it's true. The pot holds a story that I'll know when I've put all those pieces back together."

"I suspect hearing the stories is more important than the archaeology."

Anna looked up at her, fork full of tamale suspended in mid-air. She didn't answer and changed the subject, asking Minnie about her kids at school.

Minnie shared some stories about her kids and they laughed.

Anna sat back in her chair after finishing the last bite of her tamale. "Thanks, Minnie. They were delicious. Tomorrow, I'll do dinner. I'm not pulling my weight around here."

"Not at all; I'm glad for the company." Minnie looked into Anna's eyes and spoke softly, "After all, what are friends for?"

Tears welled in Anna's eyes. She stood and turned away, looking out the window over the kitchen sink, thoughtful, and once again vulnerable, as she had been when they first met. Anna had never told Minnie what had brought her to Tucson, and Minnie had never asked.

"You *are* my friend..." Anna's voice was barely a whisper. "I haven't had a friend since college."

Anna stood and looked out the window, across the parking lot and the city to the Santa Catalinas.

Minnie waited.

"When Foster and I got married, I thought I was the luckiest person in the world. I didn't have a clue... I loved him... I never loved anyone else like that in my life. He was gorgeous, intelligent, and destined for success, and I couldn't believe he had chosen me."

If Minnie was surprised that Anna had been married, Anna didn't see it. She said nothing and waited. Anna was talking more to herself and to the mountains in the distance.

"He was good to me. He was sweet and gentle—at first. He constantly gave me gifts, even though I didn't really want *things* from him. He sent flowers; he told me I was beautiful, he promised me the moon.

"But all I wanted was to be loved... All I wanted was to be me."

Anna turned away from the window. She didn't look at Minnie, but down at the floor, her hair falling forward and hiding her face in shadow. She leaned against the sink, silhouetted against the last of the evening light outside the window and continued quietly.

"Did you hear what I said? I said 'I couldn't believe he had chosen me.' That's what it was. From the beginning, I was a possession, something he selected from among all of the girls he knew. Like shopping for a car or a new suit..."

She looked up at Minnie. "We had a wonderful first year together. I didn't think I needed anyone but him, but I didn't recognize my isolation. My college friends got tired of calling with invitations to lunch or shopping. Even when Foster was at the university, he didn't like it if I went out to lunch with someone. So I just kept saying no. I didn't want to disappoint him. Or if he answered the phone, instead of telling me that I'd been invited somewhere with someone, he'd decline on my behalf."

Now she lifted her head, hooked her hair behind her left ear, and looked at Minnie. "He even declined invitations for the both of us if they came from my friends. Eventually, they quit calling." Another tear slid down her cheek, and she took a ragged breath.

"He wanted me to sell my car. I know now why he didn't want me to have a car. I'd have no choice but to stay at home—which was exactly where he wanted me.

"I can't believe how naïve I was. In spite of his efforts to isolate me, I still believed that I could be his wife and have the career I had worked so hard for. I wanted to work, but he insisted that I could only work when he could go with me, that I *needed* him. He tried to brainwash me into thinking I was a helpless twit without him. He did take me with him when he had field assignments, but it wasn't enough."

She turned back to the window and the mountains in the distance, the pink hues of sunset painting the slopes. Still, Minnie didn't speak.

Without taking her eyes off the mountains, drawing strength from them, she released the story she had been holding inside.

"I convinced myself he would finally understand how important it was to me and he'd let me do it. I believed I could persuade him to let me work."

She laughed, but without humor. "Think about it. I needed his permission." She turned around to face Minnie, anger rising in her eyes and in her voice. "I just didn't get it. I still kept telling myself he'd finally agree. Until..." She stopped talking and looked at the floor once again.

"Until when?" For the first time since Anna had begun talking, she asked a question. "What happened?"

Anna's answering laugh was tinged with bitterness. "I had offered Foster an alternative to my working. I suggested we start a family. I do want children someday, and it struck me that if I couldn't work, maybe it was a good time to..." She choked back a sob as she returned to the table to sit down across from Minnie. "When after six months I hadn't conceived, I took a job at Kimmswick, but he came and dragged me home, humiliated me in front of everyone." She looked up at Minnie. "Can you believe it? I really thought that bringing a child into our household would be a good thing. That he would settle into fatherhood and be the husband I had dreamed of."

Minnie poured her a glass of wine and pushed it across to her. She picked it up and stared into the red depths.

"In spite of what happened at Kimmswick, and because I still hadn't conceived, I thought I might be able to persuade him to let me work."

12

Evanston, Illinois, November 1984

Foster, can we talk?" He was sitting in the living room reading the evening paper when Anna came in from the kitchen. She stood in the center of the room, steeling her nerves and hoping he wouldn't get too angry. It had been some months since they had had an argument, but Anna was tired of walking on eggshells around him.

"Mmm." He didn't look up from the paper.

"Foster, please."

He rattled the newspaper as he turned the page, drowning out her plea. He continued to give his full attention to the paper.

"Foster!" She was jolted by the sound of her own voice, but he did not react at all.

Without looking up, he said, "I'm sorry, darling, you wanted something?" He carefully and deliberately folded the newspaper, and then he looked at her and smiled.

He could be so damn charming. Her spirit and determination nearly abandoned her, but she looked away from him and tried to say what she needed to say.

"Foster, I need to get out of here." That wasn't exactly what she meant. *Damn it. Why can't I say it right?*

"Indeed?" He raised one eyebrow, his dark eyes now fixed on her.

"I need to get a job." His silence only encouraged her chattering. "You don't need me here, and I've *got* to do something. For whatever reason, I'm not getting pregnant, and I can't stand being in this empty house all day—please... I want to get a job." She didn't want to beg, but she had handled it badly.

When she looked back at him, he had gone back to reading the newspaper. She was stunned by his indifference.

In the silence that followed, she could hear the ticking of the clock in the hallway and the whine of a neighbor's leaf blower. Was that what she sounded like? She was whining. She wished she could rewind and start again, but she couldn't. So she waited, trying not to touch her scar, trying not to look weak..

"No." He said it so quietly she wasn't sure she had heard him. He did not lift his eyes from the paper.

"'No'? What do you mean 'no'?"

He spoke evenly. "I said 'no.' You've done this before and you know how badly that turned out."

She remembered how humiliated she had been at Kimmswick.

"The answer is no. End of discussion." He stood up, folded the paper neatly, dropped it on the floor beside the chair, and walked out of the room.

She followed him into the bedroom.

"Foster, I don't understand. You're treating me like a child. I can't live like this." Anna stood in the doorway waiting for his answer.

He took a deep breath, and used a tone that sounded like he was, indeed, struggling with an unruly child. "Anna, my dear, I make the decisions in this house. I'm not going to chase you down at another site and drag you home. I decide where and when *we* will take field jobs. I decide where you can go and what you can do."

"You're treating me like your prisoner instead of your wife. Marriage is supposed to be a partnership."

He raised his voice a notch and she saw again how very dark his brown eyes got when he was angry. "I choose to keep you right here by my side. You will be with me on my terms. If you see that as being my prisoner, so be it. If our marriage is a partnership, you'd best remember that I'm the senior partner."

"You've made that clear, but why can't we have a normal conversa—"

"I will not share you with anyone—not anyone." By this time he was shouting.

He picked up his hairbrush from the dresser, walked deliberately toward her and shouted, "I'm sick and tired of you whining about getting out into the field, about getting a job, about having a baby." He punctuated each phrase by shaking the brush in her face. She steeled herself not to move, even though she believed he might hit her.

"Get used to it. You are not going to work unless I am with you, and you are certainly not going to have a baby!"

She took a few steps away from him, and when she was able to speak, her voice shook, "Not...? What do you mean? We were hoping I would get pregnant. I haven't been on the pill for over a year."

"No, my dear—*you* were hoping, but it isn't going to happen. I could fuck you every night of the week and twice on Sunday and you still wouldn't get pregnant."

He turned away from her and walked back to his dresser, where he put the brush down in its place.

"Why?" Anna's voice was barely a whisper.

He turned back to face her. "Because, my dear, I've had a vasectomy."

Anna's disbelief was written in her blue eyes, in sharp contrast to his dark, hateful eyes. "You got a vasectomy and you never told me?"

"I planned to tell you when the time was right." Foster's earlier loss of control had been replaced by a calm and condescending tone. "I guess the time is right now, isn't it, Anna?"

She struggled to maintain her composure, leaning against the door jamb for support. She folded her arms across her chest, hiding her clenched fists. She wanted to smash him in his arrogant mouth, but she couldn't do what her mother had done for so many years.

"When?"

Foster strode across the room until he was towering over her slender frame. For the first time, Anna returned his gaze evenly, seeing in his eyes something that had not registered for her before, and suddenly aware that it had been there all along.

"The week before we got married." He smiled at her, holding her gaze until she broke it.

He might as well have punched her in the stomach.

13

Tucson, Arizona, September 1987

One Friday morning, Anna was sitting with Nick over lunch in the shade of a paloverde tree. She had just unwrapped her sandwich when Nick asked her if she knew anything about horses. "I rode a little bit when I was a kid." She smiled at the memory. "A friend had horses and I spent as much time at her place as I could." She didn't say that she wanted to be anywhere but home, and that the horses made her feel good about herself. "I wasn't a terrible rider, but I wasn't a particularly good one either."

"I've got some horses and they get awful bored with me." He pushed his hat back off his forehead, and Anna noticed the transition from his tanned forehead to the pale skin at his hairline. He affected a cowboy twang. "I reckon they'd be mighty grateful for a little variety."

For a moment, she wasn't sure what he was saying, but she laughed at how he said it.

"That is, would you like to come out and go for a ride with me? Explore this desert without a trowel in your hand?"

It was a tempting invitation. She thought about how much she had wanted a horse more than anything in the world, a horse that she could love, and get unconditional love in return. That there was little enough money to feed the family, let alone a horse, had not occurred to her. She just kept hoping she might someday have one of her own.

So it wasn't a hard decision. It had been so long since she had gone riding and, like he said, it was a good way to explore the desert. Nick grinned when she agreed. He told her how to find his place some ten miles north of the Ramirez Ruin. Anna had to remind herself not to get involved.

I'm just going riding. What could it hurt?

On Saturday morning, she drove out past the site to the dirt road that led to Nick's place. When she turned in, she was pleased to see the back range of the Catalinas spread before her with Samaniego Ridge sweeping northward. Nice. Nick had these mountains in his back yard. She passed a few small houses along the road with horses standing in dirt-covered paddocks behind them. When she came to the house she thought was Nick's, he was just coming out the door. He waved and put on his ever-present cowboy hat. She drove through the gate under an arched sign that said, "Two Ravens Ranch." She parked her car beside his pickup.

His was a neat, single-story home built of adobe bricks. There was a bougainvillea growing up a trellis on the end of the house, and a few mesquite trees shaded the front yard. Behind the house, she could see several outbuildings and a fenced enclosure where the horses stood in a straight line along the fence, watching them. Nick laughed. "Somehow they know when I'm planning to ride. Then they compete to see who gets to go. Sometimes I have to ride them all, one right after the other. They love attention, but they can wear me out."

Anna laughed with him. While they walked to the gate, she pulled her hair back into a ponytail and threaded it through the opening in the back of her baseball cap. It was her "digging 'do," and it would work for riding, as well. When Nick opened the gate, all four horses came to them. There was a buckskin, two brown bays, and a sorrel mare. It was the buckskin that caught Anna's attention. His soft, brown eyes looked into hers and she fell in love. He stepped toward her and pressed his soft nose into her hand, not looking for a treat, but sniffing, learning her. Anna rubbed his nose and caressed his cheek. He must have decided she was okay because he nickered softly.

"He's beautiful, Nick. I've always been partial to buckskins."

"Looks like he approves of you, too. In fact, Paco's your mount today."

"Hello, Paco," Anna stroked his neck, and he nickered again.

Nick reached for one of the halters that hung on the fence by the gate and slipped it over Paco's nose and buckled it snugly. He handed the lead rope to Anna, and she waited while he haltered the mare. "This is Sadie; she was the first horse I bought after I moved to Tucson permanently. She's fifteen years old." Nick patted her neck and led her toward the gate. Anna followed with Paco, who walked respectfully beside her without crowding or pushing. The other horses followed them along the fence until they could go no further. Anna wanted to ask where he lived before, but it might lead to him asking her the same question. She wasn't ready.

Nick led the way to the tack shed and hitching rail. He tied Sadie at one end and reached for Paco's lead rope.

Instead of handing it to him, Anna said, "Let's see if I remember how to do it." She wrapped the lead rope once around the rail, then made a loop through which she pulled another loop. She did that three times and then stepped back.

Nick said to Sadie, "I think we have a ringer here." To Anna he said, "How long has it been since you rode?"

Anna laughed. "It really has been forever. I can't believe I did it right."

Nick handed Anna a curry and a brush. She turned to Paco. The sun was warm on her back and Paco's body was warm to the touch. She brushed him all over. He stood quietly, eyes half-closed, relaxed by her touch. She turned to the grooming box, putting the curry and brush back and getting a mane and tail brush. She could feel Nick watching her.

And again, without asking for assistance, she went back to the grooming box to get a hoof pick. She bent over and touched the back of Paco's front leg. He lifted his foot and she cleaned it thoroughly and then did the other three. When she was finished, she looked up to find Nick still watching.

"It's amazing how it all comes back to you."

"Like riding a bike—you never really forget how." Nick smiled and turned to pick Sadie's hooves. While he did that, Anna watched him. His shirt-sleeves were rolled—the same carelessly rolled sleeves as when he was working. She took in his tanned, muscular arms working with Sadie's hooves. *He's a good man, an attractive man.* In spite of herself she was drawn to him. The question was whether or not she could keep her distance, and she wondered if she would regret spending this day with him.

When Nick was finished, he went into the tack shed and grabbed a blanket and saddle pad in one hand and a large western saddle in the other. He stepped out and lifted the blanket and pad into place, smoothing them on Paco's back. Then he easily swung the saddle up and onto the horse. He hadn't asked Anna if she wanted to do the saddling herself.

"Thanks," Anna smiled at Nick's back while he cinched up the girth. She stepped in close to watch him handle the rigging. She liked standing that close to him, but she told herself it was only to watch him tighten the cinch.

"When I was a kid, we rode English. I could throw one of those saddles up on the horse, but I don't know about that big western one."

"You'll learn it in no time," he said. She wondered if that was an invitation to come back as many times as she wanted to.

He hung a horn bag on the saddle with a bottle of water, then hung the bridle on the horn. Anna talked quietly with Paco, standing close to his head and caressing his face, while Nick saddled Sadie. When he was ready, suddenly Anna was nervous. It had been so many years; what if she made a fool of herself?

As if reading her mind, Nick said, "Paco's a great horse; you'll be fine."

"I didn't grasp how tall he was until you put the saddle on him."

"No problem." He brought a three-step mounting block out of the tack room and put it down next to Paco. He slipped the bridle on, putting the right rein over Paco's neck and holding the left rein. Anna stepped up onto the mounting block. Nick didn't tell her what to do; he just waited.

She held out her hand for the left rein and reached up for the right one. Holding both in her left hand, she grabbed a handful of mane, stepped into the stirrup, and swung her right leg over easily. "Mane and rein," she said. "That's what I was taught."

"That's good—you never know when your horse—even a good one like Paco—might decide to move away while you've got one leg in the air."

Nick moved Paco away from the block to adjust the stirrups. He took hold of her leg and moved it forward while he adjusted the left stirrup, then drew it back so she could test its length. He did the same on the right side, then put his hand on her knee. "How's that?"

She pressed her heels down and lifted out of the saddle once or twice to test the fit. "That's good. Thanks." She noticed that he left his hand on her knee longer than he needed to.

She watched while he bridled Sadie and then swung easily into the saddle from the ground.

He rode up beside her, and for the first time, offered some advice. "Paco neck reins. You probably used direct reining when you rode English." He demonstrated one time.

ࢶ∾ऒ

They rode slowly from the barn, past an arena, and picked up a trail that headed out toward the Catalinas. After an initial burst of nerves, she settled into Paco's comfortable walk. Where the trail was narrow, she stayed behind Nick, noting details about him.

His hat sat squarely on his head with an air of authority. The back of his neck was tanned and his torso narrowed at the waist; his slim backside was settled comfortably in the saddle. She found herself comparing his body to Foster's. Foster was muscular, as well, but he was broad and tall, and he would never look this comfortable on a horse. Nick was lean and not as tall. She pictured him without his shirt. She suspected a farmer tan—untanned except where his bare arms were exposed to the sun. She smiled.

She shook her head. *God, what am I thinking?*

She shifted her focus to the horse beneath her. She patted his neck and watched his head move rhythmically with his stride. The trail widened. Nick rode slightly to the left and looked back at Anna. She squeezed Paco lightly, and he stepped up beside Sadie. They rode side-by-side in silence, with only the scrape-clop of the horses' hooves on the sandy trail to accompany them. Without Nick's back to distract her, she looked around at the desert.

The trail wound through what could only be described as a cholla forest, with hundreds of the wicked cactus, in many varieties, growing abundantly. She said, "This would not be a place to get bucked off your horse."

Nick laughed. "I'd say so. I'm not sure any place is a good one, but those cactus are particularly evil. Pay attention whenever there's one close to the trail. Paco knows how much room he needs to pass it without getting caught, but he doesn't take into account the space your leg needs."

"I'll remember that."

It was the first time they had spoken since they left the barn. For a moment, she was sorry that she had broken the spell.

The desert opened up around them, with prickly pear and barrel cactus scattered among mesquite, paloverde trees, and other desert scrub. Several of the prickly pears were collapsed and black, with pack rat middens in them—they might have their own stories to tell if you dug in to find out what the rats had stored there. Whiptail lizards raced across the trail now and then, and she looked up to see a red-tailed hawk circling above them. Cactus wrens scolded as they rode past chollas with nests in the branches. Sparrows and finches sang from the trees and occasionally a small flock of quail flew up from the scrub or doves would scatter with a squeaky fluttering of wings.

She spotted the twisted remains of several trees with their interiors burned and black. Nick told her that a fire about twenty years before had burned through the area, so most of the vegetation now at this level was relatively young.

"Tell me about Two Ravens Ranch. Is there a story behind the name?"

"Not much of a story, really. There's a pair of ravens that live and nest somewhere nearby, although I've never quite figured out where. They made friends with the horses. They sit on the fence and talk to them."

"Talk?" Anna looked skeptical.

"Not real talking—even though ravens have been known to mimic human speech, I haven't heard it. No. They have a big repertoire of vocalizations— clicking their beaks, or making a knocking sound in their throat is common, and a kind of gurgling croak. Sometimes they sound like a crow—you've heard them before haven't you?"

"That's what I thought they were when I first got here, but they were too big, and someone told me they were ravens."

"Anyway, these two ravens came so often to hang around with the horses, it's like they named the ranch for me."

"I like it. Maybe I'll meet your ravens sometime."

"I'd like that." When Nick smiled, her heart began to beat a little faster.

She shifted her gaze to the panorama of the Catalinas rising up before them. From this angle, she could see the crest of Mount Lemmon behind Samaniego Ridge and the deep cut of Ramirez Canyon at the elbow, separating the two main components of the back range, Samaniego trending northward and rugged Pusch Ridge turning toward the west, its multiple peaks and pinnacles sloping downward to where the main road swept past on the way north.

She was more at peace than she had been in a long time. She remembered when she arrived in Tucson and saw the mountains from the plane, she had had the sensation of coming home—something she had never experienced before. Again, here in this beautiful desert landscape, she had the same feeling. She was home here. She looked back at Nick and found him looking at her.

"You're happy here." It wasn't a question; it was an observation. "I'd like to think the company has a little bit to do with it."

"Oh, yes," Anna smiled and patted her horse on the neck. "Paco is great company." Nick opened his mouth to say something, but nothing came out. Anna burst out laughing and he laughed with her.

"Seriously, Nick, this is wonderful. Thank you for inviting me."

"My pleasure, ma'am," and he tipped his hat in her direction, his eyes twinkling in the sunlight.

They rode for almost two hours, sometimes in conversation, sometimes in silence, but always in communion with the desert. When they got back to Nick's and she tried to dismount, she was suddenly aware of how long it had been since she had ridden a horse. Her right leg didn't cooperate with her brain, and when she extracted her left foot from the stirrup in the manner of an English dismount, her right leg was still on the other side of the saddle.

Nick jumped off of Sadie and came running to help. He reached up and took hold of her waist and held her while she managed to get her leg over. When he lowered her to the ground, he did not step away.

His body so close behind her was frightening, yet she didn't want him to let go. She struggled to keep her breathing measured and even.

"Well, that was graceful, wasn't it? Thanks for the hand." She turned around, but Nick still didn't step back. Now she was standing with a sixteen-hand horse behind her and Nick just inches in front of her. She looked up and he lowered his face to hers. She turned her head a little so his lips only brushed her cheek. Her legs were shaking, and it wasn't from fatigue.

"Please, Nick, no." He stepped back.

"I'm sorry Anna." He turned abruptly and went to unsaddle Sadie.

Anna stood there trembling, fighting back the tears.

She took a deep breath and tried to pull herself together. Nick stood at the tack room rail with his back to her brushing Sadie. She led Paco to the other end of the rail and looped his lead rope over it.

Unsaddling him was an easy distraction. She struggled against the knowledge that she wanted to go to Nick and wrap her arms around him and allow whatever might happen. But she couldn't do that. They said nothing as they put the tack away and brushed the horses down from their ride.

After she checked Paco's hooves, she looked up. Nick was waiting with Sadie. He said, "We'll put them in the barn; it'll soon be feeding time." She followed him and Sadie and found the stall with Paco's name. She unhaltered him, hanging it on the hook, just as Nick had hung Sadie's. Then she followed Nick to the paddock to collect the other horses. They led them in and put them into their stalls.

"Thanks. I'll come out shortly and feed them." Nick's embarrassment was obvious; he looked everywhere but at Anna.

"Nick, I'm sorry..."

"Don't... Anna. Please. I'm the one who's sorry. I shouldn't have..." There was something more in his eyes than embarrassment. She wasn't sure, but she thought it was pain, and she was surprised that her refusal might have hurt him. If it *was* just her refusal...

"Nick, let me explain."

"You don't need to explain, Anna. You're not interested."

"It would be so much less complicated, Nick, if that were true." He looked into her eyes for the first time since he had tried to kiss her.

She took a deep breath and said it before she could change her mind. "Nick, I'm married."

"Married? You're married? Why did I think you came to Tucson alone?"

"I did, but it's a long story that I'd rather not go into—not now, anyway. You're a good friend and I don't want to spoil that. I just can't get involved until I can get out of the horrible mess I've gotten myself into."

He softened. "Anna, if you need me..."

"I know, Nick. I appreciate it, but it scares me."

When she looked into his eyes, she could lose herself in a way she had never done with Foster, and it was terrifying.

He walked her to her car and said, "Be careful, Anna." He put one arm around her shoulders and hugged her gently.

When she got into her car, Nick closed the door and leaned down to look in the window. "Let's ride again sometime soon, okay?"

She nodded and started the car.

She looked into the mirror and saw Nick standing there watching her drive away.

When she got to the end of the dirt road, she stopped and sat, thinking, her finger pressed to the scar. Nick was a wonderful man, and she believed he was her friend. She wasn't ready for him to be more than that—at least that's what she told herself. That she had two good friends, Minnie and Nick, was more than she had ever imagined could be possible.

14

Tucson, Arizona, September 1987

When she arrived at the site on Monday, Max was already there. Nick was setting up the level next to the pit where Anna had found the pot break.

"Hey, guys, ready for another exciting day of discovery?" Her gaze came to rest on Nick as he straightened up from adjusting the level.

Nick looked up and smiled from under the brim of his cowboy hat. His eyes caught the light of the morning sun as it peeked over Samaniego Ridge.

"Always."

Anna smiled back at him, finding the light in his eyes comforting.

Max looked at Nick and then at Anna. He frowned. "Good morning, Anna. Congratulations on finding a pot break. That was a good find."

"Thanks." She hesitated. "Can I ask you a question?"

"Sure. What is it?"

She pointed to an odd collection of cobbles scattered near the compound wall. They were separate from the old wall and the house foundation. In nature, an alignment or cluster of the same kind of rocks might be natural, but when a variety of kinds of rocks are aligned or clustered together, it suggests human activity.

"I think that's an intentional feature. The stones may have come from the old wall, just as the stones for the house had, but it doesn't look like a place where the wall had collapsed. I'd like your permission to investigate it more closely."

Max studied her for a moment. "Okay, but we've only got so much time. I'll put Margy with you, but I'm going to need her elsewhere later this morning."

"Thanks." When she turned toward the feature, she saw Nick standing some distance away. He gave her a thumbs up and turned to supervise the rectangular pit house crew.

She and Margy established the perimeter for the feature and recorded its location in their field manuals. Together, they knelt and began to systematically remove a layer of soil with their large trowels, setting the cobbles outside the perimeter. She decided that Max was probably right; it might not yield anything of interest, and she really should quit trying his patience. There was just something about this spot that she couldn't put a finger on. She decided that once the cobbles were out of the way, she would move straight down to the prehistoric level, where more interesting artifacts might be found.

"Okay," she directed her thoughts to the earth, "if there's nothing here that will open a window into the Ramirez occupation, let's just move on."

In a moment, her trowel snagged on something. *Not a sherd; not another cobble.*

"But what?" She said this last aloud, and Margy looked up and watched her as she worked to expose the find.

It was a piece of fabric, probably a discarded rag. It might provide insight into one kind of material common to the time period, and little else. Before continuing, she recorded the initial provenience, and asked Margy to help her with the horizontal and depth measurements.

She continued extricating it from the soil. The cloth had taken on the same color as the soil; there was no immediate way to determine the original color. As she exposed more and more of the piece, it became clear that it was relatively large—surely more than a rag—and quite fragile.

As she worked, she was determined not to destroy it. She was curious about finding such a large piece of material, thinking it might be a discarded article of clothing. She ruled out the idea that it was something casually discarded because it appeared to be layered, bundled, or wrapped, not simply spread out in the ground. The more convinced she became that it wrapped something, the more careful she was about extracting it.

She laid her trowel aside and ran her finger along a ragged edge, seeing for a moment the delicate, white lace that had once been a part of this garment. When she lifted the edge, she saw blood. Not the dry, brown stains of more than a hundred years later. It was red, a deep red flood that covered the ground before her eyes.

Her firstborn child was delivered at seven and a half months. When the pain and the pressure subsided, she tried to sit up to look for her baby in the terrible pool of blood and tissue. She could see the lifeless baby's head, his dark hair matted and wet. It was a boy. With great difficulty she pulled off her bloody petticoat and gently wrapped her baby and his afterbirth. She wrapped it around and around, as one might swaddle a newborn, until the cleanest parts of the white lace were on the outside.

She held her child to her breast and sang to him.

"Dulce niño, duermete ya.

Es hora de descansar."

She slept for a while, holding her infant in her arms and dreaming of watching him running in the yard and chasing the chickens.

Much later—she wasn't sure how long—she pulled herself from the bed, and carried her child outside. She did not even look at the rifle, which was still lying just outside the door. There was no sign of Armando—not yet. He wouldn't be here until tomorrow, but maybe it was already tomorrow—she wasn't sure.

She stumbled across the yard to the old compound wall near a pile of loose rocks. She lay the baby down gently, picked up a flat rock and began to dig in an area where the ground was not so hard. When she had succeeded in

*making a shallow depression, she laid
her baby gently in it. She scrubbed her
hands down the front of her skirt and
then stroked his tiny head and prayed.*

*How could she cover this child?
She wished that 'Mando were here;
she needed his strong arms to hold her
and tell her it would be all right. But
he was not here, and if she were to die,
she could not leave her baby untended,
unbaptized, and unprayed over.*

*The silver crucifix had hung around
her neck since her wedding day. Today
was the first time she had ever taken
it off. She stared at it, trying to banish
the fear that Jesucristo had abandoned
her. "En el nombre del Padre y del Hijo
y Espíritu Santo..."*

*Naming the baby Ángel, she prayed
to Santa Therése y La Virgen, to inter-
cede for his spirit. Then she touched the
cross to her lips, and tucked it gently
into the folds of the bloodstained petticoat that wrapped her stillborn child.*

*She pulled the layers up and over
his face, and tucked the dirt around
and over him as if it were a blanket.
Still on her knees, Esperanza raised her
eyes toward the mountain.*

*The Apache stood no more than fifty
yards from where she knelt.*

*Those dark eyes, hooded beneath the
red bandana that wrapped across his
forehead, those eyes, set wide apart in a
hard face that betrayed little, those eyes
looked directly into hers and penetrated
the depths of her grief. Somehow, for a*

moment, she was comforted. He shared her grief; she was not alone. Turning her attention back to the child, resting in this crude dirt cradle, she said aloud, "Mando, our baby is dead, and when you return you will find me dead as well. Lo siento, por favor."

Anna finally looked up at Margy. "Would you go ask Max and Nick if they can come take a look?"

"Sure thing."

∾∾

Margy stepped out of the shallow pit and looked around for Max. He and Nick were under the tree talking with some students.

In a few moments, both men were standing beside the pit. They watched as Anna continued to expose the fabric bundle.

Finally, it appeared that the bundle had been fully exposed. Nick ran to his pickup and came back with a blue tarp, which he spread out on the ground next to the pit.

Lifting the edges of the bundle, she brushed under it in an effort to loosen it from the last grip of the soil. In spite of her care, when she tried to pick it up, several pieces of the fabric were torn away and remained fast in the ground. She placed the bundle on the tarp and then freed the remaining scraps of cloth, adding them to the tarp. She stared wordlessly at it.

Nick squatted down and examined the bundle very closely. "Look at this. These darker stains, probably not just dirt, and there, on the edge, that looks like the remnants of lace or an embroidered edge."

"The petticoat," Anna whispered.

As a forensics anthropologist, Nick's specialty was examining the human remains they often encountered in their excavations. He began to unwrap the bundle.

The cloth was extremely fragile and in lifting the delicate layers, some of them disintegrated in his hands.

Just as he was ready to lift another layer, Anna said quietly, "The crucifix."

Nick looked up sharply. Max and Margy stared open mouthed at Anna and then looked back at the bundle.

When Nick lifted the layer, he exposed a silver chain.

He lifted the chain and the sun caught the object that hung from it. A crucifix. Again, everyone stared at Anna.

"It's a burial—likely a baby." His voice cracked and he laid the crucifix down on the tarp beside the small bundle. Nick pinched the bridge of his nose, pressed his thumb and forefinger against his eyes and put his sunglasses back on. He abruptly stood and walked some distance away, keeping his back turned to the group. He took off his hat and looked toward the mountains for several long moments.

Anna looked questioningly at Max, who just shook his head.

Nick ran his fingers through his hair and put his hat back on. He came back and picked up the crucifix again, examining it closely, and then he set it aside. He picked up layers of the cloth, noting the darker stains.

Now his voice carried the dispassionate and objective tone of a forensics anthropologist examining an artifact. "These stains could be blood. Perhaps the Ramirez woman delivered a stillborn child which they buried here, or the child died sometime after being born. I'll need to examine any bone fragments. The degree of ossification will give us a clear idea." He paused and drew in a breath before continuing. "It could tell us if it was a premature birth or a childhood death."

Disregarding the curiosity of the others about her own behavior, Anna was curious about why Nick had walked away, and now his sudden businesslike analysis of the find. She placed the chain and the crucifix on the ground next to a ruler, and Margy photographed it. Before putting it into the artifact collection, Anna drew the crucifix in her field book, noting the measurements. She sketched the pattern of the links in the chain and noted its length.

She stopped to watch Nick wrap the bundle of cloth in the tarp and label it. When he picked it up, he cradled it in his arms in the same way someone would hold an infant.

Through tears, she stared at the bundle in Nick's arms. He carried it to his truck, where he gently placed it on the floor.

15

Tucson, Arizona, September 1987

Two days later, Anna went to the lab after work and found Nick examining the fabric bundle that she had uncovered. She stood quietly and watched him.

He was using fine-point tweezers to pluck small fragments from between the layers of fabric.

He was sorting them into two containers: one appeared to be twigs, leaf fragments, and other natural materials; the other held only a very few small slivers. There was a third container, but he had covered it with a small towel. His expression was very serious.

She waited until he paused in his exacting work to speak. "You're finding bone fragments?"

"Yes. Very likely from an infant—maybe premature. Ossification is incomplete, but there has been some mummification." He laid his hand on the covered container.

Anna did not ask to see it.

Nick continued, "My guess is these slivers might be from a rib cage, and this small concave piece might be from the hip bone." His voice carried the dispassionate, professional tone again.

Anna stared at the small bone fragments. "How sad for her. She must have had a terrible ordeal." She spoke softly. "They were pretty isolated out there, with the Apache raids and no help nearby."

"Max asked Maggie to locate any descendants or family members that are still in Tucson to let them know that we found an infant burial. They may want to claim the remains and have a proper burial." His voice had softened.

Anna nodded. "That's good, Nick. Esperanza's spirit will be able to rest when her child comes to her."

Nick's expression shifted into something Anna couldn't read. He took a breath, cleared his throat and said, "There's a fresh pot of coffee in the office. How about we get some?"

She hesitated.

"Come on, Anna; it's just coffee. I won't bite." The words hit her harder than they should have, and she could only think of Foster. Involuntarily, she pressed her hand against her midsection, below her breasts.

When she looked up at Nick, he smiled, his laugh lines swallowed by his tan.

"Sure. Thanks, Nick." She walked ahead of him toward the office. They each filled a styrofoam cup. She added both cream and sugar; Nick took his black. They stepped back out into the lab and sat down at one of the tables.

Anna looked around the lab at some reconstructed pots and other artifacts that filled the shelves around the perimeter walls. Each one had a code number that identified the specific location where it had been found.

At the back of the lab were several shelves holding the collections from the Ramirez Ruin excavation. Everything was carefully cataloged and recorded in preparation for the transfer to the museum for curation.

"I know you've been to the state museum before, Anna, but have you seen the massive collection of artifacts not generally available to the public? There is an astonishing collection from Emil Haury's work at Snaketown." He paused while she was thinking. "In fact, they have one of the largest collections of Southwest Indian pottery in the nation. It's quite impressive."

"I'd love to see it, but..."

"Anna, I'm not asking for a date. Honestly, I just thought you'd like to see the collections."

"You're right, Nick. I would."

"Great! There's an open house on Saturday. We'll be able to see those collections. How about ten o'clock?"

"Sure. That works for me."

"It's a date then—sorry, I didn't mean..."

"Nick, it's okay." She laughed.

"Can I pick you up at your place?"

"I'd rather meet you somewhere if you don't mind." She was still determined to maintain a distance between her and Nick. She wasn't sure what she was starting to feel for him, but she needed to slow things down.

"Sure."

❧❦

When they came out of the museum after their tour, Nick suggested they get lunch at the student union.

"Nick, that collection is amazing! I have so much more to learn about southwestern archaeology."

"I'm impressed at how much you have learned about the archaeology hereabouts in the short time you've been here."

He smiled and, once again, she was lost in his gaze. She pulled herself together. "It's been easy, Nick. Working with Max and you and the rest of the team has been marvelous." She sighed. "I just hope I can gain Max's trust. Sometimes I think he's uncertain about me."

"Don't worry. He sees your talent. He's just not always quick to show it."

"Thanks. I hope so." She hesitated. "I'm so glad I came to Tucson. I think I've found my home." She fell silent and Nick waited. "Finally."

Changing the subject, she said, "Tell me about yourself, Nick. I've known you now for over a year, but I don't really know very much about you." This was no sooner out of her mouth when she wished she had bitten her tongue. He might say the same thing to her.

"I'm sorry—you don't have to—."

But Nick kept talking. "I grew up in Southern Arizona. In Bisbee, a mining town in Cochise County down near the Mexican border."

"I've heard of Bisbee."

"It's a fascinating town—lots of history. I'll take you sometime. You'll like it."

"That would be nice."

For a moment, Nick just looked at her. She wondered if he was trying to decide if she was serious.

"After high school, I came to the University of Arizona. I took archaeology and anthropology and then did my Master's degree, focusing on bioarchaeology and forensics. I started working with Max after graduation, and I've been there ever since."

"And your family?"

"My mother still lives in Bisbee. My dad died about six years ago." He paused. "I still miss him. He was a good man—taught me a lot. Worked many years in the Lavender Pit mining copper. It's what killed him in the end."

Anna hesitated. "And you've never been—?" She caught her breath; what was she thinking? "I'm sorry..."

"Married? That's what you were going to ask?" Nick gazed over her shoulder, but Anna thought he was looking at something far beyond the students passing by.

Anna nodded. "Yes. But I shouldn't have—"

"The answer is no, I've never been married." He paused and looked past her again. When Anna looked, among the throngs of students moving along the sidewalk, there was a couple holding hands and laughing. She looked back at Nick; he was watching them.

His voice went very quiet. Anna had to lean forward to hear him amid the noise of students coming and going around them.

"Her name was Rita. She was a freshman when I was a junior. I met her in the old museum basement. She was doing research for her intro course and I was picking up site survey files for one of my classes. She was beautiful..."

Nick stopped. His silence went on until Anna thought she should release him from saying it. "You don't have to go on, Nick."

"No. I need to talk about her. I haven't talked about her for ten years. I put her away and tried not to think about her ever again."

"I'm sorry, Nick—"

Nick raised his hand, palm outward. "I want to tell you. For some reason, I *have* to tell you." Anna waited for him to go on.

"She was beautiful. She was bright and vibrant and had a great future. I thought we were going to be a great team—something rivaling the Leakeys. We would travel the world and revolutionize thinking about prehistory.

"When I graduated, she was entering her junior year. We moved in together and I began my Master's program. She was so smart. Everyone in the department recognized her talent. She had a full ride for her Master's degree and would have easily made it into the doctoral program.

"We were going to graduate together. She with her Bachelor's and I with my Master's. We thought the world was ours." He hesitated. "But then we found out she was pregnant."

Anna struggled not to react. It occurred to her she really didn't want to hear the rest, but she couldn't ask him to stop. She reached across the table and put her hand on Nick's. He covered her hand with his other hand, holding it tightly.

"We were really happy about it. I was walking on air thinking about being a father, but I was scared. It was a lot of responsibility. I needed to get a job as quickly as possible after graduation so I could take care of her and the baby when it came. That's when I met Max and got a job lined up with him. He was kind enough to consider me more than a shovelbum. Maybe he thought I had something to bring to his company. I'd like to think so, anyway."

He drew in a deep breath before continuing.

"It wasn't an easy pregnancy, but she managed to get through her classes and her final exams. The baby was due just weeks after graduation. We believed everything would be fine, but suddenly things weren't fine. She started spiking unbelievably high blood pressure and her legs and ankles swelled so badly she could hardly stand. She had headaches and heartburn. She was miserable and there was nothing I could do to help her." His voice broke.

"The doctor decided to induce labor. Neither she nor the baby—a little girl—survived." Nick's green eyes were dry and focused on some distant scene, but Anna's tears ran freely.

"Oh, Nick. I am so sorry. I never wanted you to relive that pain."

He finally looked at her. "It's okay. I think I needed to say it. I've never talked about it. I've kept it inside for all these years. Maybe it's time for healing." He looked into her eyes. "I'd like to think you came along to help me finally deal with it."

He wrapped both hands around Anna's hand and lifted it to his lips. He brushed a kiss along her fingers where they threaded through his own. She was surprised that she let him. She lifted her other hand and brushed his hair from his forehead and drew her hand down along his cheek.

16

Tucson, Arizona, September 1987

After Margy and Anna finished working on the historic features at the site, they turned their attention to the excavation of prehistoric features. While they were setting up, she spoke to Margy. "I don't think I've ever thanked you, Margy, for helping me get started here."

"Not at all. You don't have to thank me, you brought enough talent with you that I don't think I made a big difference."

"You did. I appreciate your commitment to finding the stories buried in the soil."

Margy smiled. "I never thought of it quite like that, but, yes, that's how it is." She reached out and took

Anna's hand. "There was something about the baby's burial that really got to you, didn't it?"

Anna wondered whether she was referring to her shared experience with Esperanza Ramirez. She was not ready to talk about these things that often happened to her occasionally when she uncovered artifacts. When she was a kid, finding projectile points in the field, she thought it was just her imagination, but it was more than that. She wasn't sure how others would view her excursions into the past and the stories she uncovered, so she kept quiet about it.

"It's the idea that her baby might have died when she was out here alone. Even if her husband was with her, can you imagine going through that?"

Suddenly she was angry. "He brought her out to this ridge with no one else around... What if she didn't want to come? What if she had other plans for her life? What the hell is wrong with a man who just wants to control his wife?"

She thought Margy knew that her anger was not directed at Armando Ramirez because she said, "Anna, if you need me..."

"I know. Thanks, Margy."

They moved to the rectangular pit house that was opened the day before inside the compound wall. As they worked their way down layer by layer, they found a number of artifacts, including a tabular knife—one that would have been used to cut agave leaves or other vegetation—several good-sized potsherds, some spindle whorls, and some small fragments of shell.

She and Margy continued working in silence, each intent on their work. Suddenly, Margy called to Anna.

"Anna, come look!"

She was uncovering a shell bracelet, likely from a *Glycymeris gigantea* shell, from the Sea of Cortez, where the Hohokam often traveled to collect shells for trade goods. When Margy had released it from the soil, they saw that the circle was broken with an inch or more missing. The umbo was intact.

Using a soft brush, Margy gently brushed the dirt away revealing a horned toad etched on its surface.. Anna held out her hand. "May I?"

Margy handed her the bracelet...

> *She scanned the horizon once again, sweeping her gaze along the path the men must follow to reach the village. She rubbed her thumb along the smooth curve of the bracelet Tonrai had made for her. But there was still no sign.*
>
> *She sighed and turned around to return to the compound. Without warning, she was face-to-face with Yukui. He seemed to have simply materialized before her; she had heard nothing and his movement barely stirred the air. He gripped her wrist and locked eyes with her. Ha-wani struggled against his grip, but she could not break eye contact. A cold wave engulfed her and suddenly the village and the mountains slipped away.*
>
> *She was sliding into darkness.*
>
> *She heard a voice calling from the darkness, "Ha-wani, you are mine." She was terrified, struggling against the darkness. The voice was not Tonrai's. Only he and her parents knew her spirit name.*
>
> *Suddenly, a pain shot through her arm and the spell was broken, the spell in which Yukui held her.*
>
> *She broke eye contact and jerked her arm from his grip. She turned and ran as fast as she could, stopping only*

to catch her breath before entering the compound. She looked behind her and saw no one. She ran inside and ducked into the dim interior of her dwelling. She knelt down against the wall and tried to control her panic. She stayed there, alone and trembling. No one had seen her return.

Eventually, she heard voices outside. "Have you seen Older Daughter-in-Law?"

Then Ra-naa spoke. "She was going out on the ridge to look for the men."

Ha-wani struggled to stand and made her way to the entrance. When she stepped out into the sunlight, her mother-in-law gasped, "Daughter, what happened?"

She looked down and saw blood pumping from her arm and dripping down her hand. There was both dried and fresh blood, but she wasn't sure where it had come from.

Her sister grabbed a skin and wrapped it tightly around Ha-wani's wrist. Her mother-in-law led her to the family work shelter and sat her down by the low fire. She gave her a gourd with a little water in it. Ha-wani sipped the water.

"What happened?" Her sister gently unwrapped the skin to reveal a deep cut on the inside of Ha-wani's wrist.

"I'm not sure... I was out on the ridge looking for signs that the men were coming. I don't remember..."

Anna was breathing heavily.

"Anna, what happened?"

"I'm not sure... I don't remember." She wrapped her fingers around her wrist and squeezed.

Anna shook her head, pushing the memory away. She took a deep breath and handed the bracelet back to Margy. They recorded the provenience after Margy took pictures and drew the bracelet in her field book.

17

Tucson, Arizona, October 1987

Once the excavation was done, Max tasked Anna with teaching the volunteers and students how to clean the many potsherds that had been found during the dig. She demonstrated the steps, emphasizing the importance of protecting any designs that might be on the outer surfaces. She told them too much vigorous brushing or leaving them in the acid solution too long could erase any designs that were hidden by dirt or *caliche* deposits.

When the students finished for the day, she reminded them to organize the sherds for drying so someone else could pick up where they left off, keeping all the sherds from each collection bag together. They would later label the pieces and put them back into bags. Anna washed the potsherds she'd found at the Ramirez homestead herself.

It was a Late Rincon, maybe Tanque Verde, red-on-brown pot. That would mean it had been made sometime between 1100 and 1300, near the end of the Hohokam habitation at the site. There was some decoration on the outside, which she hadn't clearly identified in the field. For some, it was a mystery that it was found at the historical level, but Anna was certain the rancher's wife had found it intact and used it. This was a vessel that held the stories of two women: the Hohokam woman who made it, and Esperanza Ramirez, who had used it. She took to calling it Esperanza's pot.

Although she did not quite understand why she had been entrusted with these women's stories, she accepted her role as the jar's personal guardian. She was determined to see it pieced together and find out what else it had to tell her.

During the cleaning, she watched as years of dirt and caliche lifted, revealing a relatively clear pattern of red, geometric scrolls. It appeared that there might have been a second color besides the red, maybe white, but Anna couldn't be sure.

When the sherds were clean and dry, she would ink small, coded, identification labels on the inside surface of each one. Then she could begin to put the puzzle of Esperanza's pot together.

ᏤᎧ

She was pleased that Max had given her permission to work on the pot, but he had cautioned her to work on the reconstruction on her own time, not on company time. They had other projects scheduled and he wanted no delays. She believed if she could do it, she would finally have Max's approval; he would recognize her abilities as an archaeologist. No less than that, though, she needed to do it for herself.

On Saturday, she came back to the lab. Gently, she removed the sherds from their bag. She placed them on the table according to their sizes and whether they were rim, shoulder, or body pieces. There were two large pieces—the ones she had shown Max on site—several rim pieces, some undecorated ones that might have been bottom pieces, and a large number of smaller fragments, the smallest no bigger than a dime.

Anna turned each piece over, examining the inside and the decoration on the outside. Some of the pieces looked like simple plainware, with little evidence of decoration. But looking closely, she could see traces of the lines that had been there when the pot was new. As she examined the sherd for the painted design, she thought of the woman who had made this jar.

Her brown hands worked automatically, smoothing the thick coils of the crude jar resting in the puki. She picked up a river rock and gently pounded the inside of the vessel, pressing the clay outward until the sphere was close to the thickness she wanted. Then with her paddle, a flat, smooth piece of wood, she slapped the outside of the vessel while holding the rock inside to protect the shape as the sides of the jar thinned. She turned the vessel around and around, pounding the sides and the bottom, stopping now and then to pluck out a bit of leaf or a twig that stuck in the clay or to dip her paddle into the precious water and drop a bit of water onto the rock.

*She sang to the clay; she sang to her
hands as they worked; the pot would
hold her song and bring blessings to the
People.*

*The earth is our mother
Who sustains us
She honors us with gifts
We respectfully use her gifts
And honor her by giving back
The gifts of the earth
The gifts from the earth
The earth is our mother
Who sustains us*

*Ha-wani watched her hands as the
jar took shape. Her long, brown fingers
and blunt nails wore the stains of the
clay and seemed to dance of their own
free will.*

Anna felt the cool, damp clay in her hands.

⮧⮦

She picked up the two largest pieces and began the
delicate task of puzzling them together. She turned
them so that she could watch the outside decoration
and color for alignment. Holding one piece in her right
hand, she carefully turned the one in her left, testing
for a fit along the broken edge. Her hands moved slowly
and deliberately, holding the fragments gently. 'Round
and 'round she turned the piece, finding no match. She
turned the pieces over and examined the polishing
striations on the inside. They would have to match,
just like the outside decorations. Turning them edge
to edge, finding near fits, she could not find a precise
match. Maybe the key was in the rim pieces, she
thought. Holding the largest piece of the rim against a

line on a diameter template, she measured the curve of the fragment. It would be about eighteen or nineteen centimeters across when it was reconstructed—if she was successful.

Taking two of the rim pieces, she held them up, first on one side and then on the other. A rim fit should be obvious; after all, it's easy to tell which way is up. The fit should be easy to see. None of the rim pieces matched. Anna sighed and put the pieces down. She wondered if she had thought this jar would reconstruct itself. She rested her elbows on the table and massaged the back of her neck.

She looked at her watch; she had been sitting there for over an hour. She stood up, arched her shoulders back and stretched. Stepping away from the table, she bent over at the hips and alternately flattened her back and then rounded it, stretching and relaxing her muscles. Then she sat down and looked at this broken pot.

"Okay," she said, "let's get this done."

She examined the body pieces again, looking at each one carefully. She noticed some mostly undecorated sherds, some with smoke clouds from firing. They were all curved, and a few had a simple red line—it was a jar with a round bottom. It was here that the bottom of the pot began, curving downward into a rounded base. The line separated the design from the base. It would be an indicator of the jar's height if she could make a connection between these base pieces through the body to the shoulder and the rim. Identifying other base pieces would be significant in organizing the pieces for reconstruction. She would know in which direction to orient those pieces with the shoulder, the rim and other body pieces.

On a hunch, she picked up two sherds from the base, both with a red line, and began turning them in her hands, looking for a fit.

"Come on," she whispered, "talk to me." For a fleeting moment, her hands moved independently of thought. And there it was. The two pieces fit together perfectly.

> *She did not have to think about her work; her hands simply worked the clay. She dipped her fingers into the precious water, shaped the neck evenly and smoothed the rim slightly, turning the vessel as she worked. Using a small, smooth stone, she polished the outside of the jar. She was already imagining the red and white interlocking scrolls she would add to the outside once it was ready.*
>
> *When the vessel was finished, fired, and decorated, it stood apart from those of the others. It was a rounded jar with a short, straight neck and a wide mouth. The interior had been smoothed by her gifted hands...*

Just as suddenly as it happened, it disappeared. Anna was here, in the lab, and she had a pile of pot fragments before her.

She picked up the two pieces again and held them against one another. This time, her own hands held a portion of a Hohokam jar, the base from which the remaining sherds would rise. Using a small tube of adhesive, she laid a thin bead along the edge of one fragment, touched the matching edges together, and pulled them apart. Then she applied another thin bead on the edge of the opposite piece and pressed them together again. This time she held them firmly, marveling at the fit. She clipped a clothespin on each end of the seam. She stood the joined pieces in the sandbox, pushing sand around the bottom to support them while they dried.

"How's it going?"

Anna started. She hadn't heard Nick come in to work on his own project. Laughing, she turned and looked at him across the room. "I'm sorry. I didn't know you were here."

"That's a fine thing—I've spent all this time trying to get your attention, and now you tell me it's been for nothing." Nick put on a long face that failed to disguise the twinkle in his eyes.

Suddenly nervous, she stood up and began to clean up her work area. She collected the remaining pieces of pottery and put them into their labeled bags. She pushed the sandbox toward the back of the worktable and concentrated on wiping up the area, knowing that all the while Nick was watching her. When she was finished, she stuffed her journal into her bag and turned to leave.

Nick was standing there, blocking her path to the door. She was still unsure if a relationship with Nick was a good idea, and, in spite of her attraction to him, which terrified her, she didn't want to lead him on. It would be awkward, if not plain rude, to just duck around him and go, so she directed his attention to the two pieces of the pot that had come together.

"Look at this," she said, pulling the sandbox back to the edge of the table and lifting the joined pieces from their sand cradle. Reluctantly, he took his eyes off hers and looked at her work.

She watched his face; he could tell her what kind of clay it was made from, and where in the Tucson Basin the clay had been collected. She had not yet learned about the various clay deposits that had been in the area for thousands of years.

As Anna resettled the reconstructed pieces in the sand, Nick said, "How 'bout we go out for a cup of coffee?" She looked at him and then quickly averted her eyes, concentrating on cradling the potsherds in the sand. He had told her his story, and she had told him nothing. Sometimes she thought he could look at her and know what she was keeping back, and it scared her. When she looked into his eyes, it was like he was seeing more than she was ready to share.

"Nick, you know I can't."

"No, I don't know you can't, Anna. All I'm asking for is a cup of coffee. You act like I'm asking you for your soul." His words startled her. She was afraid to look into his eyes, afraid she would find every reason to give him her soul.

"You keep asking me not to say it, Anna, but I have to. I'm beginning to feel something I haven't felt for more than ten years. As much as I've tried to deny it, I can't any longer. Here you are, and I can't help myself."

He scanned her face, as if memorizing every feature. He lightly put a finger on her cheekbone just below her eye.

"What's this? How did you get this scar?"

She reached up and put her own hand on his. "I had chicken pox when I was about eight years old."

He laughed lightly. "Didn't your mama tell you not to scratch them?"

"Yes, but it's impossible not to."

Neither of them had moved. Nick kept his finger on the scar and she kept her hand on his.

"I understand impossible," he said and tilted her face upward and kissed her softly.

She relaxed into the kiss and kissed him back.

She had to force herself to step away.

"I'm sorry, I promised Minnie I'd meet her at 3:00, and it's 2:30 now." Anna picked up her bag and slipped past Nick and out the door, leaving him standing there, smiling.

18

Tucson, Arizona, October 1987

Y ou know, Minnie," Anna said, "I didn't tell you about it when it happened, but I had the strangest feeling when I was uncovering those sherds. I turned one over and on the inside there was a depression in the clay. I put my thumb on it and it fit perfectly. I touched the *thumb print* of the potter. I was overcome by the strangest feeling—a connection, a kinship somehow." She hesitated to say it, but she had to. "I was making the pot myself."

"Of course you were."

"Then today," Anna rushed on. "I know you'll think I'm crazy, but when I was having the most trouble finding a fit between the pieces, I paused for a moment and..."

Anna looked at Minnie, ready to judge if she would think Anna had lost her mind. "I spoke to the sherds, and then they went together perfectly. I don't remember consciously moving my hands to bring them together. But there they were, together in my hands."

"You're not crazy. That was real."

Although Minnie was agreeing with her, Anna still tried to convince her.

"But it was as if I had touched *her,* almost that I *was* her. For a moment everything around me disappeared, and it was just me molding the pot from the damp clay."

"You *did* touch her. The clay brought her to you. Every piece of ancient pottery on this land has a maker, and a story, and a song. They say 'the clay remembers the hands that made it.'"

Anna stared at Minnie.

"Tell the truth, Anna. This has happened to you before, hasn't it? And not just with this pot?"

She hesitated before she answered. She had never told anyone about what she privately called her little excursions into the past.

"Yes, but I'm not sure I understand why it happens."

"Remember when I told you that the artifacts you uncover have stories to tell?"

"Yes, but I didn't think it applied to me. I wasn't doubting you, but I'm not Native American. Why would I have that kind of relationship to the earth?

"You don't need to be Native American and you don't need to know why it happens. Celebrate it. Open your mind and heart to the stories the earth wants you to hear.

"Anna, you cannot doubt your kinship with the earth. Your work keeps you close to it, and you are part of it. You revere every cubic inch of soil you lift from it. Pottery is made from the earth, Anna. It is the very earth you are dedicated to. Don't dismiss what happened today. Your spirit has achieved a higher plane—your spirit and the spirit of the potter have come together."

Anna frowned. "Is it possible that I've really made that connection?"

"I don't know if the Hohokam held beliefs like those of my people, but it's likely. The Yoeme, my people, are a spiritual people. Our individual responses to the world come through the relationship of our spirit to the various spiritual worlds around us.

"Plants and animals are our brothers and sisters; we honor them for the gifts they provide." She paused a moment while Anna considered that idea.

"There are five spiritual worlds: *Sea Ania,* the Flower World, which is the essence of goodness and beauty. It is not just the physical world of flowers, but your spiritual world, where your spirit, your *hiapsi,* resides. *Huya Ania,* the Wilderness World, *Yo Ania,* the Enchanted World, *Tuka Ania,* the Night World, and *Tenku Ania,* the Dream World." Each time Minnie spoke her language, Anna heard the echoes of time in the sound.

"Everything in the physical world, and beyond, connects to these spiritual worlds. When we enter into one of these worlds, our own spiritual powers are enhanced. *Sea takaa* is part of you, it is in you. It is a special power you are born with and if you have *sea takaa,* then you will be protected from evil. It is the protective energy of your *hiapsi.*

"Your living spirit was here before you were born, and it will be here after you die. It connects you to everything that ever was, is now, and ever will be. The pot carries the spirit, the song of the potter." Minnie paused while Anna thought about that.

"You entered that world. Your spirit recognized it."
She looked at Anna thoughtfully. "Do you speak to the
earth when you are working?"

"I've never told anyone, but, yes, I do." She
laughed. "Not out loud because everybody would think
I'm crazy."

"What do you say?"

"Most often, I'm thinking, 'Tell me your stories,'
'Let me into your world.' Things like that."

"And...?"

"And I always say, 'Thank you' when the earth
gives me one of her stories."

Minnie went on to explain that among the Yoeme,
when they receive gifts from the earth, they leave an
offering—a song or a prayer. "I suspect the Hohokam
women did much the same. They may have spoken to
the earth as they took its clay and then left a prayer or
a song in thanks."

Anna nodded. "In some ways, my simple 'Thank
you' is offered in much the same way as a prayer. I will
be more direct with it now."

Minnie continued. "They also may have sung
special songs while shaping their pots, polishing them,
and firing them so it would be strong enough to last
long after the tribe was gone. Those songs remain in
those bowls and pots for eternity.

"There's a book I use in my classroom. It's called
When Clay Sings. It's by a local writer and it talks
about the songs in those ancient potsherds we can find
in our desert." Minnie quoted a line:

> *'Even now the wind sometimes finds
> one of those songs still in the clay and
> lifts it out and carries it down the can-
> yon and across the hills. It is a small
> sound and always far away but they say
> sometimes they hear it.'*

Anna drifted out of the moment into another one, remembering the song she had heard, that far away song. When the moment passed, she looked at Minnie, who was smiling.

"I heard it. I heard her song," Anna whispered. "It was as if I was singing it."

"You've been to the *Huya Ania*." She lifted her wine glass. "May its gifts be abundant and may the songs come to you on gentle breezes."

"But why would I also feel a connection with Esperanza Ramirez? She didn't make the pot."

"You told me that she had possibly found the pot and used it, isn't that right?"

"Yes."

"Well, the song and the story were in the pot when she found it."

Anna thought about it.

"Can I ask you about something else that happened, something else I saw?" Anna wasn't sure she could explain it, but she really wanted to understand what she had seen when she held the shell bracelet.

She told Minnie about her terror when she believed that someone was stealing her soul. That she could not break eye contact with those dark eyes. And thinking that he should not know her spirit name.

"I was really terrified for a few moments. What does it mean, my spirit name?"

Minnie was not surprised when Anna described what had happened.

"It's another indication of how closely your spirit is connected to the *Sea Ania*. When we are born, our parents name our spirit, but it is not for others to know. We are protected from those who might harm us by not sharing that name. Some time after birth, we are given a worldly name, that others may know.

"You've probably heard that the eyes are windows to the soul. In our belief system we take that literally.

Only those people we are closest to—our parents, and our 'soul mates'—are welcome to look us in the eyes. It is disrespectful to look into someone's eyes. For my students, this is a serious problem, because Anglo teachers will say, 'Look at me when I'm talking to you.' They don't understand that for many Yoeme children, that is a bad thing."

Anna nodded, but instead of thinking about what had happened when she held the bracelet, she was thinking about the difference between Foster's eyes and Nick's eyes, that looking into Foster's eyes was terrifying when he was angry. Looking into Nick's eyes... well, that was something altogether different.

"You said that you had a sudden pain in your wrist that broke the 'spell' as you called it?"

"Yes, that's what saved me... her..."

"That makes sense. Physical pain can overcome the unconscious situation."

Anna thought about that. "The bracelet was broken. Maybe when he grabbed her wrist, he broke it and the shell cut her."

Both of them were silent for several long moments.

"Am I really reliving moments in that Hohokam woman's life?"

The next day, Minnie brought Anna a copy of *When Clay Sings*, by Byrd Baylor. "My students love this book because it affirms their own histories. It makes them proud."

After Minnie left, Anna looked through the book. It was beautifully illustrated with drawings of ancient images often found on the artifacts of the Hohokam.

> *There are desert hillsides where ancient Indian pottery still lies half buried in the sand and lizards blink at other dusty lizards that were painted on these pots a thousand years ago.*

Byrd Baylor's words spoke to Anna. She understood her own connection to the earth, like one of those lizards who blinked at the ones painted on the pots.

> *They say that every piece of clay is a piece of someone's life. They even say it has its own small voice and sings in its own way.*
>
> *They say that even now the wind sometimes finds one of those songs still in the clay and lifts it out and carries it down the canyon and across the hills. It is a small sound and always far away but they say sometimes they hear it.*

She was comforted to know that those little pieces of someone else's life and the small, singing voices she often heard were real. She looked forward to hearing the music again.

19

Tucson, Arizona, October 1987

When Anna arrived at the lab on Saturday, Nick was already there and waiting for her.

"I thought you'd want to know. Maggie found the descendants of Armando and Esperanza Ramirez and they'd like to know more about the infant remains we found."

"That's great news, Nick. When will you meet with them?"

"We," he answered. "We will meet with them. I want you to go with me."

"Thanks. That means a lot to me."

"I know."

Rosie Espinoza was a great-great granddaughter of Armando and Esperanza Ramirez. She agreed to meet with them at Max's office before taking them to visit her mother, who was not well. "My mother suffers from congestive heart failure, which has gotten worse in recent months, so she has become more and more frail. I told her about your findings and she's eager to talk to you, but I don't want her to get too tired out. She still lives by herself, but we have an LPN who comes to see to her needs on those days that none of us can be there with her."

Anna promised that they would do their best to make their visit pleasant for Mrs. Siqueiros. She described the discovery of the child's remains, and then Nick explained how his analysis suggested that the child was probably premature, as opposed to dying as an infant.

Rosie nodded and smiled. "I think you will find my mother's story very interesting." She stood. "You can follow me, but just in case we get separated, you'll need this." She handed them a paper with an address in Barrio Anita.

Mrs. Siqueiros' house was a neat little adobe on a small lot in the historic barrio. The front yard was dirt, and a large spineless cactus grew at the corner of the house. There were two mesquite trees, neatly trimmed, on either side of the walk. The front door was bright blue. The window trim was a bright orange. Other small homes on the street were not as neat and well kept as this one, but some were painted in bright colors with a variety of colorful trims.

Anna commented on how nice the house was. Rosie laughed, "There's one thing about my mother. She insists that her house will never be an eyesore. My brothers take care of things here before they can do it at their own houses." She stepped up on the low stoop and pushed the blue door open. She stood back and let Anna and Nick enter the dimly lit living room.

The curtains were drawn against the afternoon sunlight. The interior of the house was every bit as neat as the outside, and there was the pungent, but delicious, smell of something cooking. They followed Rosie into a small sitting room just off the living room. Esperanza Siqueiros was sitting in a rocking chair with an afghan across her lap. She looked up as they entered the room. On the table beside the chair was a battered shoebox.

Rosie introduced them and invited them to sit on the small sofa. "Rosita, *por favor,* get our guests something to drink."

"Yes, *mami.*" Rosie nodded, and left the room.

Mrs. Siqueiros looked over her glasses at Nick and Anna without speaking. Anna smiled. "I'm glad to have this opportunity to meet you, Mrs. Siqueiros." It occurred to Anna that she looked much older than her 79 years.

"*Gracias.* I am likewise pleased to meet you both. Rosita tells me that you have been investigating *mis bisabuelos'* old ranch and that you found something you thought the family should know about."

"That's right," Nick answered. "We found what we are sure is an infant burial and we think it may have been a child of your great-grandparents."

"And what makes you think that?"

Before Nick could answer, Rosie came back bearing a tray with two glasses of *horchata*, a sweet Mexican beverage, and a steaming cup of tea. She put the tray down and placed the tea beside her mother's chair, then handed Nick and Anna the cold drinks.

"Thank you." Nick and Anna said it at the same time. Mrs. Siqueiros smiled.

Nick went on. "The remains were found relatively near the surface, which would indicate that it might date to the time of your great-grandparents' occupation on the site. The remains were wrapped in some lengths of cotton fabric that were likely a petticoat from that time period as well."

"I see." The old woman nodded, and then waited. "And this was wrapped in the fabric with the remains." Anna reached into her bag and pulled out the crucifix and held it up for them to see.

Both Rosie and her mother gasped. Mrs. Siqueiros' eyes watered and she closed them for a few moments. Rosie stood and reached for the crucifix. "May I?"

"Of course." Rosie took the crucifix, turned to her mother, and placed it in her hands. Mrs. Siqueiros cradled it in both palms and looked at it for a long silent moment. She looked up at Rosie and said, "Show them."

Rosie opened the box. It was full of loose pictures, some old and faded, some a bit newer. Rosie lifted one of the pictures out of the box and handed it to Anna.

It was Anna's turn to gasp. Nick leaned closer to look and quietly said, "Wow."

The picture was a wedding photo. The bride wore a long, white dress with a *mantilla* of exquisite lace draped over her head and hanging to her elbows. She was seated, and the groom, dressed in a dark suit, stood slightly behind her with his left hand resting on her shoulder. Their somber expressions failed to show their happiness, typical for photos from that time period. Hanging from a chain around the bride's neck was a silver crucifix, identical to the one Mrs. Siqueiros held.

"This is Esperanza and Armando's wedding picture?" It was a foolish question, but somehow she needed confirmation. "She was beautiful."

"*Sí. Estos son mis bisabuelos.*" Mrs. Siqueiros looked up, not at Anna or Nick, or even Rosie, but off into a distance that Anna could imagine.

Nick asked, "Can you tell us about them?"

"My great-grandfather wanted a ranch out there beyond the mountains." She waved her hand in a non-specific direction. "It was very difficult and very lonely. I don't know much about their lives there, but I do know that eventually the Apaches ran them off. They never went back, but they had a good life here in Tucson after they came back. They had several children and Armando made a very good living farming along the *Rio Santa Cruz*. *Mi abuelo*, their eldest son, claimed the land that his father had homesteaded, and he built his own ranch. Not up on the ridge, but down below, along the wash. He put up a windmill over the well that my great-grandfather dug." She paused.

"I remember going out there and playing in the wash. *Mi hermanos y mi hermanas*, we would climb the big walnut tree to see if we could get as high as the windmill blades. I can still hear the squeak, squeak of the blades as they turned in the wind. If it was very windy, it was fast—*rapido*, if not, it was a slow, lazy squeak, squeak." Her speaking slowed as she imitated the sound.

She spoke quietly, all the while pulling the silver chain back and forth through her fingers. The crucifix lay in her lap.

"The family said *Bisabuela* Esperanza never talked much about her life out there, but the family knew she had lost a child. Nobody ever said that the child had been buried there. Maybe they didn't know; maybe they thought that it was a miscarriage.

"When she was very, very old and near death, they tell me that she spoke to an angel. She would say '¿*Donde es Ángel?*' She sang a lullaby over and over again. *Mi madre* sang it to me and I sang it to Rosita, *Dulce niña, duerme ya, es hora descansar.*" As she sang it softly, Anna silently sang the words with her.

"They told me she kept repeating, '*En nombre de Dios, por favor traiga a mi Ángel a casa.*' And then she would struggle to find the words. *Mi abuelo* said she cried almost every day."

"My grandfather and my uncles and aunts liked to tell the story that *Bisabuela* Esperanza talked with an angel before she died."

"Do you think she had named the baby Ángel?" Anna thought her question brought Mrs. Siqueiros back from that far-off place she had gone.

"Yes, I suppose that could be it. But the child would not have been baptized. That must have been a terrible thing for her to take to eternity with her. It is no wonder she struggled with the child's loss when death was at her door."

Nick suggested that they talk to the priest. "We will turn the remains over to the family if that's what you'd like."

Mrs. Siqueiros was silent, sitting in her chair, rocking slightly and rubbing the crucifix. Anna noticed that the tarnished silver was beginning to shine under the constant attention of her fingers.

"Mrs. Siqueiros. May I tell you something?" Anna wasn't sure where she was going with this, but she had to say it. The older woman nodded and waited for Anna to go on. "I don't know why, but for some reason I feel very close to your great-grandmother." She looked at the photograph in her hand. "When I uncovered the baby's remains, it was as if I was sharing her grief and her loneliness."

"*Gracias.*"

"And there was something else we found during our excavation that might offer some small detail of her life there." Nick was silent as Anna spoke softly.

"*¿Que és?*"

"We found a broken vessel which probably dates back to the time when the Hohokam occupied the site, but it wasn't at the prehistoric level. It was very close to the surface. It is definitely of Hohokam origin.

I think your great-grandmother may have found it when she was digging her garden, and that she used it while she lived there. Perhaps it was broken just before they left, since it appears that the pieces were left where they lay."

Nick was staring at Anna. She glanced at him and then back at Mrs. Siqueiros. "I'm trying to put the pieces back together, trying to reconstruct it. I'm hoping that when it's finished I can show it to you."

"*Que sería muy bonito, gracias.*"

Anna handed the photograph back to Rosie who walked them to the door.

On the way to the truck, Nick turned to her. "You always surprise me, Anna."

She smiled.

Two weeks later, Rosie called them to invite them to a private service at St. Augustine Cathedral.

The priest baptized the remains Ángel Ramirez Ocoboa and arranged for a private interment between his mother and father at Holy Hope Cemetery.

When they left the church, Anna was silent until Nick looked at her and asked, "What are you thinking?"

"I'm thinking about Esperanza and her reunion with the baby she lost so long ago."

"Me, too." Nick reached over and took her hand. She wasn't quite sure what to do, but she left her hand warm in his.

20

Tucson, Arizona, November 1987

In early November, Maggie poked her head in the door to the lab while Anna was there working.

"Anna, don't make any other plans for Thanksgiving. Max and I want you to join us for dinner."

"Thank you, Maggie, but—"

"No buts allowed, Anna. I'm inviting Nick and Margy and her boyfriend Joe. We have much to be thankful for this year." Just as quickly as she appeared at the door she was gone again. Maggie had apparently accepted for her.

Her reluctance wasn't just because she was still uncertain about Max's feelings about her work, it was mostly because she didn't have many good memories about Thanksgiving, or, for that matter, about holidays in general. Her mother always had a big to-do at holiday times, inviting aunts and uncles and cousins to dinner and cooking all day. What should have been happy family time usually degenerated into a knock-down-drag-out. Anna never understood what motivated her mother to do it over and over, since they were a family that didn't particularly like one another, but that's what she did.

For that reason, she never looked forward to family gatherings or holidays. Even though her mother often insisted that she come home from college for holidays, she refused. Post-holiday phone calls usually included a play-by-play of who did what and who said what and whose fault it was. She would call and send her parents a card, and frequently a Christmas or birthday gift, but she simply didn't want to be there. Her mother understood, and her father was indifferent.

She was sure a holiday with Max and Maggie would be different, because they were so clearly devoted to one another. Even so, she was uneasy.

Nick offered to pick her up and take her to Max's house in time for dinner. She agreed, telling herself he would offer moral support if she needed it.

He called for her at two-thirty on the afternoon of Thanksgiving Day. When Nick knocked on the door of her apartment, she opened the door to see him standing there with a new Stetson in his hand, turning it around, as if he, too, were nervous. Upon seeing him, her stomach fluttered and her heart began to pound. She attributed it worrying about the inevitable social gathering.

Nick smiled, his green eyes brightening in the afternoon light. "You look beautiful, Anna." She was wearing a pair of black slacks with a pale blue pullover sweater. She had brushed her hair back on one side and secured it with a rhinestone studded comb. The other side fell loosely to her shoulder. She smiled at his generosity, but she was reluctant to make too much of it.

"Hi, Nick. Thanks for coming by for me."

"No problem. Glad to do it."

Nick placed his hand lightly on the small of her back as they went down the steps of the apartment building together. She tried to resist liking how it made her feel. As she got into Nick's pickup, she looked up to see Minnie watching from her window, her thumb raised in a friendly salute. Anna smiled at Minnie's determination that this would be more about romance than friendship.

She feared she might be right.

When they arrived at Max and Maggie's house, nestled in the foothills of the Santa Catalinas, Margy and her friend Joe were already there. Maggie greeted them at the door and led them into the family room where she introduced Joe, and invited them to help themselves from a tray of cheeses and crackers.

"I'm so glad you came, Anna," Margy said.

"Me too," Anna responded. "I'm sorry I've never told you how much I appreciated your friendship when we found the infant burial. That was very hard for me."

"I could tell that it touched you deeply, Anna." Margy placed a gentle hand on Anna's forearm.

Once again, Anna, found herself on the verge of tears, knowing that for Nick it had been just as difficult. "It was, Margy. Someday I'll tell you about it, but I'm not ready now."

"I understand," Margy assured her. "Whenever you're ready, I'm here.

"I appreciate it, Margy. And I appreciate your friendship." Again, tears gathered, but she resisted. She was damned if she was going to turn into a crybaby on Thanksgiving at Max and Maggie's house.

Maggie joined them, bringing each a glass of red wine. The word "perky" entered Anna's mind and she smiled to think that she had never applied this descriptor to anyone, but it fit Maggie. She and Max were opposites. Max was tall and Maggie was short; Max was intense and thoughtful, quiet and reserved; Maggie was energetic and loquacious. She chattered endlessly, clearly delighted at having guests in her home.

Maggie's curly, blonde hair bounced as she bustled around the room making sure her guests were comfortable. Her bright eyes sparkled as she encouraged Margy and Anna to help themselves to the *hors d'oeuvres*. Anna was grateful for the distraction; she wouldn't have to think about Esperanza Ramirez and her baby again or Nick and his tragedy.

Max came into the room, followed by Nick and Joe. He lifted his glass of wine and asked, "Do we all have something with which to toast?"

They scrambled to pick up their glasses. When everyone was ready, Max looked at each one in turn. Anna was standing apart from Nick, Margy and Joe were standing close together, and Maggie was rearranging the dishes on the table. When he leveled a glance in her direction, she picked up her glass.

"I would like to thank all of you for being here tonight. You are all an important part of our work. I offer to you my thanks for your hard work and dedication. And to whatever greater power there is, I give my thanks for good friends and family and Maggie's good cooking." Everyone laughed and moved together to clink glasses. As Anna's and Nick's glasses touched, she looked up into his eyes and found herself lost in them—again. She blinked against it and sipped her wine, thinking about what Minnie had told her about eyes; she promised herself she would not look again into those tempting eyes tonight—she wasn't sure it was a promise she could keep.

She was gratified by Max's words. For the first time since he hired her, she sensed his approval.

Dinner began with noisy and enthusiastic passing of turkey and dressing along with other familiar Thanksgiving menu items: mashed potatoes and gravy, cranberry sauce (from a can, of course—Maggie had said to do otherwise wasn't in her DNA), and green bean casserole. Anna remained quiet, watching plates fill and noting the general quiet that followed as everyone fell to eating. Early dinner conversation mostly consisted of complimenting Maggie on her cooking, then other topics were brought up. Eventually the conversation turned to the Ramirez Ruin.

Max offered a summary view of what they had learned so far. "This site is a fascinating place. We are very lucky that the state is willing to protect and preserve it."

Everyone nodded in agreement. The community had come close to losing the significant archaeology in that area.

Nick said, "Can you imagine if the developer had come in and scraped off the top of the ridge, making room for a street with houses on each side?"

"I don't even want to imagine it. I'm just glad the state stepped in and we'll still have the washes and the canyon for recreation." Margy had attended a number of the local hearings and had been a vocal opponent of the development.

Anna remembered reading the details in the proposal for the state park. In exchange for the land on the east side of Oracle Road, the developer accepted a larger tract on the west side. There were a number of prehistoric sites on that land, too, and excavation of those would result in documentation, but it would not halt development.

"In any case," Max concluded, "the state made a good bargain. The new park will protect and preserve the sensitive area of the Sutherland and the Cañada del Oro washes." He raised his glass again. "Here's to the state."

Everyone raised their glasses in agreement.

"You know, the original survey of the area revealed twenty-nine previously unknown sites and information was collected from thirteen known sites, including the Ramirez Ruin."

He paused. "Think of it. The survey covered barely one third of the eight plus square miles reserved for the new park, and *twenty-nine* new sites were found. Surely there would be many more if we could have gone further north along the Sutherland and the CDO."

Maggie chose the opportunity to interrupt him. "Max, honey, can we set business aside long enough to get some of these dishes cleared up and bring in the coffee and pumpkin pie? These folks are dying for dessert."

Max laughed. "She always knows when to shut me up."

Anna thought about how that exchange might have gone over at Thanksgiving when she was growing up. It would have been the spark that lit the fuse.

Anna and Margy helped clear the table and bring out the dessert and after-dinner coffee. When they came back into the room Max and Nick were slapping Joe on the back and laughing. Both Anna and Maggie looked puzzled, but Margy was smiling. "You told them, didn't you, Joe?"

He nodded, and while Joe, Margy, Nick, and Max celebrated, Maggie and Anna looked on in confusion. Margy turned to them and explained.

"Nick and Max have been after Joe to put his engineering degree to work somehow with their work. Joe's going to get his Master's—and hopefully his

PhD—in materials science and heritage conservation. He'll be able to stay here in Tucson and work with us during his breaks."

Both Maggie and Anna hugged Margy and smiled their congratulations to Joe for his decision. "That's wonderful, Margy," Anna said. "That means you'll stay with us, doesn't it?"

"Yes, it does." She hugged Joe and beamed at Nick and Max.

"Boy, am I glad we don't have to break in another shovelbum." Max grinned. "It took us long enough to get this girl trained."

"Stop it, Max," Maggie slapped him on the shoulder. "You know that Margy is one of your best."

"She is." Max looked at Margy and said, "You are one of our best. I would have been sad to lose you."

She smiled, and Joe hugged her close. "We really have to go, now. We promised Joe's parents we'd come to Thanksgiving dinner with them."

She laughed. "I don't know how I'll eat anything else after your wonderful meal, Maggie."

Joe laughed, too. "Don't worry, Margy, I can still pack some in." She punched him on the shoulder and everyone bade them good night.

❧❧

Maggie suggested that they take their coffee out to the patio. Anna objected because there were still dirty dishes to consider, but Maggie would have none of it. "The leftovers are wrapped and in the fridge. The dishes will be here in the morning. I could care less about getting them done tonight." She smiled, "Besides, the sky is beautiful tonight, and it would be a shame to miss it."

Together they walked out to the patio.

Max and Maggie sat in a pair of patio chairs with a side table between them. That left the love seat for

Nick and Anna. Nick laid his arm up on the cushions behind Anna. Maggie gave Max a knowing look and smiled. Max just raised his eyebrows. Dusk was falling and the cloudless sky reflected the sunset with a beauty that was typical in Tucson. None of them spoke as they watched the colors of the sky shift and darken.

Max and Maggie's patio wrapped around the southern and western sides of the house, so they had a sweeping view of the Tucson Basin with sparkling city lights as night began to fall. To the west, a golden sky brilliantly backlit the ragged profile of the Tucson Mountains. The sun had slipped below the horizon, and the darkening blue sky pushed the sunset colors, pale yellow to brilliant gold behind the mountain ridges.

Above the Rincons, a sliver of a crescent moon glowed with the evening star, Venus, just below and to the left. As darkness fell, other stars began to twinkle in the darkening sky.

Anna remembered her last Evanston sunset, giving silent thanks for Tucson sunsets now. It had been almost a year and a half, and she was safe.

"It's lovely here." Anna did not intend to speak aloud, but her whispered thought brought the rest of them out of their reverie.

Maggie passed a knowing look in Max's direction and said, "I never tire of our sunsets. I don't think there are ever two that are alike."

Max reached over, lifted Maggie's hand and kissed the back of it.

"When I asked Maggie to marry me, I promised her a lifetime of original sunsets and sunrises, with never a duplicate among them."

"He's kept that promise, too." Maggie smiled at her husband. "Truth be told, though, it's pretty easy here in Tucson. Maybe he could have promised something a little harder to deliver on, like diamonds and emeralds." She laughed and kissed the hand that held hers. They exchanged a look of mutual devotion that Anna envied.

They shared coffee and quiet conversation as darkness cloaked the patio and the city lights twinkled brightly across the basin. Finally, Anna suggested that it was past time for them to excuse themselves and leave Maggie and Max to what might remain of a quiet evening.

She and Nick rose and said their good nights.

When they got back to Anna's apartment, Nick saw her to her door, again with his hand lightly against the small of her back as they climbed the stairs. Each time he did that, a comforting warmth spread through her body. As she slid the key into the door and pushed it open, Nick reached out and turned her around to face him. "Anna," he said.

"Don't, Nick..." But even as she said it, she leaned toward him.

"I can't help it, Anna." He wrapped his arms around her and pulled her close. She didn't resist.

She looked up into his eyes, reflecting the pale gleam of the light outside her door. She had no defenses; she was lost in his eyes and it was okay.

Nick lifted her chin and brushed his lips lightly across hers. She trembled as the shockwave of his kiss spread over her and settled low in her body. She leaned closer and wrapped her arms around his neck as he kissed her with the full force of his passion. His hand slid down her back and pressed her against him. In spite of herself, she responded.

Just as she thought about taking his hand and leading him inside, she heard the steady "beep-beep" of her answering machine. She pushed Nick away gently and looked through the open door. The red light flashed with each beep; something terrible had happened.

"Thank you, Nick. I can't remember when I've had a more wonderful Thanksgiving." She smiled and stepped back just enough to let him know that things had gone as far as they were going to go tonight.

"Good night, Anna. It was a special Thanksgiving for me." Anna thought he was disappointed, and it occurred to her that she really did not want to disappoint him.

He turned and went down the steps to his truck. He stood by the open door and looked up to see her still standing there watching. He waved and got into the truck and drove away.

She watched until his tail lights blended into the others on the street. Then she sighed, trying to dismiss her disappointment. She closed the door and turned toward the answering machine. No one had her number except Max, Minnie, and Rhinehart, not even Nick. Something told her it wasn't Minnie.

21

Tucson, Arizona, Thanksgiving Evening 1987

Anna, it's Rhinehart. Foster has been crazy to find you since you left. He called me several times, but I kept saying I don't know anything. Of course, he doesn't believe me. Yesterday, he showed up at my site. He accused me of helping you and lying about it. He said I don't need to tell him where you are, that he knows. I don't know if he's bluffing or not, but you need to be ready in case he shows up. Call me."

Anna collapsed into the chair by the phone table. "Oh, God."

She jumped up and ran to the bedroom and dragged her suitcase off the top shelf of the closet; she would have to run and she couldn't tell anyone she was leaving. That way, if he showed up in Tucson and she was gone, no one would be able to tell him anything.

She pulled open her dresser drawer and gathered up a handful of lingerie and—she stopped. *Where would I go? I can't ask Rhinehart to find me another job.*

Tucson was *home*; she was finally home. She sat down on the edge of the bed and looked at the empty suitcase and made up her mind. *Be damned if I'm going to run again.*

She called Minnie. "I'm sorry I'm calling you so late"

Minnie heard the panic in her voice. "I'll be right over. Don't move!"

In a very brief moment, Minnie came through the door. When Anna saw her, the tears began to fall.

Minnie wrapped her arms around Anna and let her cry it out. "What's wrong, Anna? Did something happen between you and Nick tonight?"

Anna just pointed to the answering machine. Minnie pushed the button and listened, watching Anna while the message played.

"What are you going to do?"

"I thought about running, but I can't. I'm going to have to face him sometime. It might as well be sooner rather than later."

She called Rhinehart back.

"Anna! Are you all right? I've been so worried."

"I'm fine, Rhinehart. Thank you for warning me." She remembered that Foster had threatened him. "Did he hurt you?"

"No. He didn't have the chance. Rob is still working with me, and he brought the biggest guys on site to back me up."

"Thank God. I've been frightened that if he found out you helped me, he would do something awful. I'm going to have to face him and get it over with. I won't run again. If he shows up, I'll deal with it. I don't want you to worry anymore. I'm stronger now than I was, and you've already done more than you should have. I can't ask you for more."

"Don't worry?" She heard Rhinehart take a deep, ragged breath. "Don't worry? Anna, I've been worried about you since I first saw you and Foster together. I kept hoping you would see what a son of a bitch he is. He's a bully, and I knew if you ever stood up for yourself, he would hurt you."

He paused, and when he continued his voice broke.

"I've seen it before. My daughter was married to a man just like him, smooth and polished to the world, and mean as a snake when they were alone. Her mother and I dismissed her complaints. We encouraged her to 'work it out.' When she was the most terrified, we weren't there for her."

His voice broke again. "He killed her, Anna; he murdered her when she tried to leave him. And we hadn't paid attention. We might have prevented it if we had done something..." His voice trailed off for a moment. "I need to help you so maybe my daughter can forgive me." He paused. "Is there anyone there who can help you?"

"Yes." She looked up at Minnie. "But I'll be ready for him myself." She hoped it was true.

"I hope so, Anna. Please be careful. Keep in touch. Please."

"I will. Thank you, Rhinehart."

"Anna, there's something else you need to know."

Anna waited.

"Foster's been dismissed from university."

"Dismissed?"

"He published an article using a student's ideas, research, and conclusions, passing them off as his own."

"Hopewell."

"Yes. How did you know?"

"He mentioned something once about a student who had some radical, new theories about Hopewell."

"I see. Well, the student found out and went to the dean, who investigated. When he was confronted, Foster insisted the student was lying. He said that he had had nothing but trouble with him, accusing him of all kinds of things, like cheating on tests and plagiarizing his work. The dean didn't buy it because the student's record was good, plus he had his original research notes and rough drafts of the paper he had submitted to Foster. Other students and professors backed him up. The dean told him he was beginning the dismissal process."

"My God..."

"That's not all."

She couldn't imagine it getting worse. "After Foster left the dean's office, he went looking for the student and assaulted him—on campus in front of the student union."

"Dear God. Is the boy all right?" She spoke barely above a whisper.

"Yes, he is, but Foster was arrested and charged. With his parents' connections, though, he managed to get out of the charges with just a slap on the wrist and some community service, but he pretty much sealed his fate with the dean."

"He will blame me. He'll say it was all my fault for leaving him."

"No, it's not your fault, but I suspect you're right. That will make him doubly dangerous. If he shows up, you cannot be alone with him."

"Thanks, Rhinehart. I'll be careful." They said goodbye and she hung up softly.

∿⸅

Minnie had heard Anna's side of the conversation. "I'll be right back," and she was, bringing two bottles of red wine with her. "This is a two-bottle talk."

"Oh, Minnie, I've made a dreadful mess." She sat down at the kitchen table and put her head in her hands. "I know I took the coward's way out, but he would never have let me leave."

"I'm not surprised," Minnie said. She wrapped her arms around Anna. "If he shows up here, he's going to have to come through me to get to you."

Anna looked up sharply into Minnie's determined face. "No, Minnie, I don't want you to get hurt. And I need to be the one to confront him."

"Don't worry about me, kid; I've tangled with men like him. Someday I'll tell you about my marriage. I'll be okay. And so will you." She paused. "You should call Max."

"You're right, I've put everybody at risk."

"Comes with the territory, kid. He needs to know, and you know that Nick will stand with you."

"Nick..." *Foster will kill him.* That was more terrifying than her facing him by herself.

She dialed Max's number. "Max, I'm sorry to be calling you so late."

"Not a problem, Anna. What's wrong?"

Her voice trembled. "I owe you so much for everything you've done for me, and I hate bringing trouble down on you."

"What do you mean?"

"You hired me on nothing more than Rhinehart's recommendation, and I appreciate that you didn't ask any questions." She took a deep breath. "I appreciate it more than you know."

"I have no regrets, Anna, you're proving yourself. But that's not why you're calling. What is it?"

"It's time you knew it all, but right now I need to give you a heads-up. I don't want anyone to get hurt because of me. My husband might show up at the site and it could get very ugly."

"Your husband?" Max's surprise was evident. Nick had not told him. "Yes, my husband. I don't want anyone to get hurt, so I'll resign and I'll stay away from the site."

"Wait a minute, Anna. Are you saying that *we're* in danger?

"I'm not sure, but he's unstable and unpredictable. He will want me to come back to Chicago with him. If he thinks anyone here is standing in his way, he might..."

"Does he know where you live?"

"I'm sure he doesn't have the address."

"Does he know who you work for?"

"That's possible."

"Then you staying away from the site won't keep him from tracking us down. You aren't protecting anybody by staying away."

"I didn't think of that. I'm sorry, Max. You don't deserve this."

"That's right, I don't. But it is what it is. It looks like we'll all have to deal with it. What do you intend to do?"

"I want to stay here. I've never been more at home anywhere in my life. I won't go back." She took a ragged breath. "I can't go back."

"We'll help you." Max's voice was firm. "And you're not resigning."

"You don't have to, Max. I'm sorry to cause trouble."

"Meet me at the office in the morning at nine. We have a long weekend for the holiday, so we can put together a plan." He hesitated. "Will it be all right if I let Nick know?"

"Yes, ask Nick to join us in the morning, and Maggie, too. It's only fair that they know what's going on."

Anna hung the phone up and she came back to the table. Minnie poured them each a glass of wine, saying nothing.

Anna stared at the glass of wine for a long moment. "I thought I was doing the right thing. I thought not telling him I was leaving would keep me safe, and I believe I was right. So much time has passed since I left, I convinced myself he had accepted it and got on with his life."

She told Minnie about Aztalan and what he had done to her when they got home. "I began planning my escape the next morning."

22

Evanston, Illinois, April 1986

Anna had slipped out of bed before Foster woke up. In the bathroom she looked at her eye, swollen nearly shut and bruised. She put her finger on the scar, bruised purple and black. *I won't cry. I won't.* She pulled on a pair of sweat pants, a tee-shirt, and running shoes, grabbed a bottle of water and her sunglasses and quietly left the house.

The sun was just rising, casting long shadows along the tree-lined street. As her footfalls pounded through the pattern of shade and sunlight, she tried to make sense of her life.

She didn't want to believe what he had done to her yesterday, but there was no way to deny it. He was more than a bully, he was hateful and cruel, and he had always been that way. She had seen it with the valet in Chicago. She should have known then what kind of man he really was.

What the hell's wrong with a man who only wants to control his wife? He had a vasectomy without even discussing it with me. He knew I wanted children.

She stopped in her tracks. *Oh, my God. What if I had gotten pregnant?* She thought maybe it's a good thing he's too selfish to share his wife with children. *What would I do now if I had a baby to worry about? If I had a baby, I wouldn't have defied him about working so maybe...* No, she wouldn't even go there. He would have found another reason to abuse her. Her own father had resented his children and accused her mother of loving them more than she loved him. And eventually that was true. *But she hadn't loved us enough to leave.*

She thought about her childhood, so scarred by domestic violence, a household in which drawing blood was the favorite sport. Her father was determined to control her mother, and her mother defiantly clung to her independence. This clash of personalities led to a kind of violence that had no regard for the children who might be caught in the middle. Their shouting inevitably led to one or the other striking the first blow and then there were no rules. While her father's brute strength gave him the advantage over her short, plump mother, her mother always tried to give as good as she got, coming out on the short end, but managing to strike a few blows that left scars he wore for life. She remembered the scar on the bridge of his nose from the empty Spam can her mother had flung at him.

She remembered how her father used to check the mileage on her mother's car to find out if she had gone somewhere he didn't know about. As far as she knew, Foster had never done that, but so much of his behavior was the same. She had married a man just like her father.

She had sworn she would never stay in an abusive relationship like her mother had. She had sworn she would walk away at the first sign. But she hadn't. She had failed to recognize his domineering behavior as abuse; she had let it go when he raped her and pinched and bit her. She asked herself if she was her mother's daughter or not.

Apparently not. Should she have fought back like her mother did? Hitting him and throwing things at him? Something told her that if she had done that he would have hurt her seriously. *He's really not that much like my father—he's worse.*

She thought about her parents' relationship and wondered if they had not somehow thrived on discord and violence. She remembered how her mother stuck it out, getting black and blue and fighting back until he nearly killed her. Could she wait that long or should she look for a way to get out?

She stopped running and wiped perspiration from her forehead, tucking damp strands of hair behind her ears. She took a long drink of water and focused on the pavement ahead, which by now was painted with more sunlight than shadows. She ran on, through shadows and light, trying to put one foot in front of the other and to focus on breathing and nothing else.

When she came into sight of the house, Foster's car was gone. She breathed a sigh of relief and went inside. As she passed through the bedroom to take a shower, she stopped to look at the print from their honeymoon in Lascaux. That had been a magical place and it was a magical time. But the magic was gone and those memories were tarnished. Her marriage, like the print on the wall, was just an image, it wasn't real.

She stopped and looked at the shadow box with the seven projectile points she had found as a child. They had awakened her dream of archaeology. She was damned if she was going to suffer through an abusive marriage with a man who didn't respect her, who only wanted to own her and beat her when she disobeyed him. She would reclaim her life and her dream, whatever it took.

～◦～

After her shower, she went into the den and spent the next hour sorting through and organizing her files, throwing out what she didn't think she would ever need again. She put the most important items into large envelopes and addressed them to herself at her new address.

She picked up the phone and dialed Rhinehart's number. She listened to it ring several times and when his answering machine picked up, she hung up; he might return her call after Foster came home and she didn't want to take that chance.

She took a deep breath and opened the Yellow Pages, found what she was looking for and called the number.

"Law Offices of Warner, Cambourne, and O'Donnell. How may I direct your call?"

After a moment's hesitation, she said, "I'd like to make an appointment with Karen O'Donnell, please."

The receptionist asked her to hold for a moment, and then a voice came on the line. "Ms. O'Donnell's office. May I help you?"

Anna plunged ahead, making an appointment for early the next week. She could still change her mind if she needed to.

She dialed Rhinehart's number again.

"Wilson here." She hesitated. He might hang up if I don't say something.

"Hi, it's Anna Robinson." She tried to keep her voice from shaking.

"What's wrong?"

"I knew you didn't think much of Foster, and now I know why. I'm leaving him. I'm finished."

"Did he hurt you?" His question told her what Rhinehart had seen in Foster that she had missed all along. He probably knew better than she what Foster was capable of.

"Yes, but I'll survive. I need to get a job somewhere—anywhere—doing fieldwork. I need to get away from him."

Rhinehart's voice softened. "I had a feeling this was coming, Anna. What did he say?"

"I haven't told him. I don't dare tell him because I'm afraid of what he will do. I'll be fine as soon as I can get away."

"I'll do anything I can to help you. But you have to stay safe. Can you do that?" Although she didn't know why, Rhinehart had always been a special friend and mentor.

"I think so."

"Just tell me what you need and I'm there for you." She was so grateful, she had to blink back the tears.

"I hate to put you in this position. You've been such a good friend."

"I have my reasons, Anna. And I'll do anything I can to help you get away from that bastard."

She asked him if he could look for something on her behalf far away from Chicago and gave him her new address.

He promised to find something. "Anna, you be careful, okay?"

"I will."

She thought about what else she might need to make this work. She might be able to turn to Howard, but she hadn't seen her brother since her wedding. Now she remembered that before he left the wedding reception, he told her to watch herself. She hadn't understood what he meant, and he wouldn't explain. Like Rhinehart, he could see what she couldn't see in Foster.

No, she couldn't go to Howard, but she would at least write him a letter giving him the barest details about leaving Foster; she wouldn't tell him where she was going—even when she knew that herself. Foster would probably get in touch with him to find out where she went, and Howard wouldn't be lying when he said he didn't know.

He had once said to her, "When you turn your back, you gotta leave it all behind you. Don't look back. No regrets—ever."

She understood it then, and she thought she had done it when she left for college. Now she was right back where she started. Once again, she would turn her back, leave it all behind. No regrets.

When she left the house later, she left with a purpose. No, she was not her mother's daughter. She would not stick it out one minute longer than she had to. She could make a short-term plan. Long term would have to wait.

She drove to the post office and rented a box. Now Foster could not interfere with her communication with Rhinehart or with anyone who might be able to help her. She would erect a wall around herself that Foster could not penetrate while she considered her options.

ᕤ᠊ᕤ

When Foster got home that evening, Anna had dinner all prepared. She smiled a brief hello, and turned to setting the table. She did not ask him how his day had gone; in fact, she said almost nothing else that wasn't related to the meal.

"Pass the salt."

"Would you like more beans?"

Afterwards, she got up and quickly set to cleaning up the table, putting leftovers away, and washing the dishes. He stood in the kitchen staring at her back, but she did not turn around. She didn't look directly at his reflection in the window over the sink. Finally, she heard him walk into the other room.

She gave him no reason to suspect anything, and he probably assumed she was just sulking about last night. He simply went into the living room and sat down to read the evening paper.

Later, they got ready for bed in silence. Occasionally, she felt him staring at her, but she resisted looking in his direction. She got into her side of the bed, turned her back to him, and turned off her bedside lamp. She was pretty sure he was standing by the bed staring at her back; she was sure he was finally going to say or do something.

She was right.

"What do you think you're doing?"

"I'm going to sleep. Isn't that the point of going to bed?"

"You know damn well what I mean. You think if you pull the silent act on me, I'll change my mind about you working." Apparently, he didn't think her black eye might have something to do with it.

Without turning to face him, she said, "No, Foster, that's the last thing I expect of you. You've made yourself pretty clear."

"You're damn right." He snatched the blanket back and got into bed. Anna held her breath and waited. He grabbed her shoulder and pulled her around to face him. "You just make sure you understand who's in charge here." There would be five bruises tomorrow.

She kept her voice even. "You are, Foster. I know that."

At first, he seemed unsure of how to respond to her calm compliance. But then he pulled her hard against himself and pinched her backside hard. It hurt, and it, too, would leave a bruise, but she was determined not to react. He pushed her onto her back and climbed on top of her, forcing her legs open and himself into her. She lay still, expecting him to begin thrusting, but he didn't.

He relaxed a little and lifted his weight on one arm. Speaking softly against her neck, he said, "C'mon, Anna, let me take care of you. You need me and you love me."

He began to kiss her shoulders lightly, like a feather brushing her skin, something that had always broken down her defenses. He expected her to relax and wrap her arms around him pushing her hips upward to meet him, but she didn't. She just lay there, saying nothing, feeling nothing, her face turned away from him. He shrank inside her.

"God damn you!" He rolled off and turned his back. She was fairly sure her lack of response—neither resisting nor engaging—had rendered him impotent. She rolled over and smiled to herself. She had won that round. But she might have gone too far, and then she'd pay for it; it would be dangerous to do this again. This was not the first time she had bruises to show for his "love."

In the morning, she slipped out of bed to go running before Foster got up, but when she came out of the bathroom, he was up. He came to her and gently took her hands.

"Darling," he said softly. "I'm sorry. I shouldn't have done that last night, but you just made me so mad." His voice rose just a little, "You shouldn't do that." He smiled tentatively. "Can you forgive me?"

She looked at him levelly, knowing that he really believed what he was saying. It would be up to her to make sure it didn't happen again.

"Of course, Foster. I love you." She wasn't sure she didn't love him, but something in her had died; she couldn't live with his kind of love.

"I love you, too, baby." He kissed her hard and she kissed him back, knowing she had to. She was surprised to find that she felt nothing.

∾∾

Her meeting with Karen O'Donnell raised more questions than it gave answers. Ms. O'Donnell was sympathetic and willing to help her, but she learned that getting a divorce in Illinois wouldn't be a simple matter. One option was to claim irreconcilable differences, but Foster would dispute that. Plus, there was a two-year waiting period, unless he would agree to waive it. She could rule out any cooperation from him.

Anna thought that mental cruelty was one ground for her circumstances, but because the law doesn't define that specifically, she would need to prove the harmful nature of Foster's treatment of her, that it had happened repeatedly. The real kicker was that she would need to prove that there had been no provocation for the cruelty.

Provocation—there it was. Everything would be okay if the wife would just behave and not provoke her husband. Anna found it hard to believe just how vulnerable a woman was in these circumstances.

Finally, she would have to prove that the abusive treatment was calculated to make her miserable and was affecting her physical or mental health. She didn't doubt that Foster's efforts to control her and intimidate her were calculated to bring her into line and to behave as he wanted her to, but proving his intent would be tough. Besides, Foster probably thought his treatment of her was designed to make her a happy and obedient wife.

Even with physical cruelty as a ground, she would have to show "extreme and repeated acts of physical cruelty." Even the black eye she was still sporting wasn't enough, although the attorney encouraged her to report such domestic violence to the police. Doing that would make it worse. All in all, she would have to stay with Foster long enough "to establish a continuing pattern of both mental and physical abuse to such a degree that her mental health had been affected or that she had experienced pain and bodily harm."

To stay with him until the abuse had escalated to that point would be self-destructive. So she ruled out filing for divorce any time in the near future. Leaving him without filing was her only choice.

❧✍

While she waited and planned how to get away, she discovered just how cruel he could be. She was likely to be bruised and battered over trivial things. He was equally likely to apologize and promise it would never happen again. It was a hollow promise. Because she rarely wanted him to make love to her any more, he forced himself on her and left bruises and bite marks. Even playing the role of the acquiescent housewife didn't make a difference in how he treated her in bed.

It would require some planning, and it would require some money. That was the hard part.

Since she had it before they married, her car was in her name, so she might be able it sell it, but then again she would need it. Besides, how could she do that without Foster knowing?

He managed the checking and savings accounts but he gave her a generous household allowance. She had never used all of it, so she had squirreled away a little bit each month. She had been hiding it in the box of sanitary napkins under her sink. That was a safe place; he would never look there. Originally, she had thought she would use the money to buy him a Christmas present; she'd be able to surprise him with something really nice that he hadn't bought for himself—even though technically he had.

The only other money she had available was a small Certificate of Deposit that she purchased with the money from her mother's insurance. Even so, the CD and her "Kotex account" would not be enough to finance her escape. And she still had to pay Karen O'Donnell for her consultation.

She was not optimistic.

23

Tucson, Arizona, November 1987

Overnight, a winter storm blew into Tucson. On Thanksgiving Day, the temperature had been in the upper 70s. The next morning, it was windy and clouds cloaked the Catalinas. Where there were breaks in the cloud cover, she could see snow covering the upper slopes. On the radio, there was talk about opening Ski Valley at the top of Mount Lemmon if enough snow fell. In the meantime, the road up the mountain was closed to all but vehicles with chains until it could be properly cleared. They were also predicting snow in the city by nightfall. Anna had not yet seen snow in Tucson, and if she hadn't been so upset, she might have enjoyed the prospect of it here in the desert—she hadn't seen snow since her last winter in Chicago.

She stood at her kitchen window, her hands wrapped around her coffee mug, looking at the rapidly deteriorating weather. Low, gray clouds rolled in, blocking any hope of sunlight and a steady rain began to fall. The dismal day only served to depress her further.

On the way to Max's office, the rain splattered the windshield and the wipers swept back and forth in a monotonous rhythm—each wipe saying "run, run, run, run..."

Fortunately, she arrived at Max's office before she could obey the warning of the wipers. When she reached for the doorknob, Nick opened the door and put one arm around her and drew her gently inside, closing the door behind her. Maggie looked up from the coffee maker and smiled.

With Nick's arm around her, Anna was overcome. She was afraid her tears would begin again, and the last thing she wanted was to break down in front of these people who meant so much to her. She was still hopeful that she could protect them by putting some distance between them and her.

They went into Max's office where he pulled his chair from behind the desk around to the side. Nick and Anna took chairs in front of the desk and Maggie came in with coffee for everyone. Anna was touched that Maggie had remembered from last night how she took her coffee.

Maggie took the last chair and said, "I hope you don't mind if I stay, Anna."

"Of course not, Maggie. This really does involve you all, and I can't take any chances that you don't have the information that you need to deal with Foster if he shows up."

"Foster. That's your husband?" Max's question encouraged her to continue talking.

"Yes." She looked at Nick and saw concern written on his face. She was glad that he, at least, already knew that she was married. She didn't want to hurt him any more than she might have already.

Slowly, she told the story of her marriage and her escape. They listened quietly, asking only a few questions during her narrative; Nick took her hand and held it as she talked. When she reached the end of Rhinehart's latest revelations, no one spoke.

Finally, Max broke the silence. "The son of a bitch. I'd like to get my hands on him."

"I'm afraid you'll have the chance," Anna looked pleadingly at Max, "but I don't want you or anyone to get hurt." She looked at Nick.

He had said nothing, but she could see the tension in his face, his jaw muscles clenching and unclenching. If he wasn't holding her hand, she might have wondered if his anger was directed at her for creating this crisis.

"Nick...," Anna began. "There's nothing you can do. We just have to wait until he shows up—if he does—and then I'll deal with it."

"No." Max said. "*We'll* have to deal with it. This isn't just about you any longer, Anna," He looked at each one in turn. "Here are the possibilities: if he knows who Anna works for, and she thinks he does, he might show up here at the office before any other location; that means Maggie needs to know what to do. If he knows where the job is—which is possible, too, because we've had newspaper coverage on this project—he could show up at the site. In either case, we have to have a coordinated response. And we have to be prepared for whatever follows."

They discussed their plan and agreed that there was no doubt Foster would show up sometime. Anna gave them Minnie's phone number and a picture of Foster so they would recognize him when he appeared.

When it was done, it was as if the weight of the world had been lifted, but she felt guilty about shifting that weight to her friends.

She was the one who needed to face him.

☙❧

As they prepared to leave the office, Nick took her hand and said, "Let's go get some lunch. We can talk more about what we're going to do."

They stepped out into the gray day. The rain had stopped and the sun was shining through breaks in the cloud cover. A bright shaft of sunlight enveloped the parking lot. "See," Nick said, "even God's telling you it will be okay."

Anna laughed. "I'm not sure I have a good deal of favor with Him right now. He must be terribly disappointed in me."

"I doubt that." Nick smiled and led her to his pickup. "We'll come back for your car later."

Nick drove east on Grant Road until it ended at Tanque Verde, turning left.

"Where are we going, Nick?" Anna had never been out this way.

"You'll see." He smiled in her direction. She was surprised that he was so relaxed after the terrible details she had told them in the office.

When she saw the sign for Mount Lemmon Highway and he turned left, Anna looked over at Nick. "We're going up on the mountain? In the snow?"

"Sure," Nick replied. "How long has it been since you've had a snowball fight?"

"I'm not sure I'm dressed for it." Anna looked down at her jeans, long-sleeved tee-shirt, and sneakers. She had a light jacket on.

"There's a couple of heavy jackets behind the seat."
Nick smiled. "You'll be fine."

She hoped he was right—in more ways than one.
When they reached the roadblock, Nick got out of
the truck and put chains on the rear tires, and then
they were waved through. With each curve in the
road, a spectacular vista lay before them. Finally, they
entered the Ponderosa pine forest at the top. It was
completely different from the desert floor.

Nick told her that the drive up the mountain had
been the equivalent of driving from Mexico to Canada,
in terms of the changing life-zones and vegetation.

The rustic, winter beauty of the village on the
mountain was magical. They had lunch at the Mount
Lemmon Cafe, famous for their huge, homemade
pies. After lunch, they played in the snow, throwing
snowballs and laughing. For a short time, Anna forgot
about Foster and his inevitable arrival and disruption
of her life.

Back in the truck, she held her cold hands in front
of the heater vents, laughing. "I can't believe how
different it is up here. It's been fun, Nick. Thanks."

He smiled at her, in spite of the worry that shaded
his eyes. He said nothing.

On the way down the mountain, Anna fell silent
and Nick did not interrupt her meditation. When they
pulled into the office parking lot where Anna's car
was waiting, Nick released his own seat belt and then
reached over and released hers. He pulled her toward
him and wrapped his arms around her.

She allowed herself to relax in his arms as he
brushed his lips across her cheek lightly kissing her
scar. He whispered in her ear, "It's okay. Anna. I won't
let anything happen to you. I can't lose..."

"Don't say it, Nick. Don't think it." She looked up
into his eyes. "I'm so sorry to have dragged you into
this. It was selfish of me."

"I don't want to be anywhere but where you need me." This time, when he kissed her, she didn't want to be anywhere but in his arms, and though it still frightened her, it would be okay, just as Nick had promised.

24

Tucson, Arizona, December 1987

The weather stayed cold and rainy in the weeks following Thanksgiving, so there wasn't much work at the site. The excavations were covered with blue tarps. Either Nick or Max went out daily to check them. Even the office was quiet, as Maggie was taking a few days off. Things were also quiet on the Foster front as well, but Anna was constantly on edge, waiting for the proverbial other shoe.

In the lab, with the sherds laid out on the table before her, she could let this world disappear and focus only on the story the potsherds offered. Each time she picked up a sherd and examined it, the lab fell away and there was nothing but her and the jar. The red interlocking scrolls on the exterior of the sherds she had glued together helped her to envision the finished pot. She had drawn a sketch showing what she thought the finished pot would look like and referred to it often. It helped to see how the design would align each time she sought to find a match.

She worked quietly and carefully, so absorbed in her work that she paid no attention to either Nick or Jesse, one of the student interns. Nick was reviewing records Max needed updated for the museum and Jesse was washing and cataloging sherds.

Nick came to Anna's table and told her he was going to the museum for some papers, and that Jesse said she would be here until he got back. Anna nodded her head absently and continued to focus on her work.

Before he went out the door, he stopped and watched her work, admiring the concentration she had mustered in spite of her fear of Foster's impending arrival.

A short time later, she managed to pull herself out of the pot's spell long enough to review the work she had done. She had put several two- and three-piece sections into the sandbox, some of which included bottom edges and top rim pieces. She wouldn't be able to work with them again until tomorrow, after the glue had dried sufficiently and she could handle them without fear of breaking them apart. She removed yesterday's work from the sandbox and began to search for sherds that would enlarge those fragments.

She didn't even hear Jesse's brother come in to tell her that their father had been hurt at work and he was being taken to the hospital. Jesse explained to Anna that she had to leave. She glanced up briefly and said, "I'm sorry, Jesse. Of course, go. I hope he's okay."

Under the spell of the jar again, she worked carefully to find matching pieces. She had a reasonably good-sized sherd that would fit along the rim of the section she held, but she wanted to find the piece or pieces that would go beneath it, because if she glued the big one on, it might be too difficult to fit in the one or more smaller, odd-shaped sherds that would close the distance to the bottom edge.

She was examining each of the smallest sherds, pushing them around on the table when the door to the lab quietly opened and then closed. She didn't notice. She also didn't hear the footsteps closing the distance between her and the door.

A sudden chill ran down her spine and her hand flew to her scar. Her focus on the sherds faded and when she looked around, she found herself looking into Foster's dark eyes. She dropped the sherds and stood up so quickly her chair fell over behind her. For a moment she couldn't get her breath.

"Hello, Anna." His voice was quiet, but there was no mistaking the menace in it. She was shocked that he was much thinner than she remembered and his unshaven face was gray and hollow. She had never seen him look like this. His eyes were as black as she had ever seen them. There was no doubt they harbored unconcealed rage.

"Foster..." Anna glanced around the room, looking for Nick. She thought he was here. She moved around behind the table.

"He's not here, Anna. I saw him leave. And the skinny bitch is gone, too. I've been waiting outside for hours." He stood still and kept his eyes locked on hers.

"You know, I thought it would be warmer in the desert, but it's damn cold out there." It was a casual remark, almost conversational.

She was grateful that the table was between them, something she had the presence of mind to think about. *Where did Nick go? and why didn't he say anything about leaving?*

"What do you want, Foster?"

"'What do I want?' Why Anna, that's a silly question." Even though his voice was soft and even, he was tightly wound. "You know very well what I want. Get your gear. You're going home."

The familiar words echoed in her head. Had the intervening months since she left him even happened? It was Aztalan and Kimmswick all over again.

She would never give up what she had gained since coming to Tucson. "No, Foster. I'm not going back with you." She was surprised that she could say it so firmly. "This is my home now."

He took a step forward and started around the table. She stepped the other way, meaning to keep the table between them. She wanted to protect the pot and the work she had done, so she turned to the left and circled around another table, an empty one. He followed.

She took a deep breath and tried to think of some way to keep him talking or to distract him somehow. "How did you find me?"

"It wasn't easy. It took me a long time to track you, but the car was the key. At first I thought maybe you had sold it—you had to get money from somewhere—so I checked around. I'd call a dealer and tell them I was looking for 1981 Toyota Tercel—God, who besides you has that piece of junk anymore? Only one dealer in Chicago had one. I asked him what color it was and how long he'd had it. He said it was blue, so I knew it wasn't yours."

"Very clever, Foster. But then you were always a clever man." Anna glanced toward the door, trying to gauge the distance and if she might be able to make a break for it.

"Don't even think about it, Anna. You're not leaving here alone, and neither am I." He walked around the table and placed himself between her and the door. She moved around to keep the table as a shield.

"After I figured out that you didn't sell the Toyota, I thought you might not have gone far. That car wouldn't have taken you farther than a day or two away. After I left the university, I had plenty of time to track you down."

"Left the university?" She couldn't let him know what she knew; maybe it would keep him talking.

"Yes. I said I left the university. And it's all your fault, you bitch." It was the first time he had raised his voice and he took another step toward her. She moved around the table.

"My fault?"

"Yes. When you left I couldn't concentrate. I was frantic. I couldn't keep my mind on my work, so I resigned."

Liar.

His voice went quiet again. "Then I had plenty of time to look for you. I drove all over the Midwest looking for you. But, of course, I didn't find you.

"So I went home to think it out. I decided that you must have had your car shipped somewhere, but where would you get the money to do that? Then I figured it out. That motherfucker Rhinehart gave it to you, didn't he?"

She didn't answer.

"I finally found someone at a transport company who bought my story that they had damaged my wife's car. They looked back at their records and—what do you know? There it was: your transport manifest with the date and destination."

Anna had to admire his problem-solving ability, but she knew he was simmering just below real danger. "I'm impressed, Foster. You should have been a private detective."

"Yeah, well," he growled, "I needed to find you. Those bastards at Northwestern had no business turning me out. Dan Hamilton's research belonged to me anyway." He walked in a tight circle, raising his arms for emphasis, then stopped and glared at her. "Once a paper is turned in, it belongs to the professor. It wasn't his any longer. It was mine to do what I wanted with." He apparently didn't notice that he had revealed more about his departure from Northwestern than he intended.

He began pacing again and talking, always keeping himself between Anna and the door. He ranted about Dan Hamilton going to the dean. "I should have killed him when I had the chance."

Anna said nothing, but she tried to work her way around to the door. He seemed to anticipate her every move. Even though he might be losing control, he never took his eyes off her.

She decided to try another tack and softened her voice. "Foster, why don't you come home with me. You can go with me to my apartment and we can have dinner and talk about what we need to do next. I assume you've got a car. You can follow me."

He stared at her. "You must think I'm stupid, Anna. I'm going to follow you around an unfamiliar city? You'd lose me in no time. No, we'll go in your car."

She nodded. "Okay, whatever you say. I just need to get some things from the office."

She walked toward the office keeping her eye on him, but he didn't interfere. He watched her through the large window between the office and the lab. There was nothing she needed except time, but she began to sort through the things on Nick's desk, pretending to look for something. She kept praying that Nick would come back in.

Where did he go, anyway?

Fortunately, Foster was standing at a distance from the window, and he didn't see her lift the telephone off the hook and push the speed dial for Max's home. She heard it ringing, praying that he or Maggie would answer quickly and Foster would come no closer. When she heard Maggie's voice, she rattled the papers and called out.

"I think I have what I need, Foster. Just let me get my jacket and we'll go back to my apartment." She shoved the random papers into Nick's briefcase, and came to the door with it.

Foster looked suspicious, coming toward the office. "You didn't do anything stupid in there did you?"

"Of course not, Foster. I'm tired and I just want to go home. I like my job here and I don't want to go back to Chicago. I'll tell you about some of the work we are doing here. You'll understand when we've had time to talk it out." He pushed past her into the office, knocking her against the wall. He went to the desk and saw the receiver on the desk beside the phone. He turned around and grabbed her by the upper arms and slammed her into the wall again.

"Foster, you're hurting me! I didn't do anything. It's just off the hook. We do that when we're working and don't want to be disturbed." She prayed that if Maggie was still listening, she would hang up.

He picked up the phone and apparently heard nothing. "You'd better not be lying to me. Let's go." He grabbed her by the arm and dragged her to the door. Anna breathed a sigh of relief that he had heard only dead air.

In the parking lot, he pushed her toward her car. "Get in and drive." He went around to the passenger side and climbed in as she was starting the car.

As Anna pulled out on Grant Road, she looked in the mirror and was relieved to see Nick's pickup coming back toward the office. As she was accelerating, she lightly touched her brake pedal three times quickly, three times long, and then three times quickly again. She wasn't sure it would actually engage the brake lights because she had touched the pedal so lightly. She could only hope it worked. Foster didn't notice, but she saw that Nick stayed behind them.

She followed a round-about route back to her apartment, hoping that while she was killing time, Maggie and Max would have time to think of something. She didn't know what they could do, so she just prayed.

She didn't talk and Foster didn't seem to want to engage her. He sat there brooding silently. She wondered what he was thinking, but she decided against asking.

Nick followed at a respectable distance. She glanced in the mirror at a stoplight, and he gave her a thumbs up.

Finally, when she couldn't delay any longer, she pulled into the apartment parking lot.

Foster got out of the car and looked the building over.

"Not much of a place, is it? You'll be glad to get back to Chicago."

"It's fine, and I'm not leaving here."

"It's just a matter of time, Anna, a matter of time."

He followed her up the stairs and when she put her key in the door she panicked, realizing how foolish she had been. Now she would be alone in the apartment with him. She turned around to face him, trying to think about how to put it off. Over his shoulder, though, she saw Nick pull into a parking space in front of the next building. She breathed a sigh of relief, and pushed the door open.

25

Tucson, Arizona, December 1987

Minnie was in the kitchen, and Maggie and Max were sitting on the sofa, each with a glass of wine.

Minnie looked up at Anna and said, "I was wondering where you were. I thought maybe you had forgotten we were all coming over for dinner." She winked. "And I see you've brought another guest..."

She walked toward Foster so quickly, he almost stumbled back into Nick, who had just come in the open door behind them, his look of surprise dissolving into relief.

Minnie reached for Foster's hand and shook it firmly. "I'm Minnie, and you are...?"

He looked around at the gathering and over his shoulder at Nick and stammered, "F... Foster..." Minnie continued pumping his hand.

"So we finally meet, Foster. I've heard so much about you." He frowned, but said nothing.

While this awkward introduction was going on, Anna stepped away from Foster. Both Maggie and Max stood up. He took Anna by the shoulders and placed her next to Maggie. Nick slid past Foster and took a position next to Anna.

By now, Foster had regained some composure, but he had to forcibly extract his right hand from Minnie's because she had neglected to let go of it. He surveyed the semi-circle of people who stood before him.

He looked at Anna coldly and sneered, "I don't believe I've met your *friends*."

She smiled. "I'm happy to introduce you to my very, very good friends."

She nodded toward Max. "This is Jonathan Lomax, my employer and the Cultural Resources Manager and Principal Investigator for Archaeological Research Associates, and his wife, Maggie." They both nodded in Foster's direction but made no move to shake his hand.

Turning to her left, she said, "And this is Nick Anderson. He's a forensics anthropologist who works for the company." Nick's green eyes locked onto Foster's black ones until Foster looked away.

"And, of course, you've met Minnie, my next door neighbor."

Anna could see his discomfort. He had so successfully isolated her in Evanston, he wouldn't believe she could have friends.

His voice was suddenly polished and professional, but his wooden smile failed to reach his eyes. "I'm very glad to meet you." He nodded curtly in each one's direction. "I appreciate the support you've given to my

Anna during this difficult separation. But I'm sure you understand now that I'm here, I'll be taking care of her." He looked around at the gathered friends. "She needs me and I'm here to provide for her, so I thank you for all you've done, but I'll take it from here."

He took a step toward Anna, who stepped back and said, "No, Foster. You are not going to 'take care of me.' I don't need you to do that. I'm perfectly capable of taking care of myself."

He stopped. "Look, I'm sorry to intrude on your little party, Anna, but perhaps you could ask your friends to come back another time. We have too much to talk about and too much to do to prepare for our trip back to Chicago." He looked at Anna, barely concealing the threat in his eyes.

"No. We don't need to prepare to go back to Chicago. You will go back by yourself. I'm staying here."

Max stepped toward him. "I'm not sure you understand, Mr.... uh.... Robinson, is it? Anna is under contract to my company and she's a skilled archaeologist. I will not release her unless I know any change will be in her best interest." He paused. "Can you guarantee her a position where her talents can be best put to use?"

"You're not serious! Shovelbums move from site to site all the time. Who cares where they go and what they do next? These jobs are a dime a dozen." Foster looked at Anna and then back at Max. Neither spoke. "Are you telling me that you won't release her from her contract if she chooses to leave?" Foster's anger was escalating.

"Ah, Mr. Robinson, that might be true if Anna were only a shovelbum, as you put it, but that's not the case with her."

"What do you mean? She's not that important."

"But she is, Mr. Robinson, Anna is a valuable member of our team. She will be managing two projects that we have lined up in the next eight months. I can't let her go unless I'm sure we can replace her quickly with someone equally qualified; I have contracts to fulfill."

Anna looked at Max with grateful surprise. She thought it was a brilliant bluff.

Foster's demeanor took a softer turn. "Of course, Mr. Lomax. I understand."

"*Dr.* Lomax, please"

"Oh, sorry, Dr. Lomax. In any case, I have several contracts lined up for the company I've just begun. You see, I, too, recognize Anna's talents, and I'm looking forward to her help in building our business."

"Your business, Mr. Robinson?"

"Oh, please, call me Foster," he smiled. "May I call you Jonathan... Jon...?'

"Max."

"Thank you. Max, I know you understand the issues any new archaeological business faces when they are starting up. That's where I am right now. Anna will be an important part of my start-up team. You know how talented she is and I really need her to help put us on the map in the Midwest."

Everyone was still standing in the same position. No one said a word. Foster, with his back to the door and Anna's army almost circling him, looked awkward and off balance, something she had not seen before. But then his transformation into the smooth-talking, polished pretender he had always been kicked in, and she wondered how she had fallen for it all those years.

"Perhaps we should sit down and discuss this. I'm sure we all have Anna's best interest in mind." Foster managed something that looked like a real smile. "I'd be happy to buy out the remainder of her contract."

"Of course you would," Minnie answered, instigating a little action from everyone. "Why don't we all sit down. Foster, would you like a glass of wine?"

Without waiting for an answer, she turned and went to the kitchen.

Max turned Anna around and guided her to the sofa where he seated her with Maggie. "I'll get you a glass of wine, Anna," he said.

"Thank you, Max," Anna whispered, as Maggie took her hand.

Foster aimed for a seat on the sofa next to Anna, but Nick filled the void Max left behind, standing before the open space on the sofa, speaking quietly to Anna. Minnie took Foster's arm and steered him to a kitchen chair she had moved into the general vicinity of the end table next to the sofa.

Minnie brought Foster a glass of wine, filled to overflowing. He couldn't move without spilling it on himself.

Max returned with Anna's glass and sat down beside her. Nick took the rocking chair, and Minnie went back to the kitchen.

Except for Minnie's kitchen noises, it was silent. Maggie took Anna's hand and both Nick and Max glared at Foster.

Anna almost laughed at Foster's discomfort. Whenever he moved, a little wine sloshed out of the glass. She thought he was doing an amazing job of ignoring it; she had never seen him with any stain on his clothes. He cleared his throat, looked at Anna, and said, "Honey, please tell these folks that you're going back home with me. I promise that you can work; I won't stand in your way again. I just didn't understand how important it was to you."

Honey? Where did that come from? He usually called her "darling," unless he was mad at her. That was the only time he called her by her name. It had taken her a long time to figure that out. She was only Anna when she had displeased him. She had never been "Honey."

She could hear desperation in his voice, something else that was new for him. "You know there are lots of opportunities around Chicago. You could go back to Kimmswick if you want."

Max didn't wait for Anna's answer. "Didn't you just tell us you wanted her to work with you in your new business, Mr. Robinson?"

"Oh, Yes. Of course... th... that's what I meant." Foster appeared increasingly unsteady and the wine was still spilling. "We may have an opportunity to join the project at Kimmswick— subcontracting, you know."

Now Anna spoke. "You lied about starting a business, didn't you? You don't have a new business and you have no intention of letting me work if I go back to Chicago, isn't that right?"

Foster looked around for a place to put down the wine; Minnie had put his chair too far from both the coffee and end tables so he couldn't set it down without getting up.

Foster stood suddenly, splashing more wine on his pants. "Damn it, Anna," he muttered and walked to the table and put the offending glass down with a thump and a splash. "You belong to me. Tell these people to leave so we can get ready to go back to Chicago." He wiped his hands down the legs of his pants.

"No, Foster. I don't belong to you and I'm not going anywhere with you."

He took a step in her direction, but Nick stood and blocked his way.

Foster had both height and weight advantage over Nick, and even though she thought his agility would serve him well in a fight, she didn't want Nick to get hurt.

"Foster, stop!" Anna shouted. She started to get up, but Max put his hand on her arm.

Foster looked at her and said, "Shut up."

At that, Nick stepped forward, but Minnie stepped in between them. When Foster grabbed her by the arm to push her out of the way, she deftly brought her knee up into his groin, and when he bent over in pain, she brought her fist down hard on the back of his neck. He groaned and fell to the floor, curled up in the fetal position.

Everyone was shocked, but none more than Nick. He frowned at Minnie. But then he laughed and slapped her on the back. "Nice work! But I think I could have taken him."

She grinned. "Probably, but I didn't want to see blood all over the kid's apartment."

Anna stood, this time without interference. She looked around the room. "Max, Nick, would you please take Maggie and go with Minnie to her apartment. I'd like to talk to Foster alone."

Nick started to object, but Anna was firm. "Now, Nick. I need to do this. You'll hear it if I need help and then you should call the police. I want to talk to my husband alone. And call a cab. He'll need to go back to the office to get his car when he leaves here."

As Nick and the others left the apartment, Foster struggled to his feet and shouted after him, "God damned coward, letting a woman defend you."

Nick turned as the others went out the door. "I don't think she was defending me as much as she was making certain you could leave here with no permanent damage." He grinned at Foster, "Besides, didn't a woman just best you?"

Foster glared at him. "You've been sleeping with my wife, you son of a bitch!"

"Out! Now!" Anna stepped between them and closed the door behind Nick.

When she turned around, she pointed at Foster and said, "Sit down."

He didn't. "You're sleeping with that god damned cowboy, aren't you?" He stepped toward her, fists clenched.

"Stop. Don't come any closer." She lifted her chin and looked directly into his eyes. "And don't even think about touching me."

"I don't know what's wrong with you, why you did this. You're my wife. You belong to me."

"That's the problem, Foster. You think I'm your property, but you don't treat me as well as you treat your car. You think nothing of slapping me around when I displease you."

"Then don't displease me. You're going back to Chicago with me if I have to drag you there."

"No, I'm not going back."

He stepped forward and grabbed her arm. "You don't get to choose."

"If I scream, they'll call the police." She said it quietly.

He let go.

His voice softened. "Come on, baby. I love you and I want to take care of you. You need me." He reached up to touch her cheek but she turned her head and stepped around him.

"No. I don't need you. In fact, I don't need anybody. I can take care of myself."

"Oh yeah? What about your cowboy?"

"Leave him out of this. He has nothing to do with us. You have everything to do with us and why we are over."

"Me? I haven't done anything wrong. You were the one. You never once considered what I wanted. I gave you everything you needed, a beautiful home, clothes, jewelry. You had it all. You could have had a wonderful life if—"

"If what? If I behaved myself? If I let you walk all over me? If I gave up every dream I ever had—for a career—for a family? You said you wouldn't share me with anyone. You wanted me to think I couldn't do anything without you there to help me. You tried to undermine my confidence. You cut me off from my friends. You let me believe we could have a family..." She choked back a sob. "And you raped me, more than once you raped me."

"Raped you? You're my wife. I have rights."

"Your rights stop where my rights begin."

Just then there was a light tap on the door. Minnie said, "His cab is here."

"Thanks, Minnie." She turned to Foster and said, "I want you to leave and not come back. I'll get a restraining order and file for divorce. You'd be wise not to contest it."

"I won't give you a divorce. That will never happen."

Anna opened the door and stood back as he went out to the landing. Minnie was standing at her apartment door, which was open just a few inches.

Foster turned back to Anna. The outside light reflected in his eyes, blacker than she'd ever seen them. "This is not over, Anna. I promise you, it's not over." He turned and went down the steps.

Nick came out and stood behind Anna, watching the cab pull away. He put his hand on her shoulder. "Are you all right?"

As the taillights faded into the distance, she said, "Better than I've ever been."

26

Tucson, Arizona, December 1987

That night, Minnie insisted that Anna stay with her. In the morning, Nick came by to pick her up before Minnie left for school. He told her to bring what she needed, that Maggie wanted her to come and stay with them until they were sure that Foster was gone.

She looked into Nick's eyes and saw his concern. "Maybe for a little while. He may go, but that doesn't mean he won't come back. I won't hide from him any longer."

Nick nodded, but she knew it wasn't because he agreed with her.

Anna lay awake in the Lomax guest room, thinking about what had happened. Whatever it was that drove Foster, there was nothing she could do to change that.

She whispered a quiet prayer of thanks for the friends who had been there for her. That was what had given her the strength to confront him. She also said a quiet prayer for the strength to do battle with him when he comes back. She was sure that he would.

At breakfast, she thanked Max and Maggie for their support.

"It was easy to see just what kind of a man he is, Anna." Max said. "I understand why you had to get away from him. But I suspect he'll be back and you'll need to be prepared."

"I know. I will."

Max took a sip of his coffee. "I wasn't entirely bluffing with what I said about your work. You've impressed me, sometimes in spite of my reluctance to be impressed."

Anna smiled. "Thanks."

She could have ridden to the site with Max, but Nick insisted that he would pick her up. She said almost nothing as they walked to the truck. He opened the door and waited while she settled into the seat. Then he walked around to get in the driver's side. Instead of starting the truck, he turned toward her. "What? We're not going anywhere until you say it."

"He'll be back. I keep trying to convince myself he won't, but..."

He turned her toward him and gently took her hands. "You're right. I've known men like him before. He's a time bomb. Look what he did to that poor kid at Northwestern. And he blames you. He's the kind of man who needs to control others, and when he lost control of you he couldn't handle it. I suspect he's convinced that if he can get you back under his thumb, everything will be fine."

Whenever Nick took her hands, everything *was* fine. He leaned toward her, but she did not turn away. He brushed her lips gently with his own.

A warmth surged through her body, something different, something new. Nick's kiss was gentle, meant to comfort, not to arouse, but it stirred an entirely new emotion in Anna. She gave in to it, and as the external world fell away, Nick pulled her closer and kissed her with the passion she had missed.

> *She ran along the ridge path, laughing, her black hair flying out behind her in the wind. Her man, Tonrai, strong and brown-skinned ran behind. He reached out for her and swung her around in his arms. She felt his strength and the love that he pledged to her, knowing then that nothing could ever come between them.*

When Nick released her from his embrace and looked into her eyes, she was briefly surprised to see green eyes not brown. She blinked and smiled.

"I will be okay, Nick," she said, looking deeply into his eyes. "I will. I promise."

↲∾

It wasn't long before Anna persuaded Max, Maggie and Nick that she needed to get back to her own apartment. She told them she needed some sense of normalcy, reminding them that she needed her independence. And, besides, Minnie would be close by if she needed anything.

Nick was reluctant, but he understood.

On the way back to her apartment, they stopped for lunch at a little Mexican restaurant. Over beer and *enchiladas*, they talked about Christmases past and Christmases future. Anna didn't have a lot of happy memories, but she was filled with hope for the future.

They were nearly finished eating when Anna put down her fork and watched a young family that had just come in. They had two children and, of course, getting organized for lunch was challenging. The older child, a girl with dark curly hair, looked to be about three and the younger one, a boy, was probably less than a year old. While the waitress went to get a booster seat for one and a high chair for the other, the little girl kept asking questions.

"Daddy, when is Santa coming?"

"How does he know what I want?"

"Can I have fried ice cream?"

Her father promised her she could have the dessert after she had eaten her lunch. Finally, they were settled with the younger one stuffing Cheerios into his mouth and the three-year-old looking at the pictures in the menu.

Nick watched Anna watch the children.

She turned to him and said, "I want to see it."

"See what?"

"The baby's grave. I want to see it and know he is really with his mother now."

Nick nodded. "We can go by Holy Hope now if you want."

On the way, they stopped so Anna could buy a small bouquet of flowers. At the cemetery, they went to the office and requested a map and the location of the Ramirez plot.

They drove into the cemetery toward the neighboring Evergreen Cemetery on its southern boundary.

They got out of the truck near the fence that divided the two cemeteries, and Nick said, "These cemeteries are just about the same age and have a similar history, I think. They date back to just a few years before statehood."

"They are very different." She looked around the Catholic cemetery noting the orderly landscaping, with palm trees, a scattering of oaks, and tall, slender

Arizona cypress trees lining some of the roadways. Markers, for the most part, were flush with the ground with a few upright monuments throughout.

Nick checked the map again. "I think Evergreen is a throwback to the cemeteries so many of the founding fathers knew back east. Holy Hope looks more like the old Mexican cemeteries that many of the Mexican Catholics knew before they settled here. Most of the founding fathers of the city of Tucson are probably buried in one of the two." He directed her along the chain-link fence.

"I see what you mean. But for a civilized, eastern-style cemetery, it looks a little untamed, almost a forest of trees and towering monuments. It's easy to see why it's named Evergreen. Most of those trees look like pines."

"Those are Aleppo pines. They're not native, but I think they're thriving."

She saw that Evergreen did not actually butt up against Holy Hope. There was a deep, concrete-lined wash between them. There were bushes growing in the cracks and a fair amount of trash littered the base. The fence was in a bit of disrepair, with openings here and there along the bottom.

He stopped again to look at the map and then looked at the fence. "I suspect a lot of city coyotes make use of those openings as they travel back and forth between the two cemeteries. Saves having to climb over. Probably a fair amount of rabbits for them to hunt in all of this grass." He stopped.

"Here it is."

They stood before a modest monument inscribed with "Ramirez" along with a carved cross at the narrow top. On the wider base, side-by-side, were Armando and Esperanza's names and dates along with the typical sentiments, "Loving Husband and Father," "Loving Wife and Mother." The ground in front of the monument, close to the center, bore evidence of recent disturbance. Ángel's grave. Anna knelt and placed the flowers on the ground. Nick stood with his hand on her shoulder. Neither one spoke.

When she was ready, Nick took her hand and they walked back to the truck.

27

Tucson, Arizona, December 1987

The week before Christmas, she and Nick went horseback riding again. They had ridden several times over the past year and she had become more and more fond of Paco. Whenever she drove in to Nick's place, the buckskin would look up from the field and watch her park the car. Then he would come to the gate and stand there waiting for her, nickering softly.

He always walked right beside her, never pulling ahead or lagging behind. If she stopped, he stopped. If she walked faster, he walked faster, still never getting out ahead of her. She laughed and asked Nick if he had taught his horses to heel.

"I suppose you could call it that. A good horse knows how to walk along with his person. And I think Paco has decided that you are, in fact, his person. He's chosen you over me, I think."

Anna was pleasantly surprised at the idea that Paco might have chosen her, but she doubted he was right.

"You're exaggerating, Nick. He is your horse after all."

"No. He doesn't look up when I drive in, and he never waits at the gate for me the same way he waits for you. He joins the others at the gate, but behaves like just one of the gang when it's only me."

Anna was pleased to think that Paco saw her as special. Chalk up another good friend in Tucson.

It was a crisp morning with a brilliant blue sky and temperatures in the low sixties. Later, the day might bring low seventies—a perfect winter day for a ride. Sunlight reflected off Mount Lemmon's deep covering of snow. The upper reaches and the canyons of Samaniego Ridge held onto the snow that had fallen last week. The Tucson Basin had enjoyed a good, nourishing winter rain—a female rain, as the Indians called it. The washes were running and the rivers in Tucson had flowing water, but nothing had reached flood stage or had caused any damage.

They had ridden in all of the seasons—even in the summer when the temperatures hit 100 degrees and more by late morning. On those days, they struck out from the barn by six and were back by eight. There was something about winter and its beneficial rains that made the desert special. The naked spikes of a few ocotillos sported red blooms at the top, looking like wicked Christmas candles. Every little Christmas cholla was covered with red berries in celebration of the season and the rains.

As they rode out the trail, she breathed in the cleansing, cool air, renewing her spirit.

Anna caught Nick looking at her.

"What?"

"Just thinking."

"About?"

"You. I'm worried about you, you know." Nick pulled Sadie up and stopped. Anna halted Paco next to him.

"You don't have to worry, Nick. I'll be okay. Foster went back to Chicago. I think he'll stay away. He knows about the restraining order, and he's gotten the divorce papers by now. He should know it's over."

She had met with a lawyer in Tucson who drew up the divorce papers and recommended she ask for alimony. She refused, saying she didn't even want a division of property. She wanted nothing but out. Of course, everything depended on how Foster reacted when the papers were served.

"You know that doesn't mean he won't come back." Nick reached across the distance between Sadie and Paco and took Anna's hand. "He blames you for ruining his life. You can't trust that he won't come back. Remember, he warned you that it wasn't over."

"I remember."

"We have to be prepared if he shows up again."

For Anna, though, there was a fine line between Foster's close monitoring of her activities and the degree to which her Tucson friends were now attending to everything she did and everywhere she went.

"Really, Nick," she said, "You can't keep smothering me. I didn't trade Foster's overbearing domination for having my new friends manage my every coming and going like I can't take care of myself. I'm hoping we can relax now. Foster's gone. If he weren't, don't you think we would have known it by now? Can't we just get ready for Christmas without all of this drama?"

Paco shifted under her, impatient to move along. She patted his neck. "Paco's had enough of this standing still. Let's move on." She took her hand from Nick's. "Let's go, big boy," and she kicked him into a canter.

"Hey!" Nick kicked Sadie and caught up with her. Paco had slipped into an easy lope and the two horses settled into a comfortable pace along the old road. Anna could hear nothing but the wind in her ears and the pounding of horses' hooves. She had never before enjoyed such a sense of freedom.

As they approached the Cañada del Oro Wash, they reined in the horses and stepped into the flowing water at a walk. Anna laughed and Nick just shook his head. "I can't believe you did that. It's a good thing Paco is the boss hoss. He knows how to manage the others in his herd, or Sadie would never have caught him."

They stopped while the horses examined the water flowing around their fetlocks. Paco drank deeply, but Sadie, like many horses who aren't used to waterways in the desert, was suspicious and didn't drink.

"He's a steady boy, all right. Just perfect for my amateur riding skills."

"You didn't look so amateur a few minutes ago." He laughed.

"Why, thank you, kind sir. I'll take that as a compliment." She bowed toward him from the saddle.

"That's how it was meant, my lady." Nick returned the bow, tipping his hat in her direction.

They stepped out of the wash and rode a little further in silence, listening to the scrape-clop of the horses' hooves and to the bird songs rising from the scrub. The complex song of a curve-billed thrasher in a mesquite tree rose above the rest.

Anna stopped next to the tree to listen. "I didn't know the curve-bill could sing like that. He sounds like a mockingbird. Most of the time he just whistles for attention—kind of a 'whit-weet,' like my daddy used to call us in from the yard."

"I think they are related to the mockingbird. At least they often sound like them. Most people can identify the whistle, but not so much their song. He's staking out his territory. No doubt there's a lady he wants to impress."

Nick imitated the whistle perfectly and then trilled a little snatch of the melody. "I'm impressed." Anna smiled.

"Like our friend in the tree, I have my eye on a mate."

Anna blushed, this time enjoying the warmth of it. She wondered how long she could resist this beautiful man. It was getting harder and harder, and even worse, she wasn't sure she really wanted to.

As they rode back in to Nick's place, Anna was overcome with a feeling of serenity. "Lovely morning, Nick."

After they put the horses away, they went into the house for a late breakfast. Nick made egg, bacon, and green chile burritos and steaming coffee.

"You're spoiling me, Nick." She sighed contentedly.

"I aim to please."

Anna wondered where the light that reflected in his eyes had originated since the shades were drawn against the late morning sun. She would later think this was the moment she gave in to her feelings.

When it was time to go, Nick walked her to the car and kissed her gently before opening the door for her. She kissed him back and smiled up at him.

Their relationship had moved into a comfortable, easy commitment, and Anna was ready.

28

Tucson, Arizona, December 1987

They had finished the work at the Ramirez Ruin, and Max was working on the final report to the state. Each of them, Nick, Anna, and Margy, had been asked to read over the report and to contribute content. Nick's expertise with forensics, Anna's expertise with artifact identification, and Margy's insights into sociocultural influences were all important, and Max wanted all of it in the report. He was looking forward to helping design the interpretive trail that would finally be a part of the park.

Anna had spent a lot of time in the lab since the project was finished, working carefully and meticulously to reconstruct the pot. By now it was starting to look like the jar she had envisioned. There were pieces missing, so she went through the remaining bags of artifacts, finding two more matching pieces, and adding the code numbers to them. But there was still a sizable piece missing—a rim piece. She had not found it anywhere in the collection from the site, and assumed that the pot would always have that empty space, which was not all that unusual. Many of the pieces at the museum had empty spaces; it was just the nature of reconstruction.

By now, she was comfortable with her knowledge of the ancient potter as maker and Esperanza Ramirez as giver. The Hohokam woman had left this gift from the earth for Esperanza to find, and Esperanza had left the pieces as a gift of the earth for Anna to uncover. Each time she placed a sherd in its rightful place, she heard the distant song of the woman whose hands had crafted it; she drew strength from the potter and Esperanza Ramirez. They were women who survived in an unforgivable landscape against whatever forces of nature or man worked against them. She welcomed her communion with them during her work in the lab.

As Christmas neared, she began to get nervous. Her previous Christmas in Tucson was quiet. She had declined Minnie's invitation to spend Christmas with her family and she had spent a quiet day at home in her apartment. Even though it might have been depressing, she reveled in her aloneness, recognizing that she was nowhere near as lonely as she had been last Christmas with Foster and his parents.

❧❦

After she and Foster married, they had driven to the Gold Coast for Christmas every year. Anna was always uncomfortable around Mrs. Robinson. Even though she had been exceptionally generous in planning their wedding, Anna was suspicious of her motive. Mrs. Robinson had done it for herself, for her standing in society. No matter what Anna had done or how much she had tried to build a relationship with his mother, nothing worked, and she bore the weight of her mother-in-law's disapproval every time they visited. She wondered why Mrs. Robinson, who had never invited Anna to call her anything else, had not worked harder to persuade Foster that Anna was not good enough for him. Her enthusiasm for their wedding remained a mystery.

She hated how his mother fawned over him. She was constantly attending to Foster's comfort and his needs. She called him "my Foster" and asked him constantly if he needed anything. Did he want another drink? Of course, if he did, a servant brought it.

The last Christmas she had spent with Foster's parents, Anna had taken something up to Foster's room, and when she reached the second landing on the way down, she heard his mother say, "Foster, my dear, I just know Anna isn't caring for you properly. Is she still insisting on getting a job?" Her tone made it sound as if getting a job was disgusting, something akin to typhoid fever.

She stopped and listened.

"Don't worry, Mother, I'm teaching her and she knows now that I won't stand for it."

"That's good, darling. I'm just not sure she will ever fit in with us, you know."

"I know. You'll see. When I finish with her, you'll be pleased."

She sat down on the step. *What does he mean 'finish with' me? What is he teaching me? That it's unacceptable for a Robinson woman to work? Did he think she should emulate his mother?* She tried to put it out of her mind.

If his parents had been less affluent, she might have been able to impress Mrs. Robinson. She could offer to help with the dishes after dinner, but that was out of the question since the kitchen staff had it all in their hands. There was nothing she could have done that would have made Foster's mother see her as someone worthy of her son.

Looking back, she was glad she was not worthy of him. And she had begun to understand what Foster meant about teaching her. Too bad for him that he didn't "finish."

∽∽

On Christmas Eve, she and Nick went to Tumacácori, a small town south of Tucson, to see the *luminarias* at the 160-year old mission church. Anna had never seen *luminarias* before coming to Tucson. Minnie had told her that they were a Mexican tradition adopted by Arizonans for Christmas decorations, easily made by putting sand in the bottom of a paper bag and standing a candle in the sand.

On Christmas Eve, every year, the National Park Service staff and volunteers line the walks and every flat surface with thousands of *luminarias*—along the tops of the exterior walls, along the walks, around the doors, in the niches, and in the bell towers.

There was a festive atmosphere as they joined the long line of visitors. Many, like Nick, had been there before; others, like Anna, were unprepared for what they would see. They passed through the visitor's center, then through the museum rooms, and finally out to a patio where the first stunning glimpse of the mission was framed by an arched window. It took Anna's breath away.

She stood transfixed, looking through the opening at the paper lanterns outlining the mission and the walkways. The candle flames flickered inside of their brown paper bags, casting an ethereal glow that lit up the night.

As they stepped out of the building, overhead a dark, moonless sky held a panorama of stars, brighter than Anna could remember. When they entered the mission, they were greeted by an interior lit only by the hundreds of *luminarias* on both sides of the aisle and at the front of the sanctuary. They walked in silence down the aisle to the altar. Instead of painted walls and statues of saints, there now was only peeling plaster and vague remnants of decorations. Anna looked at the space and lifted her eyes to the domed ceiling. Feeling the press of people behind her who were seeking their own comfort at the crumbling altar, she whispered a quick prayer and took Nick's hand as they turned to follow others into the side yard.

The canopy of stars shone brightly against the dark sky above them and *luminarias* lit the walkway before them. Voices singing Christmas carols drifted on the breeze. Every now and then, there was a lantern that had extinguished itself or had set its bag on fire, but it didn't diminish the beauty.

Ahead were tables where the visitors could get hot chocolate and cookies, but they didn't stop for refreshments; instead, they made their way back to the parking lot. It was a cold night and Anna was glad to put her hands to the heater vents as soon as the truck warmed up.

"Nick, I can't remember when I've spent a more beautiful Christmas Eve. Thank you for sharing this with me."

He looked thoughtful. "It's been over ten years since I came here for Christmas Eve. It's good to be back. I'm glad I could share it with you."

They drove back to Tucson in comfortable silence. When Nick pulled into the parking lot of Anna's apartment building, he turned off the truck and turned to Anna as if he had something to say.

Before he spoke, Anna said, "Do you want to come in, Nick? We could have a glass of wine or a cup of coffee."

"I'd love that, Anna." He took his Stetson off and left it in the truck.

They climbed the steps to the second floor. Anna unlocked her door and they stepped inside. The apartment was quiet and lit only by a dim light in the kitchen. The answering machine was blessedly silent.

She turned to drop her keys and purse on the low table by the door when Nick wrapped his arms around her and pulled her to him.

She folded herself into his embrace and returned his kiss. He explored the length of her body with his hands. He drew her coat down and off her shoulders, dropping it on the floor behind her. She pressed against him and wrapped her arms around his waist.

He lifted her into his arms and carried her to the bedroom. He lay her down on the bed and knelt beside her.

"You are so beautiful." She reached up and pushed his jacket off of his shoulders and fumbled with his belt, unbuttoning his pants and pushing them down. She was surprised at herself—but not enough to stop. He helped her pull them off and then returned the favor, pulling her sweater over her head and burying his face in her cleavage. She breathed in the scent of his shampoo, and reached down his back to tug at his shirt. He pushed up to his knees and took it off quickly, looking down at her beneath him.

He hesitated. "Anna, are you sure?"

She reached for him with both hands. "I'm sure," she whispered.

Nick reached over the edge of the bed and retrieved something from his pants pocket, which he held between his teeth while he reached under her, unfastening her bra and pushing it out of the way.

She arched upward as he pulled her slacks and underwear down and tossed them from the bed. When they were both naked, he fumbled with the condom and Anna helped him. He lay down beside her wrapping his left arm under her shoulders and pulling her against him. She took hold of him and squeezed while he traced his finger lightly across her breasts, her stomach, and down. Time slowed while her desire intensified. She couldn't remember such pleasure. Even Foster, at his most gentle, had never made her feel this way. She wondered how she could be thinking about him now, and she pushed him out of her mind, letting Nick and her body take over.

He took her slowly and gently to a pleasure she had never experienced. When it was done, they lay together in the tangled sheets, spent and wet, and breathed in the perfumes of their combined scents.

"Wow." Anna smiled into the darkness. "I feel like this is the first time I've ever made love—I mean, really made love, no holds barred, anything goes." She sighed. "You are definitely something, Mr. Anderson."

"I love you, Anna," Nick whispered.

"I love you, too." Anna snuggled into the curve of his arm and his body and drifted off to a contented sleep.

❧∽❧

As Nick drifted into a dream, he heard Rita's voice. "She's good for you, Nick. It's time."

He settled into easy breathing and awoke in the morning at his usual time, thinking, "Time to feed the horses," but then he looked around and smiled.

He looked at Anna, curled up beside him. He slid out of bed and went into the bathroom. He found a towel in the linen closet and turned on the shower. He soaped himself all over and thought about last night. He was happy, finally, after years of thinking he would never love again. He thought Rita would approve.

He was rinsing off when the shower door opened and Anna stepped in. He gathered her into his arms and grabbed the soap, lathering her all over, then rinsing the soap off and holding her, wet skin on wet skin.

Nick turned off the water, whispering in her ear, "I have to go feed the horses. They'll be wondering where I am."

Anna laughed. "Is that your idea of 'sweet nothings'?"

"Get used to it. The horses come first in the morning." He kissed her, wrapped a towel around her, and grabbed one for himself. "If I don't get going now," he said, "I won't be able to."

"If I didn't care so much about the horses, I wouldn't let you go."

Nick ran back to the bedroom and grabbed his clothes from the floor. Anna stood in the bathroom door, wrapped in a towel, watching him dress.

"By the way, Merry Christmas."

"Holy cow! Today is Christmas. I totally forgot." He grinned. "Guess I got distracted." He finished dressing and took her in his arms. "I love you, Anna. I love you."

She smiled up at him. "And I love you. I tried not to, but it would have been easier to stop a freight train. You are the best thing that ever happened to me."

Nick kissed her, and said, "Let's see. We need to be at Max and Maggie's house by two-thirty. I'll be back to pick you up about eleven-thirty."

She looked puzzled. "Eleven-thirty? It doesn't take that long to get to their house."

"I know." He grinned at her, "I have something else in mind for those two hours."

"Oh," Anna grinned back at him. "Of course. You have some last minute Christmas shopping."

"Oh, yeah. I do." He looked at the unmade bed. "Right here."

He grabbed his jacket and kissed her on the cheek. She followed him to the door, still wrapped in her towel, kissed him again, and watched through the slightly open door as he ran lightly down the steps in the rising morning light. He turned and waved before getting into the truck.

She closed the door and leaned against it, thinking about last night. She was surprised that she was positively giddy.

29

Tucson, Arizona, Christmas Day 1987

Nick asked Anna if she would move in with him, but she said no. Although she was happy that she had surrendered to her feelings and that they had moved into a comfortable, easy intimacy, she thought it best to wait until her divorce from Foster was final. She had not heard anything from him, nor had her Tucson attorney heard anything. She wasn't sure how to interpret his silence, but she kept hoping he had finally accepted that their marriage was over and that she wasn't coming back to Chicago.

The holiday had been a whirlwind of joy for her. When she and Nick arrived at Max and Maggie's on

Christmas Day, they could barely disguise the change in their relationship. They had just put gifts under the tree, when she saw a knowing look pass between them and she blushed. Maggie put an arm around Anna's waist and asked her to come help her in the kitchen, leaving Max and Nick to themselves.

"Mmmm. Everything smells so good. Thank you for inviting me."

"I'm always glad to have you here, Anna. You've become a good friend."

For a brief moment, she remembered the pain of her isolation with Foster, losing all of her friends and having no one to turn to when she was most alone. Now, she had friends who had been there when she needed them the most, and, best of all, she had Nick. She looked around the kitchen. "Can I help you with something?"

"Not right now. Maybe when it's time to set the table?"

Anna nodded and sat at the counter and watched Maggie peel apples for fruit salad.

"I really am grateful to you and Max, but I worried about how Max felt about me."

"Of course. Max isn't quick to let folks know what he's thinking; he expected you to prove yourself at work and you did." She paused. "You should also know that he was worried about Nick."

"What do you mean?"

"Max has always been a little protective of Nick. He saw what he went through when he lost Rita."

"I'm glad Max was there for him."

Maggie set the bowl of fruit aside, saying, "He was, and he's spent the last ten years worried about when and if Nick might fall in love again."

"I see... and when he thought Nick was interested in me?"

"He was worried. It was the first time since Rita that Nick had shown any interest in someone, and, because none of us knew your story, he was afraid Nick was in for a hurting."

"Which became all the more likely at Thanksgiving, when Foster showed up."

"Mmmm hmmm." Maggie opened the oven door and basted the turkey. When she finished, she turned to Anna. "You're happy today." She arched one eyebrow. "You're positively glowing."

Anna blushed again. "I hope Max knows now I would never hurt Nick." She pressed her finger into the scar and whispered, "I didn't want to fall in love with him, and I tried hard not to. It scares me to feel this way when my life is so unsettled, at least as far as Foster is concerned."

"Nick's a grown man and he can handle whatever he needs to. He's not as vulnerable as Max used to think he was. He's come a long way, and he can make his own choices." Maggie went to the sink and washed her hands. "Now, let's get that table set."

❧❧

The day after Christmas, Nick took her to meet his mother. It was Anna's first trip to Bisbee, so Nick launched a running narrative, tour guide style, about the history and geography of Cochise County and the San Pedro Valley.

"Bisbee," he told her, "had been a thriving mining community for nearly a century until the copper reserves were depleted and the mining operations closed down. That's when my dad lost his job." He went on to say how the town had bounced back in recent years as an artists' community as well as a retirement community.

"When Phelps Dodge left in 1975, my dad never found another job. If my mother hadn't been a clerk

in the post office, we would have been in deep trouble.
I was at the university by then and with Rita. Then
my dad got sick —lung cancer. He died in '78. It was
a double whammy for me: Rita in '76 and then Dad.
My mom was my rock. I don't know how she did it,
working and taking care of Dad, and being there for
me when Rita—" Nick swallowed hard and looked
out across the San Pedro Valley before returning his
attention to the road before them.

Anna said nothing, allowing him the space he
needed to finish the thought for himself.

When they drove through the Mule Pass Tunnel,
she saw the city of Bisbee stretched out along the
slopes of the Mule Mountains. Houses lined the
hillsides high and low, as if they had been tossed on
top of one another. As they drove into town, Nick gave
her a quick lesson on the geography of the city.

"Houses are built on terraces and sometimes right
into the hillside. You could have a three-story house
with ground level exits on all floors. They say you can
spit off your porch right into your neighbor's chimney.
And that's probably not an exaggeration. In some
areas, houses are stacked up like so much cord wood."
Anna thought she heard hometown pride in Nick's
tone.

"It's charming, Nick. But some of those streets
look nearly vertical."

"There are lots of hills to drive up and down, but
the stairs are what Bisbee's famous for."

"The stairs?" Anna thought he might be kidding.

"Most cities have sidewalks, but Bisbee probably
has more stairs than sidewalks. I think there's
somewhere in the neighborhood of a thousand steps
that go from terrace to terrace—I don't know who
counted, but I guess they're right. They were built
during the Depression on the mule paths from the old
mining days—it was a jobs project.

"Some of them are pretty deteriorated now and could use some renovation, but I don't know if the city has the money. It would be a shame to lose something so unique to Bisbee."

Nick turned onto a side street that wound around and climbed to the upper terraces. Anna was fascinated that the houses on her left were above the street level with vine-covered retaining walls beneath porches or fenced front yards. On the right she was looking down at rooftops and back yards. A pipe fence was all that stood between them and the downhill houses. Nick steered into a pullout, got out of the truck and came around and opened her door. He reached behind the seat for the shopping bag full of gifts for his family.

He told her that because the streets were too narrow for people to park in front of their houses they had made pullouts along the streets. They walked only a short distance when Nick led her through an opening in the retaining wall. Anna was surprised that the space between the two houses couldn't have been more than five feet. Nick pointed to the house on the left, a two-story, white house, with blue shutters and an enclosed front porch.

"That's home," he said.

"Home." She paused. "Nick, you can't imagine what that word means to me." She remembered the house she grew up in. Neat? Yes. Comfortable? No. Somewhere she was glad to come back to? Never. She was glad Nick had what she never had in a place to grow up.

In front of them was a second set of stairs that climbed farther up the hill.

Nick pointed. "That leads up to the back yard and a second floor entrance." He opened the side door just as his mother was reaching for it. Mrs. Anderson was a short, round woman with graying hair, a ready smile, and green eyes just like Nick's. She dried her hands on her apron and gave Nick a loving hug.

"Welcome home, son. Merry Christmas." She turned to Anna and Nick introduced them.

"Hello, Mrs. Anderson. I'm so glad to meet you." Anna held out her hand, expecting a handshake, but Nick's mother wrapped Anna's hand in her own hands and held it.

"Pish-tush!" She shook her head. "What's this 'Mrs. Anderson'? You just call me Martha, darlin'. Come in, come in."

Anna was struck by the difference between Mrs. Robinson's artificial "darling" and Mrs. Anderson's warm "darlin'." Hers was sincere, nothing put on or snobbish about it.

Martha turned and directed them to the kitchen table where she had laid out a simple lunch of homemade soup along with sandwich fixings.

"This is lovely, Mrs. — I mean, Martha." Anna smiled at the older woman.

Nick didn't waste any time grabbing a roll, tearing it open and making a big thick sandwich. While he was doing that, his mother ladled out a bowl of soup and put it down in front of her son. She ladled a second bowl and placed it in front of Anna.

"Thank you."

"No thanks necessary, Anna, just help yourself." She reached for a pitcher. "Iced tea okay?"

"Yes, thank—" Anna caught herself and smiled. "Yes."

Martha gave them each a glass of tea, then sat down and looked across the table at Nick. "It's good to have you here, son. You might want to take a few minutes while you're here to run next door and see your Aunt Gertie. She ain't been feeling too well lately. Don't think it's anything serious. She's still grievin' for Herman, and you'd brighten her day."

"I'll do that, Mama," Nick said. "It's hard to think that both Dad and his brother are gone."

Martha turned to Anna. "Nick's Uncle Herman died about six months ago. They were just shy of fifty years together. Shame he didn't make it to celebrate with her."

Fifty years. Anna couldn't imagine it—at least not before Nick.

After lunch, Nick took Anna into the living room where it appeared that every flat surface, including the walls, had framed photographs either sitting or hanging. Nick took her on a tour of the photos, introducing her to the history of the Andersons. She saw Nick playing basketball at Bisbee High, his graduation picture, several pictures of Nick's parents at different times in their marriage, Nick's dad and his brother as young men with their lovely wives, and pictures of his sister and her family. She picked up a picture of Nick and a beautiful dark-haired woman in front of Old Main on the campus at the university.

"This is Rita." She wasn't asking. She looked at the two of them, Nick holding his hand on her round belly, this younger Nick with the love of his life and the baby they were expecting. "You were right. She is beautiful. You look so happy." There was a wistfulness in Anna's tone that alarmed Nick.

"I'll tell Mama she should put this picture away."

"No, no. Don't do that. She deserves to be remembered, along with your daughter. They are a part of you, and I love you." She looked up at him. "You don't have to pretend that she never existed or that you don't sometimes re-live the pain when something triggers a memory." Anna returned the picture to the shelf with the others. "I don't want you to ever forget her."

There was a warmth and hominess about Nick's childhood home that Anna had never experienced before—a serenity that was nourished by love. No sooner had she had this thought, when there was a sudden commotion in the kitchen.

Nick warned Anna. "Get prepared for a hurricane and a cyclone. Heather and the kids have arrived."

In the kitchen, Anna heard the high-pitched squeals of the children. "Grammy! Look at what Santa brought me!"

Then "My turn, my turn! Grammy, Grammy, lookit!"

She heard Martha laughing with them, and when she and Nick stepped into the kitchen, the children abandoned Grammy and screamed, "Uncle Nick!"

They launched themselves into his arms, nearly knocking him over as he knelt down to greet them. They covered him with kisses and hung on as he stood up, holding both children in his arms. Anna could see the delight Nick took in his niece and nephew; he would be a great father.

Between the squeals of the children, Nick introduced Anna to his younger sister and to the kids, Lucy and Danny. Heather apologized to Anna for the din the children had created.

Anna laughed. "It's okay. They're kids, it's Christmas, and Uncle Nick is here."

After the children settled down, Nick took the Christmas gifts from the shopping bag, which got the little ones excited again. They jumped up and down as Nick handed them their gifts. Lucy squealed with delight at Cookie Monster and Mickey and Minnie Mouse babies. She held Cookie Monster up to Nick and said, in her best monster voice, "Cookie!" Everyone laughed, so she said it over and over again.

Danny put his Transformer on the floor and started driving the Matchbox cars around and around it. Martha and Heather were delighted with the hand-knit, Irish wool cardigans Nick gave them.

While the children were playing with their Christmas toys, the adults had a chance to talk. While the women were talking, Nick took a moment to run next door to visit his Aunt Gertie. Later, when they were ready to leave, Nick hugged his mother and his sister, and Martha again took Anna's hand in both of hers.

"Thank you for putting the light back in my boy's eyes." Martha's eyes filled, and Anna gave her a warm hug.

"It's been my pleasure." Anna's eyes filled, too.

Nick was squatting down saying goodbye to the children. "Can you say goodbye to Anna now?" Lucy looked shy and went to hold on to her mother's legs, but Danny came directly to Anna, who leaned down to him. He put his arms around her neck and said, "Bye-bye, Auntie Anna," and he kissed her on the cheek.

Anna looked up in surprise at a laughing Nick. He raised both hands, palms out, and shook his head. "I didn't tell him to say that."

Anna kissed Danny on the cheek and said. "I hope I see you again real soon." To Lucy, still hiding behind her mother's legs, she said, "Bye-bye, Lucy." Lucy looked around her mother and wiggled her fingers at Anna.

On the way back to Tucson, Nick suggested that they go horseback riding in the morning.

"I'd like that."

"Why don't we pick up a change of clothes at your apartment and you can come home with me tonight."

She looked uncertain.

"I'm not asking you to move in with me—not today, anyway—not yet—but what's the difference? I could stay at your apartment or you could stay at my house. At least when I get up to feed the horses, you'll be waiting for me when I'm finished." He grinned at her.

"I guess I can't argue with that." She smiled.

30

Tucson, Arizona, New Year's Day 1988

Neither Anna nor her attorney had heard from Foster or his lawyer since she filed for divorce except for a cursory notice that Foster was contesting it.

Even so, she and Nick were determined to ring in the New Year with hope and optimism. They celebrated quietly at Nick's house. New Year's Day was unseasonably warm, and the skies were clear when Nick and Anna rode out into the desert together. They had packed a picnic lunch and planned to make a day of it. Nick had promised her she would see something special.

Anna looked thoughtful. "You know, when I was a kid, someone told me that whatever you do on New Year's Day, you'll do all through the year." She laughed, "Of course, as a kid, I was usually in a tree, so I probably climbed one to celebrate the New Year, and sure enough, that's where you would find me most days."

Nick smiled. "I'd like to see you in a tree sometime, but I'd have to climb up there with you." She had told him about her parents and how unhappy she had been. The trees had been her sanctuary.

She squeezed Paco a bit closer to Nick and took his hand. "This is the best New Year's ever; riding here in the desert with you is exactly what I hope to be doing all year long."

The sun had just risen above the mountain ridges when they left, and they rode in silence under a clear, cloudless, blue sky. They rode across the Cañada del Oro Wash and southward along the old road, a dirt track that still cut through the desert.

Nick turned off the road and pointed to a ridge on their right. "That's where the Apaches probably waited to ambush freight wagons taking supplies to Camp Grant. If the wagons or riders were coming from Tucson, they would not be able to see around that ridge, and the Apaches would have waited right there." He pointed to a cutback below the ridge. There were plenty of trees and scrub to hide in. "In fact, sometime in the late 1860s, somewhere along the CDO here was a pretty bad attack on one of the wagon trains. Lots of men lost their lives and lots of freight was lost to the Apaches."

Following the trail into the cutback, they climbed up to the ridge on a steep, rocky trail. When they came out on top, he turned and pointed to the ridge above the cutback. "See how the ridge parallels the road? You have a good view for quite some distance from there. That's where they would have stationed the lookouts."

Anna scanned the ridge and the old road below it. "And they would signal to the others when someone was coming?"

"Yep."

"Were the freight wagons passing through when Armando and Esperanza lived out here?"

"Actually, they were. But I don't know to what degree they made contact with them. I suppose Ramirez might have arranged sometimes for them to bring something he needed, but they were primarily hauling freight for the army when they came through here. Otherwise, I doubt that many travelers passed their way."

He spurred Sadie forward and Anna fell in behind him following the trail northward. The sweeping view of Samaniego Ridge to the east and open country to the west was magnificent.

After a short distance, the trail led toward the edge of the ridge. When Anna looked down she was surprised to see a big house in a grove of eucalyptus and pine trees. There was a long barn with stalls that opened into an arena.

"Nick, what is that place?" She hadn't known that anyone else lived in this area.

"That's an old hacienda. The road you see coming into it is the same one you use to get to my house. It's just further back into the foothills. It was built in the early part of the century by Jesús María Elías, one of Tucson's city fathers. There have been several owners and it's been kind of run down. There's a new owner now and he's fixing it up. I'm glad to see it looking better."

They continued along the trail and then turned eastward, heading toward the mountains. They followed a rocky trail leading down to the Sutherland

Wash. Nick pointed out some rock mortars on the boulders beside the trail before they got to the wash. "They probably harvested beans from the grove of mesquites."

"I suspect you're right." It never ceased to amaze Anna that they could at almost any time in the desert find evidence of the Hohokam occupation.

When they reached the wash, they crossed over a trickle of flowing water and climbed up the ridge on the other side.

At the top, Nick said, "This is it. We're here."

Before dismounting, Anna looked around. The view was spectacular. The Catalinas rose up behind them and they had a long unobstructed view to the north. "It's beautiful, Nick."

After dismounting and tying the horses, Nick carried the saddlebags to a clearing beside the trail.

Anna looked down and saw several sherds scattered across the ground. "Look, Nick. Sherds."

He smiled and said, "Let's sit here by that rock." He spread the blanket out on the ground next to a medium-sized rock no higher than four or five inches, with a deep depression in the center of it.

Anna looked at it and then at Nick. She laughed. "That rock, huh?"

"Yeah. That rock." He grinned at her. He took her hand and drew her into his arms. "You're amazing, you know that?"

She looked up at him. "It doesn't take a great archaeologist to recognize a mortar. So this is what you wanted me to see?"

"That's not all, but the other will have to wait."

They had a light lunch of cheese, crackers, and fruit, washed down with cold water. Afterward, Nick stood up and reached for her hand. He led her to the edge of the ridge, through the brush next to the trail and a short distance down the slope. He stepped around a large rock, about four feet high and maybe three feet across. "Here," he said. She stepped around the rock, bewildered.

"It's pretty hard to see the view from here. What am I looking for?"

"You'll see." He waited.

She looked around slowly. The trees were not very big, but through them you could see the Sutherland winding its way southward along Samaniego Ridge. When she turned around, she glanced down at the rock and saw it.

"Oh, my!" It was beautiful. So simple, but beautiful.

On the east face of the rock, a sun symbol had been etched. A petroglyph, left by someone centuries ago, its story known only to the artist and his people.

Two concentric circles with eight short rays extending from the outside circle. She knelt beside the rock placed her hand on its side, away from the image.

She rested her hand on Tonrai's strong shoulder, watching him work on the design. He squatted before the rock, using two hand stones to engrave the image. When he began to draw the rays around the outside circle, she knew it was the sun. A sun that would greet itself each morning when it rose over the ridge behind her.

Here, on this rock, we leave our mark, his mark.

He stood and turned; the morning rising behind her. He took her hand and drew her aside as the light found its own image, warming it with hope for the journey that lay ahead.

Together, they followed the path down and back to gather their belongings and follow the sun wherever it might take them.

She looked up at Nick.

"You were there?"

Anna said nothing and they climbed back up to where the horses were waiting.

31

Tucson, Arizona, February 1988

After the reports from the Ramirez Ruin project were finished, the company won the bid for a large project along the Santa Cruz River at the northern end of the Tucson Mountains. When Max asked Anna to take the lead on the project, she was delighted that he trusted her and respected her skills.

But because Margy had seniority, Anna was worried, wondering how she would react to the assignment. She didn't want anything to compromise her friendship with Margy. For the first time since college, she had a friend she could call and invite to lunch. Margy and Joe occasionally joined her and Nick for a movie or dinner or for hiking into the mountains. They had even been out to Nick's place to go riding.

She had finally told Margy about Foster and why the baby's burial had been so difficult for her. Margy had understood, but she had asked her a question.

"You knew about the crucifix before Nick uncovered it in the petticoat. How did you know it was there?"

"I really wish I could explain it to you," she had said. "In fact, I wish I could explain it to myself. It's just something that happens once in a while—I see or understand things about some artifacts. I don't know why, but I do know that I was very close to Esperanza Ramirez that day."

"I'm glad I was there with you, not just because something so rare happened, but because I thought you needed a friend."

There it was again. Anna was grateful for what she had gained in her move to Tucson.

Now, as they arrived on-site to begin the project at Los Morteros, she wanted to reach out to Margy and make sure she was okay with Max's decision. She tried to decide the best way to approach the conversation.

"Good morning, Margy," she said. "Can I talk to you for a moment?"

"Hey, Anna. Sure, let's talk."

They walked a short distance away from the cars and left Nick and the others to unpack the gear and carry it to the southern portion of the site where their work would start.

Margy pulled her long hair back and wrapped a pony tail band around it at the neck and put her wide-brimmed hat on her head. "What's up?"

"I just wanted to let you know that I feel bad that Max gave me the lead on this project. He really should have given it to you. You are an incredible archaeologist, and you've been working for him much longer than I have."

Margy laughed. "I really appreciate your concern. I'm flattered you think I should have gotten it. What you don't know is that he's given me the lead on another project that's due to start before this one wraps up."

"Oh, Margy, that's wonderful. I didn't know he would have two projects going at the same time."

"Yeah. He's starting to pick up contracts at such a pace that he may frequently have a couple of projects in progress at the same time. He's expanding responsibilities for all of us, and will probably add staff. He knows how good you are. You deserve it."

Together, they walked back to the cars and helped carry the remaining tools and equipment to the work area. Anna gathered the crew and the volunteers together for a quick orientation.

"Most of you already know that Los Morteros is named for the rock mortars up there in the central portion of the site. I'm not sure there are many sites that have so many mortars. As a food processing area, it's impressive.

"Our job is here in the southern portion of the site, which, by the way, provides an extensive view of Hohokam culture over the course of some 500 years. Everything here, south of Linda Vista Road, where you parked, will be covered with houses in a few years."

She looked up at Nick. "Would you give them a quick rundown of what we've done so far?"

Nick explained that they were following work done several years before by the state museum. "We've opened a few of their trenches and are using them to orient ourselves to a cluster of pit houses, along with roasting pits, cremation sites, and trash pits."

While Nick was talking, she and Margy set up the secondary datum and checked its orientation to the primary datum, which was in the central section at the mortars. They gave out the assignments and everyone went to work.

"Anna, did you bring the museum report with you this morning?" Nick wanted to check the grid they had laid out against the original.

"It's in my trunk. I'll go get it in a few minutes. Did Max say how long he thought he and Joe would be at the northern sector?"

"No, but I can call him on the walkie-talkie if you want."

"Not now. I was just wondering when he might come down to check on us—check on me to see if I'm doing things right."

Nick laughed. "He won't do that. He has confidence in you."

"I hope so. I just don't want to let him down."

"You won't." He reached up and put his finger on the scar. "I not only love you, I love being in the field with you."

"You always make me feel better. I'll go get that report."

∾∾

Foster slowed the car as he passed the site. There were several people there, but he couldn't pick Anna out from that distance. When he passed Linda Vista Road, he saw her car parked not far from the corner; she was here today. He had driven by the site twice before, but it looked like there was only a prep crew there with a backhoe opening some trenches. Even if she saw him drive by, she wouldn't recognize the car. When she left, he still had the red one. His new, dark blue Mercedes wouldn't attract attention. He pulled off the road just below a rock outcrop on the west side of the road.

He got out and walked to the barbed wire fence that marked the boundary between the pull-off and public land. He took a pair of wire cutters from his pocket and, after he cut through the fence, he climbed up the hill to get a better view of what was happening across the road. On his previous passes by the site, he had noticed the outcrop about halfway up the slope. It would be a good vantage point. He carried a rifle and a pair of binoculars hung from his neck. When he reached the rocks, he propped the rifle against the wall next to the opening of what appeared to be a small cave.

"Jesus, I hope there are no snakes in there," he muttered as he turned around to see if he could find Anna.

He trained his binoculars on the group of workers. There must have been about eight people there. He saw Nick talking to a woman whose back was turned toward him. Anna.

Her ponytail was drawn through the back of a baseball cap, like she always wore it in the field.

"Fucking cowboy. You won't get in my way this time." He lowered the binoculars and picked up the rifle, raising it to his shoulder and looking through the scope until he focused the crosshairs on Nick.

He whispered, "Bang."

Not now. That pleasure would have to wait. He needed to get to Anna and bring her home.

But then the cowboy reached out and touched her cheek.

Through clenched teeth, he said, "You son of a bitch..." His heart pounding in his ears, he focused the cross hairs on Nick again and squeezed the trigger.

Nothing happened.

"Damned safety."

He lowered the rifle without taking his eyes off Anna. It was just as well the safety was on. If he shot the cowboy now, it would ruin his plans. He'd deal with him later.

He looked again; Anna was heading in his direction.
Did she see him? No... She couldn't have.

He looked around. She was heading toward her
car.

She's going to the car!

He scrambled down the slope, slipping through the
gravel and sending small avalanches of stones down
before him. He was only dimly aware that he dropped
the wire cutters in his rush. He didn't care. He needed
to get to her before she saw him.

While much of the area they were working in was
cleared of vegetation, there was a thick line of trees
and brush along the road between him and where
her car was parked. He trotted along Silverbell Road
toward the intersection, confident that she could not
see him. Just as he turned the corner, he saw her
standing behind her car. She opened the trunk and
leaned in.

When she stood up straight with a knapsack in her
hand, he grabbed her. Pulling her back against him,
with one hand over her mouth and the other holding
the rifle where she could see it, he said, "Don't make
a sound. If that cowboy comes over here, I'll kill him."
When Anna quit struggling, he loosened his grip and
let her turn to face him.

"My God, Foster, you look..." She stopped. "Let's
talk, Foster. You don't want to do this. I know you
don't."

"You don't know shit. Let's go." He grabbed her
by the upper arm and dragged her with him. She
struggled briefly looking over her shoulder toward
Nick and the crew.

Foster pulled her around behind the line of trees
and brush and stopped to catch his breath, but he
didn't loosen his grip on her arm.

"You're hurting me."

"Go ahead. Scream. This time, I have the advantage." He held the rifle up. "If this can stop an elephant, it sure as hell can stop your cowboy. Now, move."

He pushed her toward the Mercedes.

When they got there, he threw open the driver's door and said, "Get in. You're driving." She got into the car and he slammed the door. When he started around to the other side, she opened the door. He spun around and pointed the rifle in her direction. "Don't be stupid; if I have to kill you now, I will. Like I said, I won't share you with anyone."

She got back into the car. When he got into the passenger seat, he angled the rifle so the stock was against the floorboard and the muzzle was aimed at Anna's head. He handed her the keys and said, "Let's go."

"It's been a long time since I drove a stick shift, Foster. I don't remember how."

"You, darling? My independent-doesn't-need-a-husband-to-take-care-of-her wife might have forgotten how to do something? Not fucking likely. Move."

Anna started the car and put it into gear. When she started to turn north on Silverbell, he said, "No, go right."

As they drove by the southern sector, Nick glanced up to see the Mercedes drive by. When he turned back to lean down over the trench, Foster smiled.

32

Tucson, Arizona, February 1988

Margy climbed out of the trench and looked around. "Hey, Nick, did Anna get the museum report?"

Nick looked in the direction Anna had gone. He frowned. "She hasn't gotten back yet." He was glad Margy had been filled in on Anna's situation and he could count on her.

"I'll go check." Margy headed in the direction of the cars. "I'm sure there's nothing wrong."

Nick watched Margy walk away, but his gut said that there was, indeed, something wrong. He should never have let her out of his sight.

In a few short minutes, Margy came running back, alone and shouting. "Nick!" He turned and ran to meet her.

"The trunk was open..." Margy paused.

"What?" Nick was ready to panic. "What?"

"The knapsack was on the ground behind the car, the trunk was open with the keys in the lock, and Anna was nowhere in sight. I called her and ran down to Silverbell Road and looked. I didn't go up toward where Max and Joe are, because... why would she go up there?"

"Jesus—" He could only imagine the worst.

He grabbed the walkie-talkie and called Max. "Situation serious—get down here, NOW!" He handed the walkie-talkie to Margy and started toward the cars at a run.

Max and Joe pulled onto Linda Vista where Nick was circling Anna's car as if he expected her to simply materialize at any moment. She had to; she just had to. He was frantic.

After Nick explained what had happened, Max sent Joe to help Margy close the southern sector. When he and Margy and the crew got back to the cars, he sent the crew home and told them he'd let them know when they could come back. Then Margy and Joe went to the northern sector to close that one down.

Max told Nick, "Come on. Get into the truck. We're going to call the sheriff's department."

"What about Anna's car?"

"I asked Margy to bring it to the office."

They drove to a convenience store near the site and called from the pay phone. The deputy they spoke to was patient and asked several questions to clarify the circumstances of Anna's disappearance.

"Look," Nick said, hanging on to his last thread of patience, "her husband was here in November and he vowed to come back and get her. She has a restraining order. We can't take a chance; he's dangerous."

Nick and Max returned to the site and met the two deputies who arrived shortly afterwards. Deputy Chavez, interviewed Nick and Max while Deputy O'Neill went to investigate the area.

Nick told Deputy Chavez he had seen a car drive by the site around the time Anna headed back to her car, but he hadn't noticed anything peculiar about it. He gave the deputy Foster's name and description, along with what had happened at Thanksgiving. "I'm not sure what kind of car he's driving. He had a rental in November."

Chavez said they would do a background check and see if he could be located in Chicago or Evanston, which could rule him out.

Nick frowned, but didn't say anything. He was certain they would find no trace of Foster Robinson anywhere in the Chicago area.

When O'Neill came back, he reported to Chavez. He had taken pictures in the immediate vicinity of the car, and then drove up Silverbell Road, noting the vegetation along the road was a good screen.

"There's a pull-off area up under that rock outcrop." He pointed at the jumble of rocks up the slope from the road. "I stopped and took a few pictures of car tracks. But there are probably too many to identify any one set.

"While I was doing that, I saw the fence had been cut. The wire was old and rusty, but the cut ends were shiny. New."

None of this made Nick feel any better.

O'Neill continued. "I went through the fence and climbed up there." He pointed. "From there, I had a good view of your work area here. Got some pictures from there, too."

He reached into his jacket and pulled out a plastic evidence bag. Inside was a pair of red-handled wire cutters. "Coming down the slope, I found this beside the path. Brand new. Couldn't have been there very long."

When Deputy O'Neill was finished his report, Chavez turned to Nick and said that Anna's absence did, indeed, sound suspicious. He gave them his card and asked them to call if they heard anything from her. "I'll let you know what we learn."

33

Tucson, Arizona, February 1988

Anna drove east on Interstate 10 as Foster had demanded. She was a little relieved that they were heading back toward Tucson, but she wondered if they were just going to pass through on the way to Chicago.

How will Nick know which direction we went? Will he assume we're going to Chicago? How long will it take for him to figure out what happened?

She could feel panic rising like bile in her throat. Foster had said nothing after telling her to get on the Interstate.

She wondered if getting him to talk might help, but she was afraid he was too irrational to make any sense.

She looked at him. He had his head back and his eyes were closed. His appearance was shocking. He had lost even more weight and his clothes hung on him. He had not shaved for days. It was hard to believe this was the man she had married. He was nearly unrecognizable.

She remembered the look in his eyes when she turned around at the car. She had seen hatred in his eyes before, it was nothing compared to what was there at that moment.

The muzzle of the gun still pointed at her head. She lifted her foot from the accelerator and he opened his eyes.

"What the hell are you doing? We're not stopping here."

"I need to go to the bathroom, Foster. There's a gas station at the next exit."

Foster chuckled. "You must think I'm an idiot..."

Then he frowned, his voice softening. "I can't believe you think I'm an idiot... You used to think I was smart."

"Of course I did, Foster. You're the smartest man I know. You're brilliant—"

"Shut up. I know what you think."

They drove in silence for a few miles and then he said, "Get off here."

It was the Miracle Mile exit, only one way to go, in toward town. She was relieved.

This will give Nick some time, I hope.

They passed through the first traffic light, and Foster said, "Turn in there—second entrance." It was the Ghost Ranch Lodge. Anna had seen it a number of times and only knew that it was an historical landmark. Now it was a little run down and seedy.

She looked up at the big, neon sign with a cow skull in front of the main building, and hoped that the name and the skull didn't foreshadow what was to come.

For no particular reason, she pointed at the sign and said, "Georgia O'Keeffe designed the cow skull for the sign."

Foster looked at her and said, "We're not here for the art."

She turned into the second entrance and drove toward the back of the motel. "Park there." There were no other cars nearby.

She stopped behind one of the casitas and waited for Foster to make the first move. He opened the glove compartment and pulled out a pistol and slid it into his belt.

He came around to her side of the car and opened the door. When she hesitated, he reached in and grabbed her by the arm and dragged her out. He pushed her ahead of him around the casita to the door. "After you, my lady." She was relieved that he left the rifle in the car, but the pistol did nothing to make her feel better. She looked around the central courtyard, hoping someone would see them and see that she was in trouble. But she saw no one. He reached past her and unlocked the door.

It took a few moments for her eyes to adjust to the dim interior. He flipped on the light. The unit was on the periphery and far enough away from Miracle Mile that the car wouldn't be seen from the street. It must have been nice at one time. The brick walls were painted white —probably not a lot of sound carried through to the neighboring unit—if anyone was in it.

She had to come up with something. Foster would have to sleep at some point. Maybe she could get away. Then she saw the duffel bag on the end of the bed.

There was a rope in it. *Jesus.*

"Foster, is it okay if I go to the bathroom?"

"Why, Anna, my dear, are you asking my permission?" He smiled and sounded like he was genuinely curious. "I thought you had a mind of your own. I thought you didn't need me to tell you what to do." He glared at her.

She glared back. "Yes, Foster, I'm asking your permission. You are, after all, the one with the gun."

He laughed.

He wrapped his hand around the butt of the gun and pulled it out of his belt. "If only I had known that this was all it would take to win your obedience." He aimed the gun at her head and smiled.

"Go on. Go to the bathroom, but leave the door open."

She went in and turned on the faucet full blast. She looked around. There was shaving cream and a razor on the sink. The sink was dirty and towels were thrown over the shower rod and on the floor. There was only a small window near the ceiling.

He's been here for a while and he's not letting housekeeping in.

She sat on the toilet and as she was pulling her panties back up, Foster stepped into the doorway. When she jumped, he laughed.

"Really, darling. You're not embarrassed, are you? You can use the bathroom in front of me. After all, I am your husband." He smiled. "You do remember me, don't you?" His tone changed and his voice hardened. "Your husband."

She pulled up her jeans, buckled her belt and flushed the toilet. Turning to wash her hands, she said nothing.

He stood back and allowed her to walk past him. He had placed a chair in the middle of the room facing the foot of the bed. The rope was no longer in the duffel bag, but tossed loosely on the unmade bed.

"Foster—you're not going to—"

"No, not yet anyway. He drew back his arm and swung quickly. He connected with her jaw. When she fell, she started to curl into a ball and wrap her arms around her head. He kicked her in the stomach. While she lay there, writhing in pain, he went into the kitchenette and came back with a glass of red wine.

"Get up."

She struggled to her feet, and tested her jaw, moving it back and forth. It clicked and was a little out of place, and it hurt like hell, but she didn't think it was broken.

He pointed to the chair. "Sit."

"After what you just did, you still think you need to tie me up?"

"If only I could trust you, darling. But I can't." He smiled again. "You give me no choice."

He pushed her to the chair and tied her hands behind her, drawing the rope down and around to the front, tying her legs to each of the chair legs. Several times she flinched when he pulled the rope tight, but it only seemed to please him, so she tried to be quiet.

He sat down in another chair and propped his feet up on the bed and picked up the glass of wine.

"To you, my darling, and to us." He raised the glass in a mock toast and then took a drink.

∾∾

Nick was beside himself. They were back in Max's office and Nick was pacing back and forth.

"What's taking them so long? They have to know something by now." The police had promised to give them an update as soon as they knew anything about Foster's possible whereabouts.

When the phone rang, Max answered it quickly and Nick looked hopeful. Max nodded to Nick and pushed the speaker button.

"Mr. Lomax, this is Deputy Chavez, Pima County Sheriff's Office."

"Yes, please go on, Deputy."

"Based on the information you gave us, we asked the Chicago and Evanston Police Departments to check into the whereabouts of Foster Robinson. Evanston PD told us he had assaulted a student at Northwestern last year, but the charges got squelched. They got a warrant to search his residence, but they didn't find much there. The place was a wreck. Looked like someone had gone on a rampage.

"Chicago PD interviewed his parents. They have not seen their son for over two weeks—they weren't too worried about him even though they admitted he was distraught the last time he had been there. They had bigger things on their mind. Apparently, his father is involved in a financial scandal. His only concern is minimizing the harm to his bank account. In any case, we have the description and tag number of his car. It's a dark blue, 1988 Mercedes 500."

Nick reminded the deputy, "It's possible he's taking her out of state—maybe heading back toward Chicago."

"We have an APB out for the vehicle, so if he's heading east, we'll be looking for him."

When Deputy Chavez hesitated, Nick said, "What? There's something else you haven't told us?"

The deputy cleared his throat. "The Chicago police asked if Robinson had access to any weapons. They said no. But when they followed up with a question about any weapons on the premises, his father admitted that he had a collection in the garage. He balked at allowing them to look, but when the detective offered to get a warrant, he caved."

"And?" Nick was afraid to hear the rest.

"There were two guns missing from the father's collection, a Weatherby 9-Lug Mark Five big-game hunting rifle and a pistol."

"Jesus." Nick was terrified.

"Dear God." Maggie was standing in the doorway. She had heard the entire conversation. Max looked at the phone and said, "Is there anything else, Deputy?"

"We've alerted the city police in case he's taken her inside the city limits—that is, if they aren't already headed for Chicago."

The deputy rang off and Max got up and put his arms around his wife.

"Jesus, Max. What are we going to do?" Nick paced back and forth. "I should never have let her out of my sight."

"It's not your fault, Nick. She didn't want to be cloistered by us and she sure as hell wouldn't want you blaming yourself, so knock it off. Now."

Nick collapsed into a chair. "I know, but damn it, Max, I feel so helpless. I can't lose her."

Max laid his hand on Nick's shoulder. "We'll find her. Whatever it takes, we'll find her." He sat back down at his desk and unrolled a large map of the Tucson area. "We don't have to sit and wait for the police to do everything. Let's look at his options."

He tapped a marker on the map. "Let's assume he doesn't intend to head straight back to Chicago. If he's dumb enough to be driving his own car, he's not so dumb that he doesn't know the police will have its description, so he'll probably want to keep out of sight for a while." He looked up at Nick. "That could work to our advantage."

Nick leaned forward to look at the map.

Max went on. "Let's assume that he's still somewhere in Tucson with Anna as his prisoner."

"So where would he go?" Nick looked hopeful for a moment. "He'd have to hole up somewhere locally."

"That's what I was thinking." Max stared at the map. He marked the location of Los Morteros and the route from there to the Interstate.

"If he turned west, he'd be heading for Phoenix, but how likely would he be to choose Phoenix? He's been here before. It might be more reasonable that he'd head toward Tucson."

Nick nodded and, with his finger, traced the route that would bring them back toward Tucson. From Los Morteros, along Silverbell Road..." He remembered seeing a car drive by the site. It was dark blue.

"Let's assume he wants to get back to the freeway. He could get there via Ina Road, but he has to have a place to stay—a motel or hotel. I'm pretty sure there's nothing at Ina Road."

"My guess is he might not have driven as far north as Ina to find a place to stay. He would have passed lots of opportunities coming in from the east."

Nick traced his finger east along the highway, pausing at each interchange. There were no motels anywhere along the route until you got to Miracle Mile. There were several there.

He looked up at Max and held his finger on the map at Miracle Mile.

"This would be the closest place for a number of motels to choose from. There are others along the highway across from downtown, and more on the east side. Their sheer numbers could complicate things, so it's a matter of where he chose to stop. "

Nick grabbed his hat and started for the door.

"What are you doing, Nick? You can't do this by yourself."

"I've got to go look. If I have to check every motel between here and Chicago, I'll do it."

Max shook his head. "Okay, but keep me informed—and call Deputy Chavez if you see anything. Be careful."

Nick was already out the door.

34

Tucson, Arizona, February 1988

She tried to steel her nerves, but the discomfort of the ropes, the ache in her midsection and her jaw didn't make it easy. She would have to get through to him—to a reasonable Foster, if there was one still inside of this man. But she would not cower and she would not beg.

"How long are you going to keep me here?" She tried to keep her voice steady.

He looked at her for a long moment and put his wine down on the bedside table. He leaned forward and rested his elbows on his knees, lacing the fingers of both hands together between them.

"I'm not sure, Anna. I don't want to hang around in this damn hick town very long. The sooner we get on the road, the better, but I want to make sure we understand each other."

"I think I understand you, Foster, but I'm quite sure you don't understand me."

"The only thing you need to understand about me is how much I love you and how much I need you to come back to Chicago with me. When we get home, back to our house in Evanston, everything will be fine. I can go back to the university and we can get back to our lives again and be happy."

"Get back to our lives again? Foster, do you think things can go back to what they were? After you kidnapped me at gunpoint? After you hit me and kicked me and tied me up?" It was the wrong thing to say. She wanted to reason with him, not make him angrier.

"I didn't want to do those things, Anna, but you made me. You know I don't want to hurt you. I love you."

Anna said nothing. She had no answer that wouldn't enrage him.

"How could you just leave like that?" He sounded genuinely curious. "You don't know what I went through when I came home and read your note. It was a nightmare. Why didn't you talk to me? We could have worked it out." She detected a little-boy sadness in his tone.

"I tried to talk to you, Foster, but you wouldn't listen. And I told you in November." She said it carefully, betraying no anger.

"You didn't talk to me; you just whined about going to work, getting 'out in the field.'" He drew air quotes around the words. "You sounded like a broken record and I couldn't put up with it."

"Doesn't that prove my point?" She was determined to keep her voice even and calm.

"Anna, I only wanted what was best for you. I wanted to protect you and take care of you."

"I didn't need to be taken care of. I didn't want to be protected."

Foster frowned. "You don't mean that, Anna. You're lost and confused. We were happy together. You were perfect for me."

She tried to maintain a reasonable tone. "It's true that we were happy for a time and I did love you, but when you started to isolate and suffocate me, I couldn't go on like that."

He stood up and moved around to sit on the end of the bed, right in front of her. He reached out and touched her cheek gently. When she turned her face away from his hand, he grabbed her chin and turned her back to face him. The pain shot through her jaw again.

"Foster that hurts—please..." He squeezed even harder.

"You were standing there with him. He... touched your cheek." His eyes bored into hers. "You didn't turn away from *him*."

He was describing what had happened just before she went back to her car. He had been watching.

But, of course, he had been watching. That's how he managed to intercept her so easily.

"You listen to me, Anna. We're going to stop this nonsense and you're coming back to Chicago." He stood and leaned in closer, wrapping the fingers of one hand around her neck, his thumb pressing into the hollow of her throat. With the other hand, he grabbed her hair and held her while he kissed her on the lips, pushing his tongue past her teeth. When she struggled to turn her face away from him, he let go and stood up looking down at her.

She was coughing and gasping for breath when he slapped her.

The pain shot through her head and rippled throughout her body as it tensed against the ropes.

"Do we understand each other now?" Foster's voice had gone deadly soft.

Anna said nothing.

He turned and went back to his chair, picking up his wine and watching the reflected light as he swirled it in the glass.

He kept his eyes on the wine. "Tell me about your cowboy. How long have you been sleeping with him?"

"I'm not going to talk to you about Nick. This is not about him."

Nick. He must be terrified.

❧

Nick drove west on Grant Road from the office, white knuckles gripping the steering wheel in an effort to maintain control. At Oracle Road, he turned north along what used to be part of Miracle Mile and drove the few blocks to the stretch of Miracle Mile between Oracle and the Interstate. Most of the motels were along this stretch on the south side of the street. Many of them dated back to the earliest days of motels along U.S. highways. By the late '70s and early '80s, the street had begun to deteriorate into an area of illicit activity. At night, prostitutes trolled for clients along its stretch and many of the motels were known for hourly rates.

Most of the motels were open court styles, where u-shaped buildings surrounded the parking lot, allowing guests to park in front of their unit. It was easy to see if Foster's car was there. He drove down the side streets to get a better look at parking areas that might be behind the units. He didn't see a blue Mercedes anywhere.

At Ghost Ranch Lodge, not all of the guest units were visible from the street. Going around the block didn't help because the motel was almost completely enclosed by a high wall. He entered a driveway into the complex from the side street and drove slowly, looking at every vehicle. When he turned toward Miracle Mile at the eastern corner, he saw the Mercedes. He stopped the truck and looked around, half expecting to see Anna running toward him. It took all of his willpower to stay in the truck.

When he got himself together, he drove to the front and stopped at the office. Getting out of the truck, he took off his hat and wiped perspiration from his forehead with his sleeve. He settled his hat on his head and walked into the office.

The young woman behind the desk was talking on the telephone. She barely acknowledged his presence so he waited, noting the nametag, Amanda, on her low-cut blouse.

"You won't believe what he said next." She twirled her hair around her finger and popped her chewing gum while she listened to the response on the line.

"No... No. He said *you* were lying and that he had never slept with her. But I know now he's the liar—"

Nick rapped on the counter impatiently. She looked up.

"I gotta go. Talk to you later." She hung up the phone, glaring at him. "Can I help you?"

"Yes, you can." Nick tried to smile, hoping to disarm her annoyance with him. He leaned down over the counter toward her and smiled again, this time allowing his smile to reach his eyes.

"I hope you'll forgive me for interrupting you, Amanda," he spoke softly. "I'm looking for a friend of mine. He was supposed to get here sometime this past week and I'm positive he was going to stay here. We went to college together and he's notorious for losing phone numbers. He drinks a little, you know, so I thought I might check to see if he's arrived."

Amanda gave Nick an appraising once-over and apparently decided his good looks were credentials enough for her.

"What's his name?" She dragged the registration book across the counter and opened it. "Foster Robinson—he's from Chicago."

Amanda ran her long, red-polished fingernail down the register, pausing at one line. She looked up through her eyelashes at Nick and smiled, leaning forward so that he had a good view of her cleavage. "You know, I'm not supposed to give out information about our guests." She batted her eyes at him.

Nick tried to force down the nausea and smile again. "Of course you aren't, but maybe you could make an exception for me. I don't know anybody who loves to party any more than he does, and I'm just itching for a good time like we used to have." He smiled again and this time Amanda smiled back. He looked around, and lowered his voice as if sharing a secret. "You wouldn't happen to have any friends who might be interested in having a good time with us?" He winked and gave Amanda an inviting look, lingering just a bit too long on her cleavage.

"Like I said, I can't tell you whether he's here or not, but..." She slid the registration book around on the counter so Nick could read it.

The name was there. "F. Robinson, Chicago, IL, Unit 127."

He sucked in his breath and tried to disguise his excitement. He casually reached over and patted Amanda's hand softly, lingering on it just one short moment.

"Thanks, beautiful. I'll be in touch." He winked again, smiled, and walked out the door to his truck.

Inside the truck, his hands began to shake and the nausea rose again. He had to get under control. He reached into his shirt pocket for the deputy's card.

At the convenience store on the corner, he called from the pay phone. He left an impatient message for Deputy Chavez and then called Max. "I'm not going to leave here, Max. I don't want to take a chance that he'll take her somewhere else. I'm staying here."

He parked beside the store where he had a good view of the motel's front entrances and the side street entrance. About twenty minutes later, Deputy Chavez pulled in.

35

Tucson, Arizona, February 1988

After speaking with Nick, Deputy Chavez called in a report. A short time later, someone from the Tucson Police Department arrived. Although Nick was interested in what the deputy and the policeman were saying, he continued to lean on the front fender of his pickup, his eyes locked on the Ghost Ranch entrances.

The two policemen joined Nick. Deputy Chavez introduced Detective Murchek, who told him the Pima County Sheriff's Office would take the lead on the incident and TPD would provide backup. "We will have officers on hand to assist as it becomes necessary."

"When can we go in?"

Chavez shook his head. "First, it's not 'we;' *you* will not go in." Second, your friend's safety is what's important here. You suggested she was in danger, and from all indications, she is. Let us do our jobs."

Nick nodded. "I'm sorry. Can you tell me what you're planning?"

"I can't tell you everything right now, but we're getting personnel into position. We'll have units on Laguna Street behind the motel, and on Fairview as well as two within range east and west on Miracle Mile. If he tries to leave, he has to use the Miracle Mile or Fairview exits."

Nick panicked. "So you just plan to wait until he makes a move? What if he's already hurt her? What if—?"

"Calm down, Mr. Anderson." Deputy Chavez put his hand on Nick's shoulder. "No, we're not going to wait, but we're also not going in with guns blazing. Trust us."

"I'm sorry. I appreciate what you are doing." He turned and walked toward the pay phone.

He heard Chavez say to the detective, "He's a bit of a time bomb."

"Can't say as I blame him," the detective replied.

Nick called Max and updated him on the situation. Then he dialed the phone again. "Damn," he said when her answering machine picked up.

"You know the drill—leave a message."

Nick waited for the beep and started, "Minnie, it's Nick." At that moment, Minnie picked up. "What's wrong?" He had barely disguised his panic.

He told her as much as he could.

"Jesus, Nick. Do you think he will hurt her?"

"He's got guns. I don't know if he knows how to use them."

"Thanks for letting me know. I'm on my way."

Before he could tell her not to come, she had hung up.

When he left the phone booth, Chavez told him he was going to talk to the motel manager. "You can come along. I don't have a problem with you knowing what we're doing, but I need to know you will stand back and allow us to do our jobs."

Nick nodded his head.

When he came in the door with the deputy, Amanda looked up and stared at him. Chavez asked her to call the manager. Nick suspected she thought she would be fired for letting him see the register, and maybe she would. He couldn't worry about that.

After speaking briefly with the deputy, Mr. Macias told Amanda to go home for the rest of the day.

"Are you firing me?" Nick wasn't sure if she was scared or angry.

"No. I just need you to go home now."

She went behind the desk and picked up her purse and a jacket. On the way out the door, she glanced back and gave Nick the finger.

The manager agreed to have undercover operatives stationed at the motel, one acting as a groundskeeper, trimming the shrubbery outside the suspect's unit, while another pair would take up residence in the adjoining room.

"He's had the "Do Not Disturb" sign on the door since he checked in. Not even housekeeping could go in." Mr. Macias introduced the head of housekeeping to the deputy.

Mrs. Soto, nearly as wide as she was tall, pushed her shoulders back and drew herself up to her full four-foot-eleven inches. "I knocked on his door two days in a row. I wanted to change the sheets and clean the bathroom.

"It's not right. It gives us a bad name. I work at Ghost Ranch twenty-two years, and there are no dirty rooms on my watch—I don't care what nobody says." She shook her head. "He'll just go and tell everyone

'*Qué motel san sucio.*' ¡*No es correcto*! ¡*Es* mi *motel*!"
She turned and marched her short, round frame from
the lobby, leaving them standing there smiling.

Even Nick almost smiled.

"I could use about ten more like her," the manager
said, spreading a layout of the motel complex out
across the desk. "The unit has only one entrance and
none of the windows open far enough for anyone to
climb out."

"So if the captive had a chance to escape, she'd have
to come out the door." The word, "captive," echoed in
Nick's head. He wanted to shout, "It's Anna," but he
forced himself to remain silent.

Deputy Chavez looked thoughtful.

"That's right, but your suspect won't have another
exit when you close in on him, either." The manager
pointed to the small unit on the map. "There's no way
in or out except into the courtyard.

"That means we have to be very careful. He'll be
even more dangerous once he knows he's trapped."

Nick's stomach clenched and he tried to suppress
the images that came to mind with those words.

When Deputy Chavez ordered him to go back to
the convenience store and wait—and to stay out of the
way, Nick reluctantly did it.

⁂⇛

Foster returned to his chair, picked up his glass of
wine and again propped his feet on the bed. He tilted
the chair back on two legs and lifted the glass to Anna.

She thought about how drawn and tired he looked.
She was not used to seeing Foster in any kind of
disarray. This, the man who lined his ties and cufflinks
up carefully to avoid wearing the same thing two days
in a row; the man whose clothes were always clean
and crisp; the man who would have been mortified to
be seen in public with five-o'clock shadow. Here he

was, unshaven and rumpled. His khaki slacks were wrinkled and stained. His shirt was tucked loosely into his pants. The shirt was missing a button on the cuff.

Anna refused to feel sorry for him.

Even though her throat hurt and her jaw popped when she spoke, she tried to shift his focus. "How are your parents, Foster? Do they know you're here?"

Anna shrank against her bonds when he jumped up and threw the glass across the room, shattering it, leaving red rivulets running down the white bricks. She tried not to see them as blood.

"Fuck them! They don't care about me!" He dropped back into his chair and leaned over and put his face into his hands, his elbows resting on his knees.

Anna wasn't sure what to say. This was the last reaction she expected. She thought his parents—especially his mother—would be 100% behind his efforts to bring her home. She decided to say nothing.

"My father," he said it with a sneer, "is in some kind of trouble with the Securities and Exchange Commission—something about the way he's been helping his clients rip off their investors and filing manufactured audits of their books. It's a pretty sweet deal he cooked up, helping himself and them to big fucking profits. But now that the SEC is on to him—on to the whole company—they're falling over one another to point the blame. If anyone goes to jail, it will be him; it was his division and his project. All the higher ups knew what he was doing and profited from it—they'll stay clean. They'll say he was acting on his own.

"He doesn't give a flying fuck about what's going on with me... Not that he ever did. He's got to protect his bank account."

Anna remained silent.

"And Mother," he paused, and Anna could have sworn he was about to spit. "Dear, sweet, Mommy dearest—she's so fucking busy trying to pretend nothing is wrong, trying to maintain her 'social status.'" He made air quotes again. "She can't stand the idea that she might be *un*registered from the social register.

"She's fucking gone off the deep end. She won't even talk to me. She has more important things to deal with."

He went back to the kitchenette and poured himself a new glass of wine, gulping it down and pouring another.

When he sat again, he lifted his glass, he said, "So here's to us, darling. It's just you and me."

She said nothing and waited. Maybe it would help to let him keep him talking.

He put his glass down and reached over on the nightstand to pick up the handgun. He ran his fingers up and down the barrel, looking almost lovingly at it. Anna had to turn away.

"Remember when I told you I wouldn't share you with anybody?" He continued to caress the gun barrel. "I meant that. I'll do whatever I have to. If I can't have you..." He pointed the gun at her. "So you need to make a decision, darling. Come back to Chicago with me, or..."

She tried to persuade herself that he wouldn't kill her. Even with everything else he had done, he surely wasn't a murderer.

"You know," Foster said quietly, "it was easy to get into Father's gun safe. He was too preoccupied with his career crisis to pay any attention to me. I've always known where he kept the key." He ran his finger down the gun barrel. "I used to sneak this gun and the ammunition out and go with some friends up-country to shoot rabbits and anything else we could find. I shot a dog once... a retriever I think it was. He just came up to us, wagging his tail. He was a pretty dog, friendly." He laughed. "One of the boys poured beer in his hand and the damn dog drank it. I didn't know dogs drank beer. It was my beer, and I didn't want to share it. So I shot him."

He never took his eyes off the gun while he told the story. Anna was stunned and when he looked up at her, he laughed.

"Actually, Anna, you don't know me at all. My family? We're fakes—phonies. We were nobody until my mother saw that my father's job—his career—was going to lift us into the best circles. The more he helped the 'upper class' sock away money, the more money he made and the more important he, and she, became. She made it work for them."

He stopped talking and looked off into a distance that Anna couldn't fathom. She waited for him to go on.

"Remember once you asked me if I lived on Elm Street all of my life? I told you that life before Elm Street was another story altogether."

He picked up the wine glass again and swirled the wine around, watching the lamplight dancing in it.

"Me? I was Tommy Robinson." He watched Anna's expression change again. "Foster is my middle name, my mother's maiden name. I was a real handful for a sales clerk at Marshall Field's." He appeared to enjoy it each time he added new details that she didn't expect.

"That's where she learned how to fit in with the upper classes. She worked on the top floor, waiting on the real cream of Chicago society. My father was working his way up through the accounting firm. I was always in trouble at school, suspended more times than I could count. They didn't pay a lot of attention, especially after the money started coming in.

"When my mother could finally give up her job, she dyed her hair and started joining exclusive clubs. It's funny, not one of those rich bitches she had sold clothes and furs to ever recognized her. She laughed about it. She said peons like sales clerks were invisible to the rich. Suddenly, I had all the money I wanted, drugs were cheap, and I could keep the other kids at school supplied, even making a tidy profit for myself."

Anna understood now. The crude, nasty Foster she had glimpsed from time to time was the real Foster. The suave, sophisticated intellectual had been a façade, the image he had groomed for the public.

"Oh, yes, darling. Don't look so surprised. I could do whatever I wanted whenever I wanted, and if I got caught, Mother could get me out of it. It's amazing what a little money can do. One of my best friends went to reform school, but I went to Lake Forest Academy.

"After she got me into Lake Forest, Mother took me aside and told me how important it was that I learn proper manners because she would not tolerate any embarrassment I might cause. We were going to move to the Gold Coast, and she made it clear that if I handled myself well, I could have anything I wanted. If I didn't, then she would cut me off.

"It sounded like a good deal to me, so I went along."

He laid the gun down on the bed, with the barrel pointing directly at Anna. She tried not to look at it. "I learned. I learned very well. Mother was proud of me. She was pleased when I could meet her circle of friends and impress them with my sophistication and manners. As long as Mother was happy, I had it all."

Again, Anna didn't know what to say.

"Then I met you. You were perfect. You were exactly what Mother said I needed. A poor girl like you would be grateful to marry 'up.'"

Anna was shocked.

He went on. "Mother assured me I could mold you into the wife I needed. That's why you have to come back to Chicago with me. I can't do what I need to do if you don't, be what I want to be. I need to finish you."

Anna remembered the conversation she had overheard between him and his mother: that Foster needed to "finish" her. Foster was silent.

"I'm sorry, Foster. I'm sorry for what's happening with your parents, and I'm sorry that I'm not the wife you thought I would be. But I don't think you understand the kind of trouble you are in."

"Trouble?" He looked genuinely puzzled. "What do you mean?"

"Foster, look at us. You kidnapped me, dragged me here at gunpoint, you beat me up, and now I'm tied to a chair and you've been waving around a pistol. Don't you think you'll be in trouble when this is over? That what you've done is against the law?"

"Kidnapped you? You're my wife; that's not kidnapping. That's asserting my marital rights. You belong to me." He paused. "Besides, Mother will get me out of any trouble that comes up."

Anna nearly laughed, considering what he had just told her, but he was perfectly serious. She tried to keep her voice even.

"I do not 'belong' to you, Foster. I told you that in November. A wife is not the property of her husband. That's not how it works. It's supposed to be a partnership."

"So you say. But you also said 'look at us.' I'm looking, and from my point of view, I'm in charge and you'll do whatever I tell you to do. And we're heading for Chicago, whether you like it or not. Now."

He got up and gathered some things from the bed and the bathroom and threw them into the duffel bag. He slipped the gun into his belt, and untied Anna.

He hung the duffel bag over his shoulder with his hand inside, holding the gun. "We're going out the door and around the corner and you're going to drive us home."

He pulled open the door and looked outside. It was nearly dark, but the only person out there was a groundskeeper trimming the hedges.

"Don't make a sound." When he shoved the duffel bag against her back, the cold, hard steel of the gun pressed against her. She was no longer confident that he wouldn't kill her.

36

Tucson, Arizona, February 1988

As they approached the Mercedes, two policemen stepped around the corner of the casita, each with a gun trained on him.

"Stop where you are, Robinson, and let the woman go."

For a brief moment, Anna was relieved, but the gun at her back told her it was too soon.

"You want me to let her go? How about I let her go dead? Back off or I pull the fucking trigger now." He lifted his gun hand out of the duffel where the police could see it.

They continued to point their guns at him. "You don't want to do this, Robinson."

"Oh, yeah? Watch me."

She hoped he was going to get into the car because it would give her a chance to run. Then she saw the boot on the rear wheel. The car was not going anywhere.

"Okay, gentlemen. This is what I'm going to do. I'm going to walk away from here and she's going with me. You might kill me, but she'll be dead before I hit the ground."

He started walking toward the street, pushing Anna ahead of him. The policemen followed at a distance, keeping him in sight, one of them talking into his radio. When they reached the street, Anna saw police units sitting a short distance in both directions. He swung the duffel off his shoulder, threw it on the ground, and pushed her ahead of him into the traffic. Tires screeched as a car swerved to miss them.

"Through here." When he pointed to the pipe fence, Anna realized he wanted to head across the open field into Evergreen Cemetery. When he started to run, instead of pulling against him, she ran, too, no longer trying to get away.

Something told her that Nick was watching. That Nick could see what was happening.

"There's a drainage up there, Foster. It looks deep, but if we can get across we can take cover in the cemetery." She grabbed his hand and pulled. *I need to take over, tell him what to do, like his mother would.*

He had lost his grip on her arm, but she held his hand, running with him. If he thought something was up, he didn't question her. They ran to the edge of the drainage and slid down in.

At the bottom, she said, "Put that gun away or we can't get out of this ditch. You need both hands."

He hesitated, but he shoved it behind him into his belt.

They clawed their way to the other side. In fact, Anna made it to the top before he did, and she turned to help him up.

"This way." She grabbed his hand and ran around the mortuary building at the western end of the cemetery. "Into the trees."

Once in the cemetery, she stopped to catch her breath. Foster grabbed her arm and swung her around to face him. He was gasping. They were standing in the shadows of the large pine trees. Her midsection ached where he had kicked her, but she was determined to go on.

"What's going on? You could have gotten away back there at the drainage. Why didn't you?" He was bent over, holding his side.

"Yes, I could have tried to get away back there, but, remember, you have a gun. Why would I take that chance? Besides," she reached for his hand, "I don't want to see you hurt. Those policemen mean business, and for whatever reasons, I remember why I fell in love with you." She hoped he would buy it.

He stood, one hand in hers. There was nothing threatening in his manner at that moment.

"But you left me—you had it planned. How could you do that if you loved me?"

"Foster, I said I remembered *why* I fell in love with you; I didn't say I was still in love with you."

"But—"

Just then, a spotlight wheeled through the trees above their heads. Red and blue flashing lights were coming from two directions where the police were entering the cemetery.

"This way!" Anna grabbed his hand and started off at a run. Foster fell in behind her.

They dodged trees and tombstones, pausing only long enough for Anna to decide where they were and where she wanted to go.

"We've got to get through this open space and back into the trees over there." She looked at him. "Are you ready?"

"Yes."

"Go!"

Once in the trees, she stopped and looked back. The spotlights were still wheeling about behind them. They reached the paved wash between Evergreen and Holy Hope. Anna didn't know whether or not there was a bridge anywhere they could cross, but she remembered holes under the fence.

"We need to get over to the other cemetery if we can," she said. "They won't think we can get across. They'll expect us to stay in Evergreen."

When they got to the boundary, Anna slowed down and tried to find the best place to get across the wash.

"This way," Anna said. She grabbed his hand and pulled him along the boundary, trying to remember where she had seen a break in the fence on the other side.

Finally, she found the opening in the fence. They slid into the wash and climbed out of it on the other side, grabbing the lower edge of the fence and pulling themselves under.

Anna stood up and looked around. She had to find the right spot.

"This way."

❧❧

Nick was standing by his truck at the food store when he saw Foster pushing Anna across the street. He held his breath when a car barely missed them. He took two steps forward as they ducked under the fence. He watched them disappear into the drainage and when they came up from the drainage, he saw her grab his hand and start running into the cover of the cemetery trees.

"Damn it," he said to Minnie. "What the...? It looks like she's leading him!"

Before Minnie could answer, he took off at a run. He ducked under the fence and fell into the drainage.

He rolled to the bottom and then, pulling himself up on the other side, he ran toward Evergreen Cemetery.

Just as he reached the trees, he stopped. Evergreen is so damn big. All these trees.

Police cars were swarming the cemetery and a number of policemen were moving cautiously through the trees.

Jesus. If they see me, they might think I'm him.

He had to figure it out.

She was leading him. Somehow she had taken control, but where would she go? What is she thinking?

Then it hit him.

He turned and sprinted along the western edge of the cemetery, staying just outside the trees, heading for Holy Hope as fast as he could get there. He had to get there first.

He hit the paved wash between the two cemeteries at a dead run, nearly falling head first into it.

He didn't have time to look for the openings. He grabbed the chain-link fence, and scrabbled up and over it into the Catholic cemetery.

He stopped and looked around. Where was the plot? Where had they buried the baby from the ridge? It was almost dark, nothing like the day they were here, so he had to think. It wasn't far from the fence, somewhere between here and Oracle Road, he thought.

He worked his way along the fence, stopping to read some of the markers in the gloom. When he found the tall, narrow monument, he prayed she was bringing him here, to Esperanza.

What else could it be? If she thought he was watching, if she hoped he would figure it out, she would come here. Nick prayed that he was right. That she would remember where they had seen the breaks in the fence.

If I'm wrong, I'm going to lose her. Please, God...

He hunched down on the north side of the monument and waited. He tried to control his breathing and still his pounding heart.

He heard Anna's voice.

"Let's go this way."

"Where are you taking me? How do you think we're going to get out of here?"

"Calm down, Foster, and let go of me."

If Anna hadn't answered right away, Nick might have made his move.

"We can get out of the cemetery on the north side, on Prince Road. The police think we're still in Evergreen—hiding in the trees. Look, the lights are still over there. Not one is aimed in this direction. If we can get to Prince Road, we can get to a pay phone. We'll call a cab."

"You want to call a cab?"

"Do you have a better idea, Foster? We need to put some distance between us and the cops."

They stood on one side of the monument while Nick crouched on the other.

Anna softened her voice, "Listen, Foster. Let's just get out of this and we'll talk more about what we need to do. I don't want to see you hurt, but I can't—I won't—come back to Chicago with you."

"It's that cowboy, isn't it? I knew it. The son of a bitch!"

"Nick has nothing to do with my decision, Foster." She took his hand. "I needed to leave you a long time ago."

"But Anna, I needed you."

"That's just it, Foster. Listen to yourself. You needed me—not that I needed you. I didn't need you the way you wanted me to need you. I needed a husband who loved me and—"

"I loved you, Anna. I love you." Foster's voice cracked.

She let go of his hand.

"And I loved you, once, but you didn't respect me. I didn't need you to make me a successful archaeologist. You needed me to believe that I couldn't do anything without you there to make it happen. What you really wanted was for me to make you the man you wanted to be, but I can't do that. I know the woman I want to be, and I don't need you or anyone else to make that happen. I'm sorry, Foster, but it would have never worked out for us."

He was quiet for a moment.

"No, you're coming back with me. You have to come back with me."

"For now, let's just see if we can get out of this mess."

As they stepped past the monument, Anna in the lead, Nick lunged out and tackled Foster.

When they hit the ground, Foster rolled on top of Nick. Even though he had lost weight, he was still the heavier man.

He grabbed Nick's throat and squeezed.

"You bastard. I'll kill you."

Nick struggled. He wrapped his hands around Foster's wrists and pushed. Hard.

He swung and connected. Foster fell back and rolled away from Nick, reaching behind him for the gun.

Nick dove at him.

When the gun went off, Anna screamed.

"Nick!" She stepped toward the men on the ground, and put her hand on Nick's shoulder. He pulled himself up and took her in his arms.

"Are you all right?" Blood was running from his forehead. "You're hurt."

Nick shook his head. "I'm fine, but I think Foster's hit." Foster lay on the ground moaning.

They heard the sirens and saw police cars speeding down Oracle to the entrance to the Catholic cemetery. The spotlights wheeling through the trees went dark.

They waited.

When the first policeman arrived, he aimed his gun at them. "Don't move!" He didn't take his eyes off of them as he spoke into his radio. "Man down. 10-45."

৵৽৽

The black and white dropped Anna and Nick at the convenience store. Max and Maggie, Margy and Joe, and Minnie, were all there. Maggie and Margy hugged Anna and they cried together.

Max grabbed Nick by the shoulders and pulled him into a bear hug. "We saw the ambulance. Thank God you're both all right." He stood back and looked at Nick. "Foster?"

Nick nodded. "He'll recover."

"What happened?" The question came from everyone. Nick told them that Anna was the hero. She led Foster to the Ramirez plot where Nick was waiting.

Anna looked at him. "Thank God you figured it out, Nick. I didn't know what else to do."

"When I saw you take the lead into the cemetery, I couldn't imagine you had any other destination in mind."

Margy looked at Anna's bruised and swollen face. "I'm going inside to get you some ice for that."

Minnie stepped forward and took Anna by both hands. "I told you," she said, "you have *sea takaa*. It protected you."

Anna laughed and Minnie wrapped her arms around her.

Margy came out and gave Anna some ice in a cup and some paper towels.

"Thanks, Margy." Anna wrapped some ice in the paper towel and held it gingerly against her face.

Detective Murchek and Deputy Chavez approached the group. Chavez looked at Anna and said, "Glad to see you're all right, ma'am."

The detective spoke to both of them. "We'll need you to come down to headquarters tomorrow."

Anna and Nick nodded and spoke at the same time. "Thank you."

Nick took Anna in his arms and said, "No arguments. You're coming home with me tonight."

"No arguments."

37

Tucson, Arizona, March 1988

Foster was out of the hospital, but still in jail. He was scheduled for arraignment and would be charged with kidnapping, illegal possession of a gun, and attempted murder.

Anna was not looking forward to the trial; a conviction and prison might be the only way she would be safe from him. Could he plead temporary insanity? She suspected he might. She wondered if his parents would try to pull strings to get him off. They didn't have any influence in Arizona, and she wasn't sure if they would have the money left when the SEC got finished with them. It remained a question she couldn't answer.

❦

A week after the arraignment, Rosie Espinoza called her at the lab.

"My mother wants to see you. She's not doing well and she said it's urgent that she talk to you."

"Of course, I can come right now if you wish." Rosie agreed.

Anna remembered that she had promised Mrs. Siqueiros that she would show her Esperanza's pot. She packed it in a box and cushioned it with crumpled newspapers.

A short time later, she parked in front of the neat little house in the barrio. She tapped lightly on the blue door and Rosie let her in, thanking her for coming on such short notice.

Before they went into the older woman's bedroom, Rosie said, "She's weak, but her mind is remarkably good. I don't know what she wants to tell you, but it's important to her. I'm worried about tiring her out, though."

Anna nodded. "I understand. I brought Esperanza's pot for her to see."

"Thank you. She'll like that."

The bedroom was neat like the rest of the house, although the bed was a standard hospital bed. The same afghan that she had spread across her lap when Anna first met her was on the bed. Anna thought she looked tiny and very frail.

"*Mami*, Ms. Robinson is here."

Anna put the box down on a chair near the bed.

Mrs. Sequeiros opened her eyes and lifted one hand to her throat. She coughed and Rosie plucked a tissue and wiped the edges of her mouth.

Anna stepped up beside the bed and took Mrs. Sequeiros's hand in hers. "Hello."

The old woman turned her head in Anna's direction. "*Gracias por venir.*" She turned toward her daughter. "Rosita, *por favor*, the box." Rosie turned and lifted a box from the dresser. "Tell her."

"She wants me to tell you that there is something in this box that belonged to her great-grandmother Esperanza. And she made me promise not to look into the box until you were here." Rosie laughed. "I'm glad you could come today, because I'm dying of curiosity."

Mrs. Sequeiros laughed lightly. "It's a family secret, *mi'ja*. One you must swear to keep, just as my mothers before me. Do you promise, Rosita?"

"*Sí, mami, prometo.*"

"The leather pouch." She began to cough again. Rosie put the box on the bed and wiped her mother's mouth again. She took a cool cloth from a basin and wiped her forehead.

"The box."

"*Sí, mami,* I have it here." She opened the box and found the rawhide pouch among other things inside. Anna was surprised to see a small, fringed pouch with an intricate, beaded design.

"Open it."

Rosie turned the pouch up. Three things fell into her waiting hand.

Anna was astonished. She looked at Rosie and at Mrs. Sequeiros, who was smiling.

"When you were here, when you came to tell us about the baby, you said you had a pot that you thought *Bisabuela* Esperanza might have used while they lived there." She coughed again, this time harder and longer.

Anna was alarmed and looked up at Rosie. Rosie dabbed her mother's mouth and told Anna it was all right.

The old woman continued. "When you told me about the pot, I knew my great-grandmother had kept a piece of it. I don't know why, but it was important to her or she wouldn't have put it into the pouch with the other." Her voice was getting stronger. Anna marveled at her memory.

Rosie said, "You told us you were trying to glue the pieces back together."

"Yes. I brought it for you to see." She turned to the box and lifted the pot for Mrs. Sequeiros to see."

The old woman's eyes brightened. "You will need this piece to finish."

Anna was overwhelmed. "Thank you. The finished vessel will be a lovely tribute to your great-grandmother's legacy." She returned it to the box and placed the missing sherd inside the bowl.

Mrs. Sequeiros moved her hand in Anna's direction, and when she took it again the old woman held it tightly.

"Show her." Mrs. Sequeiros was talking to Rosie. "Show her the other. Show her the secret things."

Anna had been so surprised to see the sherd, she hadn't noticed the other things that were in the pouch. "I don't know how these relate to *Tatarabuela* Esperanza."

Rosie handed them to Anna.

> *Her heart pounded in her ears.*
> *He stood very still, watching her*
> *without any change of expression. There*
> *was nothing threatening in his posture,*
> *and he did not speak. When he took a*
> *step forward, she stepped backward.*
>
> *He was wearing a loose, cotton shirt*
> *with a brown, wool vest; his leggings*
> *were loose and hung in folds around*
> *his ankles, covering the top of his*
> *deerskin boots. A large knife was held*

*fast to his side by a wide belt. A bead
and bone medallion hung at his throat.
Two pouches, a small one and a larger
one, both with beads and fringes hung
from the belt. His tangled hair, lightly
streaked with gray, was chopped off
unevenly around his shoulders. The
red bandana was tied around his head,
covering his forehead and shading his
dark eyes.*

*Deep lines etched his coppery face;
his mouth stretched in a straight line,
intimating neither a smile nor a frown.
A light breeze carried his mildly sour
body odor to her.*

*He took several very slow steps, and
although he kept watching her, he did
not walk in her direction. He walked
toward Ángel's grave. She held her
breath.*

*Not until he was standing in the
middle of the yard, did he take his eyes
off her. He looked toward the meager
pile of rocks and the small cross, and he
began to chant quietly. For a moment,
she thought she was imagining it. As he
sang, the pounding of her heart slowed.*

*When he stopped singing, he pulled
the small pouch from his belt, knelt
down, and laid it on the ground. He stood
and looked at her. She had not moved.
She could not read his expression, but
she knew he intended no harm.*

"*Gracias,*" Anna whispered and looked into Mrs.
Sequeiros's watery eyes.

The old woman smiled. "*Era su amigo.*" Then she
sighed and said. "I am tired. I will sleep now."

Anna looked down at what she was holding in her hand. One was a metal point, blackened with age. Only the Apaches were known for their metal points. The other was a short length of rawhide with a metal cone hanging on one end—a tinkler, a decoration from a ceremonial outfit. Apache.

She handed them back to Rosie and picked up her box. They left the bedroom.

"What do you suppose this means?" She looked at the point resting in the palm of her hand. "Why would this be a secret to be held by generations of the women who descended from my great-great-grandmother?"

"If I'm not mistaken, it's an Apache point. It's made of metal. The Apaches actually made arrowheads and spear points from metal. They probably used old tin cans to make them. It would have been a good weapon. And the other is part of a decoration used on Apache ceremonial outfits and cradleboards, among other things. Sometimes they're called 'tinklers' because they make a jingling noise when the person dances."

Rosie frowned. "If these are Apache, she must have known it, and that's why she didn't want the men to know. The Apaches were always raiding and stealing their cattle, and Armando's hatred of them was legendary. He passed that hatred along to his sons and grandsons. In fact, he was with Bill Oury and the so-called Committee of Public Safety that attacked the Apaches at Camp Grant. Even though the Indians were under the protection of the U.S. Army, it didn't matter. Most of those in the camp were women and children, and the elderly—the men had gone hunting. They killed almost all of them." She shook her head sadly.

"There are those of us in the family—the women—who think it was a terrible thing and others—the men, of course—who still think it was a good thing. I don't believe that Armando would have allowed her to keep such a thing if he had known about it."

She looked up at Anna. "She found the pot; might she have found these as well?"

"I'm inclined to doubt it. The Apaches never lived at the site, and there were no Apache artifacts recovered in the surface collection or in the excavations. I suppose the point might have been left after an Apache raid, but the tinkler? That's even more unlikely. I don't think the warriors wore them when they were raiding—the jangling might have given them away. I wish I could give you answers." She did not tell Rosie what she and Esperanza Siqueiros had shared when she held them.

Rosie returned the point and the tinkler to the pouch. "I suppose the secret will continue through another generation."

Anna thanked Rosie again and walked to her car.

&&*

When she got back to the lab, she carried the pot to her worktable. There were a few openings where very small sherds had not been recovered, but, with the final piece in place, it might be a museum piece.

She lifted the sherd and turned it over in her hand. She put her thumb on the inside of the piece, in the nearly imperceptible depression, and once again, the potter was there with her.

She drew a bead of glue along the edges and did the same to the pieces already in place. She waited a moment, then slid the piece into place and gently tugged the pieces on each side toward the new entry. When she was confident that they were holding, she clipped a clothespin on each of the joints.

She sat back and reached out with both hands, cupping them around the jar; she closed her eyes and listened.

The earth is our mother

Who sustains us
She honors us with gifts
We respectfully use her gifts
And honor her by giving back
The gifts of the earth
The gifts from the earth
The earth is our mother
Who sustains us

Epilogue

Tucson, Arizona, May 1992

Nick parked in the small parking lot. They got out and Anna reached into the back seat and lifted Hope from her car seat.

Together, she, Nick, and Hope walked across the wash, through the sand, and up the steps fashioned from railroad ties that wound upward around the curve of the ridge. Hope managed a few of the steps, holding their hands, but then reached up to Nick.

At the top, there was a bench and an interpretive sign. They stopped and stood Hope on the bench while they read the sign. The sign said the ridge was a perfect location for an agrarian people centuries ago, mentioning the multiple waterways that surrounded the site—the Sutherland, the Cañada del Oro, and the Montrose washes.

Walking along the path, Hope holding each of their hands, Anna stopped and bent down to pick something up. She handed it to Hope who turned it over and over in her own tiny fingers. "This is a small piece of pottery, Hope."

"Pot–try," Hope said. Anna looked into her daughter's trusting green eyes, feeling an overwhelming sense of gratitude and love.

"Someday, if you are lucky, you will hear its song." Anna quoted Byrd Baylor's words as best she could:

> Each piece has its own small voice and sings in its own way.
> Even now the wind sometimes finds one of those songs and lifts it out and carries it down the canyon and across the hills.
> It is a small sound and always far away but they say sometimes they hear it.

Hope took the small piece of pottery and held it to her ear. She listened. She frowned and then held it to her mother's ear. Anna laughed gently.

When Hope put it back to her own ear, her eyes lit with wonder and she smiled.

She handed the sherd back to her mother who said, "We need to return this to where we found it. We can't keep it."

Hope pouted as Anna put the sherd back on the ground away from the path.

They walked on, stopping from time to time to read the interpretive signs that explained to park visitors how the Hohokam had lived so many years ago.

When they reached the Ramirez Ruins, Anna picked her daughter up and pointed to the old rock walls that made up the foundation of the house and the shed.

"This is where Esperanza lived, Hope. She was a very special lady."

"Es-panza," Hope whispered.

If you enjoyed my book, won't you please write a review on Goodreads, Amazon, Barnes & Noble, and/or other online retailers' sites.

Preview: The Clay Endures

Arizona Territory, Winter 1865

Every morning, Armando fed the horses and saddled them. Normally, he rode the mare, Sofi, when he went out to check on the cattle, leaving the gelding there at the ready in case Esperanza needed him. Before leaving, he checked Esperanza's rifle. He wanted to make sure it was fully loaded, clean, and in good working order. It was a .44 caliber, rim-fire Henry repeating rifle, like his own.

He had paid dearly for the rifles, but he knew they needed to be prepared to do battle with the Apaches. Even though Henrys were known for their hair trigger, repeaters were necessary; a single-shot rifle would be worthless out here. The Henry held at least sixteen cartridges in the magazine, more than enough to send the Apaches packing if they were bold enough to come to the house. And Esperanza was an excellent shot. They had spent a great deal of time in target practice before coming to the ridge. It was another reason for his mother to criticize his wife. He could hear her voice. "Ladies do not handle firearms." It always made him smile.

Sometimes the Apaches were bold enough to stage daylight raids, and when they did, he rode out to defend his property. One man against a party of five or seven Apaches. It seemed like a game, but a very dangerous one. They could have killed him any number of times, but they did not. He often returned from these forays bleeding and battered, having retrieved only a few of the stolen stock. He often said that might be their intention: steal six and let him retrieve two. Whatever it was, they always came out ahead.

One morning, shortly after he had saddled the horses, he glanced out toward the bajada and saw three Apaches working their way through the herd. He yelled for Esperanza, grabbed his rifle and mounted the mare. When Esperanza ran out of the house carrying her rifle, he shouted, "¡Los bastardos hacen de las suyas! I will get them this time!"

She watched as he spun the mare and kicked her hard. Standing in the cloud of dust he left behind, Esperanza made the sign of the cross, and watched the chase unfolding across the bajada. Armando had cleared the base of the ridge and was pushing the mare through the desert scrub toward the cattle.

When she lost sight of him in the brush, she lifted her gaze toward the Apaches. She thought it was strange that they were moving around in slow circles instead of driving the cattle they had separated from the herd. She knew they were watching Armando as he emerged from the brush and closed in on them.

"*Madre de Dios,*" she thought, "*protogerlo.*" They were setting a trap. They normally kept out of range of his rifle, which was better than their guns. They would have to close in tight to get a good shot at him. She heard the shots, the sound bouncing off the mountains and echoing across the desert. She could not tell who had fired nor when.

Just as she made another sign of the cross and began a second prayer, she saw Armando fall from the mare and disappear into the brush. She turned and ran to the gelding, shoved the rifle into the scabbard, and mounted, throwing her right leg all the way over the horse and loosening the layers of her skirt and petticoat. She jammed her feet into the stirrups and swung the gelding past the house and down the trail in the direction Armando had gone.

They dashed through the brush, ignoring mesquite branches and acacia grabbing and shredding her skirt and petticoat. She kicked the horse even harder each time a branch reached out to slow her. She had tried to keep her eye on the spot where Armando went down, but here below the ridge on the bajada, the trail—what there was of it—went up and down and around larger trees and cactus. In spite of that, she thought she knew where he had fallen.

As she rounded a turn in the trail, the mare came thundering toward her, dragging her reins. "*¡Jo!*" Esperanza turned the gelding across the trail and raised her arm. "*¡Sofi, mi niña! ¡Jo!*" Sofi slid to a stop, heaving and blowing. She sidled up to the gelding as if seeking shelter. Esperanza leaned over and grabbed Sofi's reins. She pulled her around and started in the direction the horse had come from. At first, Sofi resisted. That was the direction of danger and she didn't want to go.

"*¡Vamanos!* Sofi, come on!" Choosing not to be left alone, Sofi ran along beside Pepe. "'Mando!" Esperanza began calling. She had to find him. "'Mando!" She drew Pepe up and tried to settle him and Sofi so she could listen.

Then she heard him. "*¡Espe, estoy aquí!*"

She worked her way through the brush, stopping to listen now and then. When she found him, he was sitting on the trail, blood dripping from his forehead, and looking a little dazed.

"*¿Estás bien?*" Esperanza started to dismount, but Armando raised his hand and told her to stay in the saddle.

"*Estoy bien,* Esperanza. *Nada duele pero mi orgullo,* only my pride." He picked up his rifle and pushed the butt against the ground to help him stand. He slid the rifle into the scabbard and climbed into the saddle. "They missed me, and then I fell off of Sofi."

Had she not been so relieved, she might have laughed.

"How many cattle did they take?"

He pulled himself into the saddle and dragged a forearm across his forehead, and then looked at the blood on his sleeve. "I'm not sure. It was hard to see what they were doing when I was lying on my back in the trail."

She was glad he was able to joke. "It does not look bad, 'Mando, but you'll probably have a headache." It could have been so much worse.

He looked at her and smiled. "*¿Qué haría yo sin usted?* What would I do without you?"

"We will be all right, 'Mando. We have each other." She reached for his hand and he sidestepped Sofi closer to Pepe so he could lean over and kiss her.

"Let's go count cows."

They turned their horses and headed across the bajada.

∽•∽

The Clay Endures will be published in late 2015. To learn more about it and to get regular updates and previews, go to www. sharonkmiller.com and join my e-mail list.

The Clay Sustains, the story of the Hohokam woman who made the pot Anna so lovingly restores, will be published sometime in 2016.

Author Notes

Many Tucson residents will recognize Ramirez Ruin as the Romero Ruin in Catalina State Park. Sometime in the mid-1800s, Francisco Romero (1822-1905) and his wife Victoriana Ocoboa (1833 or 1834-1908) established a homestead some fifteen miles north of Tucson in the Territory of Arizona. He built a simple home on the site of an ancient Hohokam village.

Certain events in the lives of my fictional characters, Armando and Esperanza Ramirez, are based on historical accounts of Francisco and Victoriana Romero. For example, while they lived at the site, the Apaches constantly raided, stealing cattle and threatening their safety. He did, indeed, chase after them armed with pistols and a rim-fire carbine, which gave him an advantage over the weapons of the Apaches. His son reported that he bore multiple scars from his battles with them. They built their living structure from rocks and cobbles from the ancient Hohokam compound.

The history of their time there is confounding, with different sources suggesting different dates. Some sources place them there as early as the late 1850s and others around 1879. I chose to place Armando and Esperanza at the site in the mid to late 1860s and to provide a fictional backstory for them. The lullaby that Esperanza sings to her child is, in fact, not from that time period. It is a modern lullaby, written to the tune of the theme from "Pan's Labyrinth."

Esperanza's story is told in Book 2 of The Clay Series, *The Clay Endures*. In Spanish, *esperanza* means "hope."

The Romero Ruin site has been the subject of archaeological interest for more than one hundred years. In the early 1800s, the site was marked on the map as *Pueblo Viejo* (ancient village) and the first description was written in 1910 with photographs by geographer Ellsworth Huntington.

In the 1920s, interviews with long-time residents said that it was the site of the Lost Mission of *Cirú*. For many years, people believed that there was a fortune in gold that had been left behind when the mission was abandoned. Because that mythology persisted into the 1950s, the site was frequently vandalized by both pot hunters and gold hunters.

Romero Ruin is among the largest and most important ancient sites in the Tucson area. Data from various archaeological studies suggest that the site was occupied by the Hohokam from approximately 550 CE through 1450 CE.

It is important for readers to understand that the archaeological excavations conducted by my fictional characters at the site are not based on actual excavations; the same is true of their work at the Los

Morteros site in Marana. Southwest Archaeological Associates is a fictional company.

Some artifacts uncovered in the story are typical of those that may have been collected in actual excavations, but the pot break and the infant burial are the products of my imagination.

Book 3 in The Clay Series, *The Clay Sustains,* is the story of the Hohokam woman who made the pot during the declining years of her village.

The manner in which Foster's university handled his plagiarism is not based on any university policy that I am aware of. I created the policy based on what I think *should* be the response of a university for such a blatant theft of student work. Interestingly, a situation arose at a prominent university in 2014, long after I had written about Foster's plagiarism and its outcome. A professor took the work of one of her students and used it, verbatim, in a paper she presented at a conference. She did not cite the student nor did she credit him for any contribution to her paper.

After an investigation confirmed the material was, in fact, the work of the student, the university declined to reprimand the professor and allowed her paper to stand as published. Unfortunately, when students commit similar acts of plagiarism, at a minimum, they fail the course and possibly face further disciplinary action. I am outraged that a student should be so victimized by both the professor and the university. One additional note: I have actually encountered educators who, like Foster, believe that student work belongs to them and they can use it as they please.

The Elm Street house on Chicago's Gold Coast is a real house built by the developer Potter Palmer in 1888. After the Great Chicago Fire, he purchased swampland along the Lake Michigan shoreline, filled it in, and built a forty-two room castle-like mansion. He persuaded the city to build Lake Shore Drive, and later he built a subdivision of brownstone houses along Lake Shore Drive that was one of the most affluent neighborhoods in the United States at the time. Specifically, the house at 74 E. Elm Street is a narrow brownstone of five stories with four bedroom suites, six baths with heated floors, seven fireplaces, and an indoor heated two-car garage. Several years ago it was on the market, and I downloaded the floor plans and pictures of the interior. In the summer of 2014, I visited Elm Street and had my picture taken in front of the house.

The Gold Coast Gun Club, of which Foster's father was a member, is a fictitious club, although many trap shooting clubs throughout the United States previously held, and may continue to hold, live pigeon shoots. The big-game rifle, the Weatherby, 9-Lug Mark V, is a rare, collectible rifle.

The accounting company, Arthur Andersen, was a real company in Chicago that was involved in a scandal much like that described in the book. The company was accused of falsifying audits on behalf of big corporations, which increased the profits of the corporations and the accounting company that was supposedly conducting independent audits. I have placed the scandal several years before it happened in reality.

I have no idea whether or not Marshall Field's ever had a top floor sales salon for wealthy customers, but I have heard and read of such services.

Evergreen and Holy Hope Cemeteries in Tucson were established early in the twentieth century because of development in downtown Tucson. The remains of Catholics who had been buried in the old Church Street Catholic Cemetery, among them the Romeros, were moved to Holy Hope Cemetery.

Remains from the Alameda-Stone Cemetery were moved to Evergreen. Sadly, not all of the burials in the downtown cemeteries were moved. Many still lie beneath the streets and modern buildings.

Archaeological Site Etiquette Guide

State Historic Preservation Office Arizona State Parks

Welcome to the past! Arizona contains some of the nation's—and indeed the world's—greatest archaeological sites. Please take a few minutes to familiarize yourself with this site etiquette guide that will facilitate an enjoyable visit for you, AND for others who follow you!

Archaeological sites in Arizona are the remains of a long occupation of prehistoric, proto-historic, and historic cultures. They are a fragile and non-renewable resource. You are responsible for the stewardship of these ruins, both for public enjoyment and education, and for preserving their scientific values. The following guidelines will help you minimize impacts to archaeological sites:

1. Walls are fragile and continually deteriorating. That is why they are called "ruins." Climbing, sitting or standing on walls can damage them. Also, picking up or moving rocks alters the walls forever.

2. Artifacts, where they lay, tell a story. Once they are moved, a piece of the past is destroyed forever. Digging, removing artifacts, or piling them up changes what can be learned from these pieces of the past.

3. Cultural deposits, including the soil on an archaeological site, are important for scientific tests and are used in reconstructing past environments. For instance, from such information we can learn what kinds of plants were be used by the past inhabitants. Please carry out any trash (especially organic remains) you may have while visiting a site.

4. Fragile desert plants and soils that are part of archaeological sites are destroyed when you stray from the trail. Also, snakes and other small desert animals make their homes in the bushes and under rocks and in burrows... you may disturb them. Please stay on trails... they are there for your protection and the protection of fragile cultural remains.

5. Fire destroys prehistoric organic materials, ruins the dating potential of artifacts, and damages or even destroys rock art. Absolutely no fires, candles, or smoking should occur at archaeological sites.

6. Oils from even the cleanest hands can cause deterioration of prehistoric drawings and ruin the dating potential for future scientists trying to unravel the meaning of symbols painted and pecked on stone. Please refrain from touching rock art.

7. Graffiti (drawing/painting, scratching, and carving) is destructive and can destroy rock art, as well as deface wooden/stone buildings. Graffiti destroys rock art as well as other values.

8. Pets damage sites by digging, urinating and defecating in them. They can destroy fragile cultural deposits and frighten other visitors and native animals. Please do not bring pets onto archaeological sites.

Finally, be aware of your surroundings when you are outdoors. Avoid driving or riding your bicycle through sites; pitching your camp in a site; dismantling historic buildings for firewood or any other use; and, camping, or making campfires, in historic buildings.

All archaeological sites on public (federal and state) land in Arizona are protected by the Archaeological Resources Protection Act and state laws that prohibit digging, removing artifacts, damaging and/or defacing archaeological resources; these laws provide for both felony and misdemeanor charges with jail time, confiscation of property, and large fines. Arizona state law also protects graves (human remains) and grave goods located on state and private land.

If you see people vandalizing sites, please report it as soon as possible to the public land manager (e.g., the Forest Service, the Arizona State Land Department, etc.) or their law enforcement entity.

Archaeological site locations are also protected under federal and state laws. Please do not disclose information about where sites are located, as it could potentially lead to those sites being vandalized or looted.

By following these simple guidelines, **YOU** can help preserve these unique and fragile remains of **OUR** American heritage. Remember, **THE FUTURE OF THE PAST DEPENDS ON YOU!** Thanks for your cooperation, and we hope that you enjoy visiting archaeological sites in Arizona!

Reprinted with permission of the Arizona State Historical Preservation Office Arizona State Parks, 1300 W. Washington Street, Phoenix, AZ 85007.

Download a copy of this guide at http://az-stateparks.com/shpo/downloads/SHPO_Site_Etiquette.pdf

Glossary

alluvial fan: a fan- or cone-shaped deposit of sediment; often found where a canyon drains from mountainous terrain onto a flatter plain.

anthropology: the scientific and humanistic study of man's present and past biological, linguistic, social, and cultural variations. Archaeology is a sub-field of anthropology.

archaeological record: the physical remains produced by past human activities that are sought, recovered, studied, and interpreted by archaeologists to reconstruct the past.

archaeology: The scientific study of material remains of past human life and activities

artifact: any object manufactured, modified, or used by humans that can be picked up and moved.

Aztalan: a Mississipian culture site that flourished during the 10th to the 13th centuries. The Mississippian people built massive earthwork mounds for religious and political purposes. The site, in Wisconsin, is a state park and a National Historic Landmark.

bajada: a geological term (from Spanish) for a foothill slope generally made up of alluvial fans that have formed into a single apron of deposits against the slope.

ballcourt: a large, elliptical feature defined by earthen or stone embankments and a flat floor. Archaeologists think they were used by the Hohokam for a version of a Mesoamerican ball game or for other public ceremonies and activities.

barrio: a Spanish word for neighborhood.

BCE/CE: before the Common Era/Common Era; used to denote dates as an alternative to BC (before Christ) and AD (*anno Domini*—in the year of our Lord).

caliche: deposits of calcium carbonate that occur throughout the Tucson Basin. Caliche creates a seemingly impervious layer a fraction of an inch to several feet in thickness in the soil.

Camp Grant Massacre: During the winter and spring of 1871, Jesús María Elías and William S. Oury, prominent citizens of Tucson, formed a Committee of Public Safety that blamed every depredation in Southern Arizona on a band of Apaches who were under the protection of the U.S. Army at Camp Grant. Historical documentation confirms that these Apaches were not involved in the raids that had been attributed to them. On the afternoon of April 28, 1871, six Americans, 48 Mexicans, and ninety-two Tohono O'odham gathered along Rillito Creek and set off on a march to Aravaipa Canyon. At dawn on Sunday, April 30, they surrounded the Apache camp. The O'odham were the main fighters, while the Americans and Mexicans picked off Apaches who tried to escape. Most of the Apache men were off hunting in the mountains. All but eight of the corpses were women and children. A total of 144 Aravaipas and Pinals were killed and mutilated, many of them scalped. Thirty or more children were missing, likely taken captive by the attackers. Efforts to restore the captive children to their Apache families were unsuccessful. Some captors quickly baptized the children and claimed it would be against Christianity to return them to a heathen lifestyle. Other children were absorbed by Tohono O'odham families; still others were sold as slaves in Mexico. President Grant informed the territorial governor that if the perpetrators were not brought to trial, he would place Arizona under martial law. In October 1871, a Tucson grand jury charged 100 of the assailants with 108 counts of murder. The trial, two months later, focused solely on Apache depredations; it took the jury just 19 minutes to pronounce a verdict of not guilty.

ceramics: clay (often fired) artifacts including vessels and objects such as figurines and spindle whorls.

cholla: (*Opuntia* species) (pronounced *choy-a*) any of several species of spiny cactus having cylindrical stems and branches. The jumping cholla looks soft and fuzzy from a distance, but when you touch it, a segment "jumps" off the plant and attaches itself to you. Actually, tiny barbs on the ends of the spines embed in your skin and when you pull away, the action brings the segment along.

Clovis point: projectile point used by the first human inhabitants (Paleo-Indians) of North America, who arrived here between 10,000 and 12,000 years ago. Paleo-Indians hunted with spears tipped with Clovis points.

context: the provenience of an artifact or feature; the relationship of one feature or artifact to other features or artifacts.

cordones: From Spanish, referring to long finger ridges.

datum: a reference point or surface against which vertical and horizontal measurements are made.

Emil Haury: (1904-1992) archaeologist who specialized in the Southwest. His work at Snaketown helped to define the Hohokam tradition.

excavation: systematic and controlled digging into a site.

feature: any object or structure made or modified by humans and typically incorporated into the ground. A feature cannot be removed from its location without compromising the integrity of the object or structure.

field school: a hands-on opportunity for archaeology and anthropology students to learn a variety of field methods. Field schools are offered at archaeological sites around the world.

forensic archaeologist: also forensic anthropologist, uses knowledge of anthropology to help identify human remains, often in medical or legal situations. In forensic archaeology, forensic anthropologists employ archaeological methods to assist in the excavation of human remains.

Glycymeris **and** **umbo:** *Glycymeris gigantea* is a large, saltwater clam found in the Gulf of California (Sea of Cortez) which can be as large as ten centimeters. The Hohokam frequently traveled to the sea to collect shells for trade goods and for making bracelets and rings. Glycymeris bracelets are among the most common, finished shell artifact found in Hohokam collections. The center of the shell was removed, creating a circle, and the **umbo**, or the thick, hinge of the bivalve, was often carved or etched with designs.

hearth: the remains of a fire pit.

Hopewell: near Chillicothe, Ohio, it is the site of the Hopewell culture, indigenous peoples who lived from about 200 BCE to 500 CE and built enclosures made of earthen walls, often in geometric patterns and shapes. It is a National Historical Park.

Kimmswick: a Paleo-Indian site located south of St. Louis where, in the 1800s, mastodon bones were unearthed; in 1979, a stone spear point made by hunters of the Clovis culture (13,500 to 12,500 years ago) was found embedded in a mastodon bone. Additional points were found in subsequent excavations. This was the first solid evidence that humans co-existed with mastodons. It is now known as Mastodon State Historic Site.

kohtpul: Tohono O'odham word for cicada.

Lavender Pit: part of the Copper Queen Mine in Bisbee, Arizona. Copper was mined from the pit by Phelps Dodge Corporation from 1879 to 1974. The abandoned pit covers 300 acres and is 950 feet deep. (The Center for Land Use Interpretation, www.clui.org)

Los Morteros: a site in Marana, Arizona, which is one of the largest and longest occupied villages in the Tucson Basin. Including communities that surrounded it, the area was settled for more than 1000 years (from around 100 CE to 1200 CE). The phrase is Spanish for "the mortars," and is named for a number of rock mortars at the site. Pima County has preserved a large portion of the site.

luminarias: small lanterns made with a candle set in sand inside a paper bag; in the American Southwest, they are popular Christmas decorations.

mano: Spanish for "hand," a milling stone used to process materials on a metate.

metate: a block-shaped stone on which materials are processed with a mano.

midden: a trash deposit from a prehistoric culture that provides rich evidence of cultural practices and lifestyles; also, the nest of a packrat (woodrat), which, through the items the rat collects over time, often provides insight into the rat's environment. Fossilized packrat middens can provide a record of the plants and animals that lived within the rat's range.

mortar: a rock with a concave area of varying depths on which materials are pounded, crushed, or ground.

Mount Lemmon: the highest point in the Santa Catalina Mountains north of Tucson, Arizona. The summit is 9,159 feet high.

nopales: the pads of the prickly pear cactus, a popular vegetable in the southwest.

ossification: the natural process of bone formation.

outcrop: surface exposure of rock layers.

paddle and anvil: a technique used to build and smooth a clay vessel. The potter holds a smooth rock inside the vessel and uses the paddle to beat the exterior, thus raising, smoothing, and thinning the vessel walls.

petroglyph: a rock drawing created by incising, picking, carving, or abrading the surface of a rock.

pit house: a semi-subterranean habitation structure.

plainware: a generic term for pottery that has not been slipped, painted, or textured. This is the most common type of pottery found in the Tucson Basin. In the Tucson area, plainwares were made from clays that turned brown or tan when fired.

post-processual theory: a theory that arose in the late 1970s and early 1980s that challenges processual archaeology. *Processual archaeology*, which was developed in the 1960s, involves the scientific method, using artifacts to determine how the people who created or owned such artifacts lived and thought. A key tenet of processualism is that by using the scientific method to analyze the data, completely objective conclusions can be drawn. Post-processualists believe that because processual archaeology interprets data through a modern lens, its conclusions are unreliable; it challenges the notion that we can *objectively know* the lifestyle and belief systems of an ancient culture. Even so, processual archaeology is the most commonly practiced.

potsherd: a piece of broken pottery. Also called shard or sherd.

provenience: the three-dimensional location of an item (artifact, feature, or eco-fact) in a site

puki: a shallow vessel used to shape a pottery vessel; thought to be an invention of the Hohokam (see www.palatkwapi.com/2004/12/pottery-without-pukis/).

red-on-brown ware: ceramics made from the same brown-firing clay as the plainwares, but which have been decorated with designs painted with a red, iron-based paint.

Romero Ruin: a feature in Catalina State Park, north of Tucson, which includes the remains of a historic ranch built by Francisco Romero in the 19th century and the prehistoric Hohokam village in the same location. There is an interpretive trail through part of the site.

Rincon Mountains: one of the five mountain ranges that surround Tucson, situated to the east. Redington Pass separates the Rincons from the Santa Catalinas.

saguaro: (*Carnegiea gigantea*) one of the largest cacti, the saguaro has one central trunk with one or more upward curving branches. This tree-size cactus played an important role in the economy of the Hohokam, as well as historic and modern Native Americans in the region.

Santa Catalina Mountains: one of the five mountain ranges that surround Tucson, situated to the north. It is the most prominent of the ranges and is Tucson's signature range. Pusch Ridge is part of the mountain range and provides a rugged, striking backdrop for the Romero Ruin interpretive trail.

Santa Rita Mountains: one of the five mountain ranges that surround Tucson, Arizona, situated to the south. The highest point in the range is Mount Wrightson at 9,453 feet.

sherds: pieces of broken pottery. Also called shard or potsherd.

shell bracelets: usually made from *Glycymeris*, a bivalve. Shells were collected from the shores of the Sea of Cortez (Gulf of California) or acquired in trade from other communities.

shovelbum: a field technician, often the first job an archaeologist gets. Most jobs are temporary, as the field technicians may work for multiple cultural resource management firms or government agencies, traveling around the country from one project to the next.

site: a geographic place where there is evidence of past human activity.

slip: a liquefied suspension of clay particles in water used by the Hohokam to cover the surface of their pots. Slip is applied after the ceramic has been formed and allowed to dry to "leather hard," but before firing. It is often polished.

Snaketown: a Hohokam archaeological site thirty miles southeast of Phoenix, thought to have been inhabited between 300 CE and 1200 CE, and excavated by Emil Haury in the 1930s and again in 1964.

Sonoran Desert: the hottest desert in North America, it covers 110,00 square miles in southern Arizona, southeastern California, and much of the states of Sonora, Baja California, and Baja California Sur in Mexico. It is characterized by tall-growing cactus such as saguaros and bean trees such as mesquite and paloverde. Tucson is near the eastern edge of the Sonoran Desert.

spindle whorls: disks or beads that were used to weight a spindle when spinning thread. Disk-shaped whorls were made from old potsherds or flat pieces of slate. Bead-shaped whorls were modeled from clay, slipped and polished, and fired.

survey: a systematic examination of land to document the archaeological resources located on it.

tabular knife: a worked stone tool used to cut yucca, sotol, bear grass and agave. It was also used to scrape tissue from the agave leaves.

temper: organic or inorganic agents added to ceramics to reduce shrinkage or cracking during firing.

Tohono O'odham: literally "Desert People." They are a Native American people who live in the Sonoran Desert of southern Arizona and northwestern Mexico. They claim descendancy from the Hohokam.

Tortolita Mountains: a small mountain range northwest of Tucson, and at the northern boundaries of Oro Valley and Marana. Much of the range is protected within Tortolita Mountain Park.

Tucson Mountains: one of the five mountain ranges surrounding Tucson. It is a minor, but rugged, range with odd-shaped volcanic peaks that create a profile unlike any of the other mountains surrounding Tucson.

Tully-Ochoa Freight Ambush: In May 1869, teamster Santa Cruz Castaneda along with fourteen men, nine 16-foot Murphy wagons (Murphy wagons could haul between four and eight tons depending on their length) and eighty mules left Tucson early in the morning on their way to Camp Grant. Shortly before 8 a.m. they arrived near the Canyon del Oro and saw signs of Apaches, so they circled the wagons. They were attacked by approximately 200 Apaches. A small contingent of soldiers from Camp Grant happened along and helped some of the teamsters escape on some of the mules. The Apaches took the freight and burned the wagons, costing Tully-Ochoa Freight Company around $12,000 and the lives of three teamsters.

umbo: see *Glycymeris*

Yaqui/Pascua Yaqui: a federally recognized tribe in southern Arizona. They migrated to southern Arizona from Mexico in the late 19th and early 20th centuries. Having converted to Christianity with the coming of Spanish missionaries to Mexico, they are still predominantly Catholic but retain much of their native Indian practices and culture in their religious ceremonies.

Yoeme: the historic, or cultural, name of the Yaquis, meaning "people." The Yoeme are a highly spiritual people, believing in five spirit worlds: *Sea Ania* (the Flower World), *Huya Ania* (the Wilderness World), *Yo Ania* (the Enchanted World), *Tuka Ania* (the Night World), and *Tenku Ania* (the Dream World). The Yoeme believe that when you enter into any of these worlds, your spiritual powers are enhanced.

References

All Books in The Clay Series

Alcock, John. *When the Rains Come: A Naturalist's Year in the Sonoran Desert*. Tucson: University of Arizona Press. 2009.

Arizona Engineer. "UA Engineers Help Save and Reconstruct the Past," Vol. 29 No 1. Tucson: University of Arizona College of Engineering and Mines. Spring, 2006.

Ashmore, Wendy, and Robert. Sharer. *Discovering Our Past: A Brief Introduction to Archaeology*. Mountain View, CA: Mayfield. 1996.

Bahr, Donald, Juan Smith, William Smith Allison, and Julian Hayden. *The Short Swift Time of Gods on Earth: The Hohokam Chronicles*. Berkelely: University of California Press. 1994.

Baldwin, Gordon C. *The Warrior Apaches: A Story of the Chiricahua and Western Apache*. Tucson: Dale Stuart King. 1865.

Ball, Eve, with Nora Henn and Lynda A. Sanchez. *Indeh: An Apache Odyssey,* Norman, OK: University of Oklahoma Press.1980.

Barnett, Franklin. *Dictionary of Prehistoric Indian Artifacts of the American Southwest,* Flagstaff: Northland. 1973.

Baylor, Byrd. *And It Is Still That Way: Legends Told by Arizona Indian Children*. El Paso: Cinco Puntos Press. 1998.

Baylor, Byrd. *When Clay Sings*. New York: Aladdin. 1987.

Bernard-Shaw, Mary, Henry D. Wallace, Linda Mayro, and William H. Doelle. *Archaeological Testing at Los Morteros North and a Mitigation Plan for the Site of Los Morteros,* Technical Report No. 87-10. Tucson: Institute for American Research. 1987.

Bezy, John V. *A Guide to the Geology of Catalina State Park and the Western Santa Catalina Mountains*. Tucson: Arizona Geological Survey. 2002.

Bowden, Charles. *Frog Mountain Blues*. Tucson: University of Arizona Press. 1994.

Colwell-Chanthaphonh. *Massacre at Camp Grant: Forgetting and Remembering Apache History*. Tucson: University of Arizona Press. 2007.

Cornett, James W. *Indian Uses of Desert Plants.* Palm Springs, CA: Nature Trails Press. 2011.

Cremony, John C. *Life Among the Apaches,* San Francisco: A. Roman and Company, Publishers. 1868. (Digital reproduction by Digital Scanning, Inc., 2001.)

Crider, Destiny L., Cathryn M. Meegan, and Steve Swanson. *The Hohokam Preclassic to Classic Transition Part II: Modeling Socioeconomic Changes.* Tempe: Arizona State University Department of Anthropology. n.d.

Dancey, William S. *Archaeological Field Methods.* Edina, MN: Burgess. 1981.

Doelle, William H., and Deborah L. Swartz. "Hidden Times: The Archaeology of the Tortolita Phase," in *Archaeology in Tucson: Newsletter of the Center for Desert Archaeology,* Vol 11, No. 2. Tucson: Center for Desert Archaeology. Spring, 1997.

Ferg, Alan, Ed. *Western Apache Material Culture: The Goodwin and Guenther Collections.* Tucson: University of Arizona Press. 1987.

Fish, Suzanne K., and Paul R. Fish, eds. *The Hohokam Millennium.* Santa Fe: School for Advanced Research Press. 2007.

Fontana, Bernard L. *Entrada: The Legacy of Spain and Mexico in the United States.* Tucson: Southwest Parks and Monuments Association. 1994.

Giddings, Ruth Warner. *Yaqui Myths and Legends.* Tucson: University of Arizona Press. 1959.

Gregonis, Linda M., and Karl J. Reinhard. *Hohokam Indians of the Tucson Basin.* Tucson: University of Arizona Press. 1979.

Gronemann, Barbara. *Hohokam Arts and Crafts.* Scottsdale, AZ: Southwest Learning Sources. 1994.

Hanson, Roseann Beggy, and Jonathan Hanson. *Southern Arizona Nature Almanac: A Seasonal Guide to Pima County and Beyond.* Tucson: University of Arizona Press. 1996.

Hayden Papers. Francisco Romero Documents. Arizona Historical Society. Tucson.

Heilen, Michael. *Uncovering Identity in Mortuary Analysis: Community Sensitive Methods for Identifying Group Affiliation in Historical Cemeteries.* Walnut Creek, CA: Left Coast Press. 2012.

Hernandez, John. *Blood Along the Cañon del Oro— Tully & Ochoa Wagon Attack.* April 4, 2013. http://www.copperarea.com/pages/blood-along-the-caon-del-oro-tully-ochoa-wagon-attack-2/ (Retrieved January 9, 2015).

Hester, Thomas R., Harry J. Shafer, and Kenneth L. Feder. *Field Methods in Archaeology,* Seventh Edition. Mountain View, CA: Mayfield. 1997.

Homes in the Gold Coast Historic District of Chicago, http://www.74elm.com/photo-gallery/ (Retrieved 8/10/2012).

Huckell, Lisa W. *Archaeological Assessment of the Proposed Catalina State Park.* Archaeological Series No. Tucson: Arizona State Museum. 1980.

Illinois Grounds for Dissolution of Marriage http://www.divorcesource.com/ds/illinois/illinois-divorce-laws-674.shtml,http://www.illinoisdivorce.com/family_law_articles/grounds_for_divorce.php (Retrieved 7/18/2012).

Kane, Charles W. *Medicinal Plants of the American Southwest*. Lincoln Town Press. 2011.

Kessel, John L. *Friars, Soldiers, and Reformers: Hispanic Arizona and the Sonora Mission Frontier, 1767-1856*. Tucson: University of Arizona Press. 1976.

King, Dan. *General Hohokam Pottery Descriptions*, July 2004. http://www.rarepottery.info/protect/articles.htm (Retrieved 7/19/2010)

Lavin, Patrick. *Arizona: An Illustrated History*. New York: Hippocrene Books. 2001.

Malville, J. McKim, and Claudia Putnam. *Prehistoric Astronomy in the Southwest*. Boulder: Johnson Books. 1993.

Martin, Patricia Preciado. *Beloved Land: An Oral History of Mexican Americans in Southern Arizona*. Tucson: University of Arizona Press. 2004.

Martin, Patricia Preciado. *Images and Conversations: Mexican Americans Recall a Southwestern Past*. Tucson: University of Arizona Press. 1996.

McNamee, Gregory, Ed. *Named in Stone and Sky: An Arizona Anthology*. Tucson: University of Arizona Press. 1993.

Molina, Felipe. *Yoeme History and Culture Personal Communication*. 2014.

Muehrcke, Phillip C. and Juliana O. Muehrcke. *Map Use: Reading, Analysis, Interpretation*, 4th edition. Madison: WI: JP Publications. 1998.

Nahban, Gary Paul. *The Desert Smells Like Rain: A Naturalist in Papago Indian Country*. San Francisco: North Point Press. 1982.

Nabhan, Gary Paul. *Gathering the Desert*. Tucson: University of Arizona Press. 1985.

National Register of Historic Places. *Registration Form: Ghost Ranch Lodge*. U.S. Department of the Interior. 2012.

Officer, James E. *Hispanic Arizona: 1536-1856*. Tucson: University of Arizona Press. 1987.

Olin, George. *House in the Sun: A Natural History of The Sonoran Desert*. Tucson: Southwest Parks and Monuments Association. 1994.

Overstreet, Daphne. *Arizona Territory Cook Book: Recipes from 1864 to 1912*. Phoenix: Golden West. 2004.

Pablo. "Duerme Ya" (Sleep Now), Lullaby written to the theme from "Pan's Labyrinth." https://answers.yahoo.com/question/index?qid=20080918102717AAFdsjU (Retrieved 1/25/2010)

Phillips, Steven J., and Patricia Wentworth Comus, eds. *A Natural History of the Sonoran Desert*. Tucson: Arizona Sonoran Desert Museum Press. 2000.

Potter, Lee Ann, and Wynell Schamel. "The Homestead Act of 1862." *Social Education* 61(6): 359-364. October, 1997.

Record, Ian W. *Big Sycamore Stands Alone: The Western Apaches, Aravaipa, and the Struggle for Place*. Norman, OK: University of Oklahoma Press. 2008.

Reid, J. Jefferson, and David E. Doyel. *Emil W. Haury's Prehistory of the American Southwest*. Tucson: University of Arizona Press. 1986.

Reid, Jefferson, and Stephanie Whittlesey. *The Archaeology of Ancient Arizona*. Tucson: University of Arizona Press. 1987.

Saxton, Dean, Lucille Saxton, and Susie Enos. Dictionary: Papago-English, O'otham-Mil-gahn, English-Papago, Mil-gahn-O'otham, second edition. Tucson: University of Arizona Press. 1983.

Shelton, Richard. *Going Back to Bisbee*. Tucson: University of Arizona Press. 1992.

Shelton, Richard. *Hohokam*. Tucson: Sun/Gemini Press. 1993.

Spicer, Edmund H. *Cycles of Conquest: The Impact of Spain, Mexico, and the United States on the Indians of the Southwest, 1533-1960*. Tucson: University of Arizona Press. 1962.

Stein, Pat H. *Homesteading in Arizona, 1862-1940: A Component of the Arizona Historic Preservation Plan*. Phoenix: Arizona State Historic Preservation Office. 1990.

Stockel, H. Henrietta. *Women of the Apache Nation: Voices of Truth,* Reno, NV: University of Nevada Press. 1991.

Sutton, Mark Q., and Brooke S. Arkush. *Archaeological Laboratory Methods: An Introduction*. Dubuque: Kendall/Hunt. 1998.

Swartz, Deborah L. *Archaeological Testing at the Romero Ruin,* Technical Report 93-8. Tucson: Center for Desert Archaeology. 1993.

Swartz, Deborah L. *Archaeological Testing at the Romero Ruin,* Technical Report 91-2. Tucson, Center for Desert Archaeology. 1991.

Thiel, J. Homer. Winter-Spring, "People of the Presidio—Family Records from the Tucson Presidio." *Supplemental Media Content for Archaeology Southwest,* Vol. 24, Nos 1-2. Tucson: Center for Desert Archaeology. 2010.

"Traditional, Processual, and Post-Processual Archaeology," *Stephanie Hatch: Archaeology, Art History, Religion, Ancient Cultures, Anthropology, and Nature,* http://stephaniehatch.blogspot.com/2010/02/traditional-processual-and-post.html (Retrieved August 12, 2014).

Underhill, Ruth Murray. *Papago Woman.* Prospect Heights, IL: Waveland Press. 1979.

Underhill, Ruth Murray. *Singing for Power: The Song Magic of the Papago Indians of Southern Arizona.* Tucson: University of Arizona Press. 1993.

Underhill, Ruth Murray. *People of the Crimson Evening,* Palmer Lake, CO: The Filter Press. 1982.

Van Ness Seymour, Tryntje. *The Gift of Changing Woman,* New York: Henry Holt and Company. 1993,

Ward, Andy. *Palatkwapi: True Southwest, www.palatkwapi.com.* 2014.

Weatherby 9 Lug/Magnum, http://en.wikipedia.org/wiki/Weatherby_Mark_V (Retrieved 8/20/2012)

Weaver, Donald E, Susan S. Burton, and Minnabell Laughlin, eds. *Proceedings of the 1973 Hohokam Conference.* Ramona, CA: Acoma Books. 1978.

Wechel, Edith te. *Yaqui: A Short History.* http://www.lasculturas.com/aa/vs_EdithYaqui.htm (Retrieved 5/17/2012)

Yetman, David. *Sonora: An Intimate Geography.* Albuquerque: University of New Mexico Press. 1996.

Book Club Discussion Questions

1. What is your initial impression of Anna? What do you learn about her relationship with her husband?

2. What is your initial impression of Foster? What do you learn about him and his attitude toward Anna? What do you make of his comment to his reflection in the mirror?

3. What is it about Anna that makes her the perfect target for Foster's predatory nature? In the flashbacks related to their early relationship, there were red flags she failed to recognize. Discuss.

4. How does Anna's family background influence the choices she makes?

Discuss her relationship with her brother and her reaction to his remark before he left the wedding.

5. Was Anna's decision to run away appropriate? Should she have stayed to work at resolving the difficulties in her marriage? Should she have sought help from social agencies working with victims of domestic violence?

6. Archaeologists often agree with Byrd Baylor's idea that "the clay remembers the hands that made it" and that touching a fingerprint is like touching the hand of the potter. Why would they agree with this idea?

7. They might also agree that the songs still in the clay are lifted out by the winds and that sometimes they can be heard. Is this a far-fetched idea, or do you think it has merit?

8. There is an emphasis on the stories that the artifacts tell. In what way does it seem that archaeology is the practice of story finding?

9. Discuss the character of Minnie. What is her role in the story?

10. Discuss the character of Nick. Is he as vulnerable as Max thinks he is? What is it that draws him to Anna?

11. Discuss Anna's relationship with men in the story: her father (to the extent you know about him), Foster, Nick,

Max. Are there parallels in any of these relationships?

12. Is Anna's relationship with Nick altered because of her experience with Foster?

13. What does Anna learn about Esperanza through the artifacts she finds? What is your impression of Esperanza as a frontier wife?

14. What does Anna learn about Ha-wani through the artifacts she finds or handles? What is your impression of Ha-wani's role in her Hohokam community?

15. Throughout the story, there is an emphasis on the eyes as windows to the soul. Contrast Foster's eyes with Nick's and what they imply about these men. In what way are Ha-wani's experiences similar to Anna's?

16. Why is reconstructing the pot so important to Anna?

17. Explore the relationship between Foster and his parents as described in flashback chapters. Again, are there indicators of trouble that Anna fails to recognize? Is she just naïve?

18. Are you surprised by Foster's revelations about his family and his past? Were there events that foreshadowed these revelations throughout the story? Discuss.

19. How does the character of Esperanza Siqueiros contribute to the story?

20. In the story, it says that "Anna drew strength from the potter and Esperanza Ramirez. They were women who survived in an unforgivable landscape against whatever forces of nature and man worked against them." Even though you only meet them briefly in the story, how is their strength illustrated? How does this affect Anna's own struggles?

21. Anna's story illustrates a number of opposing themes; for example, Anna is dedicated to uncovering secrets and Foster and his parents are dedicated to burying them. Explore this and others you find in the story.

22. Where does Anna get the strength to take charge when she is most vulnerable to Foster's threats? Is she trading Foster's domination for dependence on Nick?

23. How does the backdrop of Tucson and the Santa Catalina Mountains affect how the reader perceives the book? If you live in the area, does having a local setting impact your perceptions? If so, how?

24. In what way does this story describe the legacy of the past as a means of understanding the present?

About the Author

Sharon K. Miller is an author and freelance editor in Tucson, Arizona. The Clay Series has been a long-time project for which she has done extensive research into the archaeology, history, and prehistory of the Tucson Basin, including the history of the Spanish *entrada* into the Southwestern United States. Her affinity for the Sonoran Desert inspired the characters and the events in these books.

Connect with me

Email: sharon@buckskinbooks.com
Twitter: @authorskmiller
Blog: boxeldersandblackberries
about.me/sharon.miller
LinkedIn